INSPECTOR FRENCH
AND THE CRIME AT GUILDFORD

Freeman Wills Crofts (1879–1957), the son of an army doctor who died before he was born, was raised in Northern Ireland and became a civil engineer on the railways. His first book, *The Cask*, written in 1919 during a long illness, was published in the summer of 1920, immediately establishing him as a new master of detective fiction. Regularly outselling Agatha Christie, it was with his fifth book that Crofts introduced his iconic Scotland Yard detective, Inspector Joseph French, who would feature in no less than thirty books over the next three decades. He was a founder member of the Detection Club and was elected a Fellow of the Royal Society of Arts in 1939. Continually praised for his ingenious plotting and meticulous attention to detail—including the intricacies of railway timetables—Crofts was once dubbed 'The King of Detective Story Writers' and described by Raymond Chandler as 'the soundest builder of them all'.

Also in this series

By the same author

*with other Detection Club authors

FREEMAN WILLS CROFTS

Inspector French and the Crime at Guildford

COLLINS
CRIME
CLUB

COLLINS CRIME CLUB

An imprint of HarperCollins*Publishers*
1 London Bridge Street
London SE1 9GF
www.harpercollins.co.uk

This paperback edition 2020
1

First published in Great Britain for the Crime Club
by Wm Collins Sons & Co. Ltd 1935

This novel is entirely a work of fiction. It is presented in
its original form and may depict ethnic, racial and sexual prejudices
that were commonplace at the time it was written.

A catalogue record for this book is
available from the British Library

ISBN 978-0-00-839324-3

Set in Sabon Lt Std by Palimpsest Book Production Ltd, Falkirk, Stirlingshire

Printed and bound in Great Britain
by CPI Group (UK) Ltd, Croydon CR0 4YY

MIX
Paper from
responsible sources
FSC
www.fsc.org
FSC C007454

This book is produced from independently certified FSC™ paper
to ensure responsible forest management.

Find out more about HarperCollins and the environment at
www.harpercollins.co.uk/green

TO
DR J. MORRIS WALKER
In cordial acknowledgment of an idea suggested by him
and developed in this book.

Contents

1

The Stage is Set

Sir Ralph Osenden, of Brookhurst Lodge, Ryde, Isle of Wight, stepped briskly from the train at Waterloo Station and turned towards the nearest cab rank.

He was a dapper little man in the late fifties, spruce in appearance, natty in dress, and precise, if not pedantic, in manner. His bow-tie was mathematically symmetrical, his spats, of a dazzling whiteness, fitted as if they were a part of himself, and the umbrella he carried hooked to his left forearm was rolled smooth as a steel tube.

Sir Ralph did not now often honour Town with his presence. He had been a worker all his life, and having amassed a moderate fortune, had decided to sell his business and go in for certain artistic hobbies in which his soul delighted.

He had not, however, given up all association with the City. He still retained his directorship of certain companies, and on their boards he proved himself a shrewd and helpful adviser. He was looked up to by those in the know and out of it, and his name stood a synonym for success, straight dealing and stability.

Today he had come up to attend a regular though informal meeting of certain of the directors of Nornes Limited, a large firm of working jewellers which did business all over the world. It was by far the biggest firm with which he was connected, and had been one of the most prosperous. The depression, however, had hit it hard, and in spite of all that he and his fellow directors could do, profits had continued to shrink till now an adverse balance threatened. It was, indeed, to consider its very serious position that the present meeting had been called.

The Company's offices were situated on the upper two floors of a block of buildings in Ronder Lane, a cul-de-sac near the Aldwych end of Kingsway. Sir Ralph paid off his taxi, and crossing the marble entrance hall, was wafted upwards by one of the building's six lifts. Reaching the eighth floor, he passed along a corridor, knocked at a door marked 'Private', pushed it open, and entered the room.

A pretty girl seated before a typewriter smiled up at him.

'Good morning, Miss Barber,' said Sir Ralph. 'Is Mr Norne disengaged?'

'I think so, Sir Ralph. I'll see.'

She jumped up, went to a second door, and put her head into the adjoining room. Then she threw the door open. 'Will you please go in?'

Sir Ralph passed through into a larger and more ornately furnished office. A man sitting at the big table desk in the centre nodded.

'Glad you were able to come, Osenden,' he said. 'Sloley and Ricardo are here. They'll be in directly.'

Sir Ralph carefully placed his hat and umbrella on a side table. 'I suppose it's still the same question, Norne?' he asked as he moved to a chair.

Claude Willington Norne was the managing-director of the firm and chairman of the board. He was a tall, athletic-looking man with features set in a hawklike mould, graying hair brushed back from his forehead, a brown skin due to years passed in the East, and the lightest of blue eyes. He was a man of great ability and force of character. In the City his keenness and efficiency were universally admired, though faith in his absolute straightness under all circumstances was not so strongly marked. Now he leant back in his chair.

'Still the same,' he answered dryly: 'merely what we're going to recommend at the next board. I think we should agree on our policy—if we can.'

'We've got a fortnight to make up our minds.'

'I know we have, but I'd rather settle it now than wait till the last moment.'

'Does Sloley still want to borrow?'

'So far as I know. He's said nothing more to me.'

Sir Ralph's reply was interrupted by the entrance of two other men. Both were of middle-age and gave the impression of physical and mental fitness, though one was tall and fair and the other small and dark. These were two more of the directors, the Reginald Sloley and Anthony Ricardo who had been mentioned. They also were men of ability and force of character. These four dominated the policy of the Company. When difficult or controversial matters were coming before the board they invariably held a preliminary meeting to decide their policy. The present was one of these. If all four were agreed on a line of action, it seldom failed to go through.

The newcomers nodded to Sir Ralph. 'Thought you were going to Paris, Osenden?' Ricardo remarked. Sloley flung himself into an armchair and lit a cigarette.

'I'm going tomorrow, but only for a week. I'm going to fly—my first experience.'

'I shouldn't think of going any other way,' Sloley remarked. 'There's no comparison.' He turned to Norne. 'Go ahead, Norne, like a good chap, will you? I'm going down to Brighton and I want to start as soon as may be.'

Norne pushed some papers from before him, replaced them with a pencil and pad, and then leaned back in his chair.

'Today,' he began, 'we have really only one question before us. I think all of you know as much about it as I do. This is Wednesday, and on this day fortnight we have our board. At that board a decision vital to our entire future must be taken. I think we ought to be agreed as to our line of action. I may say, incidentally, that I arranged this meeting a week earlier than usual on account of Osenden going away.'

'You say we know as much about the matter as you do,' Ricardo interrupted, 'and you may be right. At the same time, the whole question's so important that I for one would like you to go over the facts once more, just to be quite satisfied I've got them all correct.'

Sir Ralph nodded approval. 'Yes, Norne,' he urged, 'I think that would be wise. There may be some small point overlooked by one of us, which would affect our judgment.'

Norne glanced at Sloley, who also nodded. 'Well,' he agreed, 'I can run over the facts easily enough. Unhappily, they're only too simple. It's when we come to consider the conclusions that we should draw from them that the difficulties begin to arise.' He opened a drawer, took out a box of cigars, helped himself, and pushed the box towards the others. Then he went on.

4

'The main fact is, as we all know, that owing to the depression and one thing and another which I needn't mention again, our business has been going steadily down for over four years. I'll not go into the figures, because you have them on the sheets before you. I need only say that from the normal twenty to twenty-five per cent dividends which we were accustomed to in prosperous times, our returns have dropped gradually until last year we were thankful to get three per cent. This year there will be no dividend at all, and if things go on as they're doing, we shall end up with a pretty considerable adverse balance.'

'Is there no improvement at all?' Sloley put in. 'No response to the general improvement in trade?'

'There is,' Norne answered, 'so far as this country is concerned—a slight improvement. But as you know, Sloley, our foreign business is larger than our home, and abroad there's very little improvement showing so far.'

'Unemployment has gone down abroad, same as here,' Sloley persisted.

'The probable degree of prosperity to be expected at home and abroad is naturally one of the factors upon which we shall base our judgment,' Norne agreed smoothly. 'If we knew that we should have less difficulty in coming to a decision.'

'Suppose you go ahead with your statement, Norne,' Osenden suggested.

'With regard to our present liabilities, as you can see from your sheets, we owe something like three-quarters of a million, of which, of course, the largest item is for stones. Then for the future there is the running of this office and the workshops, fresh purchases of stones, overhead, bad debts, and so on. I needn't go into it?'

'No,' Osenden remarked. 'We have all that before us.'

'Of our assets the major item is our stock of stones. As you know, it's extremely high—higher, I think, than ever before. We have in the safe there,' he motioned with his head across the room, 'over half a million's worth of stuff. Then there our plant, goodwill, and so on, as you see.'

Osenden moved uneasily. 'Do you think we're wise to keep all those stones in the safe?' he asked. 'Half a million sterling is a tidy bit of money.'

'I'm not entirely happy about it,' Norne admitted, 'but we must have the stuff where it can be got at. The workshops are always wanting special stones. Besides, it's a pity not to take the good stuff that's coming cheap on the market.'

'I agree,' said Osenden.

'Well, that's a rough summary of things, and we may now turn to the object of our meeting. That is, quite briefly, whether the circumstances demand any special action, and if so, what?'

'Just let me be sure of one point first,' Ricardo interrupted. 'We are now definitely solvent?'

'At the present moment absolutely. It's the future we're concerned about.'

'Right. I understand.'

'It seems to me,' continued Norne, 'that we have a choice of four alternatives. The first is to carry on as we're going.'

'Which you think will lead us to bankruptcy?'

'I think so.'

Sloley moved impatiently. 'You needn't waste time over that. We're all agreed we must do something.'

Glancing at the other two men, Norne resumed:

'The second is to shut down: to wind up the business.

6

As you know, we've got a first-rate offer for our stock of stones. We'll certainly never get a better. But that only stands open for a fortnight. If we closed with it, we should come out all square.'

'But leaving nothing for ourselves and our staff?'

'Practically nothing.'

Osenden looked round. 'We'll have to keep that offer in our minds, of course, but I think we might leave it to the last. If we're able to hang on till the depression's over, I think we'll get our dividends again.'

'I agree,' said Ricardo, 'but, as you say, we mustn't overlook the offer. I'd rather come out of the thing square now, even without a profit, than have to go into liquidation later.'

'We'll not go into liquidation,' Sloley exclaimed roughly. 'Go on to something practical, Norne.'

'The other proposals are that we should either go into voluntary liquidation and reconstruct, or that we should issue more stock and carry on.'

'But,' Ricardo objected, 'why should we go into voluntary liquidation if we're all square? I don't follow you there, Norne.'

'It's unhappily very simple. Put very crudely, if we meet our liabilities, we use up all our assets to do so. That leaves us with no capital to carry on, and we can't carry on without capital.'

Norne paused and surveyed his companions with a saturnine expression. None of them spoke, and he presently went on.

'Unhappily we are not agreed as to which of these two last policies we should advocate. Osenden appears to favour the first and Sloley the second. If I'm right, I think we should get these two to put their views forward. Will you get on with it, Osenden?'

Sir Ralph slowly drew his cigar up to redness. Then he began to speak.

'I rather look at it like this. If we go into voluntary liquidation and reconstruct, there's not a great deal of harm done. I don't know what we could pay, but it would probably be fifteen or sixteen shillings in the pound. That would be a nasty loss for ourselves and our share-holders, but nobody's ruined. If we carry on, it seems to me we're heading for a crash and we may lose everything. Personally, I'd prefer a small loss now to a larger one in a year or two.'

Sir Ralph paused and looked round his audience. Then, with some appearance of embarrassment, he continued:

'There's another thing which I want to say—without any intention of throwing mud.' Again he glanced round with something of apology in his manner. 'If we don't go into liquidation and have a reconstruction, we must, of course, appeal to the public for more money—your last alternative, Norne. Now, if we go to the public for more money we can't show them those figures which you, Norne, have just given us. We should therefore have to, shall I say, "select" the figures we publish. Now, I question the wisdom of that. In fact, it would in my judgment be getting perilously near the fraudulent balance-sheet. Not,' Sir Ralph smiled crook-edly across at the tall director, 'that I'm accusing Sloley of advocating fraud. I just want to put up the point of view and see how he answers it.'

'Not hard to do that,' muttered Sloley.

'Well, I'm open to conviction,' Sir Ralph went on. 'Then there's the other more general point of view. Even supposing we could get the cash in a perfectly correct and legal way, I don't know that it's the game to take a lot of money from people unless we're pretty sure we can pay them a dividend. That's all I have to say.'

Norne once again glanced round the three faces.

'That's straight enough, Osenden,' he said, 'and all the better for it. Now, Sloley?'

'Apart from the pleasant suggestion that we're a bunch of crooks,' answered Sloley, grinning back at Sir Ralph, 'I suggest that none of all that touches the point at issue. If this were a question of fraud versus straight dealing, there would be no more to be said. Unfortunately, it's not so simple. I, for one, believe that some more capital might very well see us through. Trade's bucking up, and that's going to help us. I suggest that if we could carry on long enough—as we could if we issued more stock—things would right themselves.'

Sloley paused to draw up his cigar.

'If you want to consider the morality argument, here it is. Osenden wants to destroy part of our shareholders' capital—20 or 30 or 40 per cent, or whatever the figure may be—without hope of return: for what? To save himself and us from the results of our bad management. I propose to offer them the chance of getting all square.'

'Then you're definitely for the issue of more stock?'

'Definitely.'

'And how would you answer Osenden's argument of the fraudulent balance-sheet?'

'It doesn't arise. The whole thing depends on what we put down as estimated profits. I think the improvement in trade would justify us in putting out an attractive prospectus.'

'And I don't,' Osenden put in. 'That's the difference between us in a nutshell.'

Norne turned to Ricardo. 'Well, Ricardo?' he questioned. The small dark director moved uneasily.

'Personally, I feel the question of a voluntary liquidation in connection with our Company is so horrible that I should be against it unless everything else had proved impossible. What do you say yourself, Norne? If we had some more capital, should we pull through?'

Norne did not answer at once, and when he spoke it was deliberately, as if he was weighing every word. The others listened as to an oracle.

'That really is what we're here to discuss. Personally, I sympathise a lot with what both of you two say. I agree with Osenden—and I think we all agree—that unless we believe that the raising of fresh capital will see us out of our difficulties, we shouldn't try to raise it. I agree with Sloley—and again I feel sure we all agree—that if we think raising the capital would save the Company, then we shouldn't hesitate. The point on which we differ—whether or not extra capital would save us—is very difficult to decide. My own personal view is that if things continue as they are, we'd only be getting deeper into it. In fact, not to put too fine a point on it, under present conditions we haven't a dog's chance. On the other hand, we all know that Sloley's right when he says it depends on trade. If there was a boom we might get out of it all right.'

'Then,' said Ricardo, 'it's a question of foretelling whether or not there's going to be a boom?'

'Partly that,' Norne returned. 'But also I think we must get down more closely to actual figures. I've got here some quite rough notes of our probable position in various actualities,' he indicated some sheets of paper on his desk, 'which might serve as a basis of discussion.'

The others nodded their approval and Norne, having picked up one of the sheets, went on: 'Now, to take first the current year. Suppose, instead of paying the whole of Molloy and Dobson's account—' and he began a highly technical exposition of various possible actions and their problematical results. His three companions listened carefully, and when he had finished broke into an equally technical discussion.

Soon, however, it became apparent that in spite of the illuminating—or befogging—influence of figures, agreement was no nearer attainment. The talk dragged on, but grew steadily more aimless and unprofitable. It was evident that the difference between Sloley and the others was fundamental and that neither side was prepared to give way.

At last Sloley jerked himself round in his chair.

'Look here,' he exclaimed, 'we're getting no-where with all this. Tell you what, Norne. Suppose we drop it for the present and have another meeting? We've a fortnight to make up our minds, and a bit more thought about the thing wouldn't do any of us any harm.'

This produced another difference of opinion. While Ricardo and Sir Ralph welcomed the proposal, Norne advised caution.

'We should be very careful,' he declared, 'about holding extra conferences at the present time. You know as well as I do that already there are rumours going as to our position. As a result, our stock is dropping. You may bet we're being watched, and if we keep on having emergency meetings someone will tumble to it and our chance of raising fresh capital will be gone for good.'

Ricardo seemed impressed with this argument, and Sir Ralph nodded his agreement. But Sloley gesticulated impatiently.

'Well,' he returned, 'if you don't want our meeting to be known, let's hold it on Sunday. Not here—someone would be sure to get to know. I'll tell you. Come to my house. It's not very big, as you know, but it'll be big enough for all we want. Come along after breakfast and I'll put up a spot of lunch.'

'And have Mrs Sloley's eternal curses on our souls?' Norne returned. 'It's jolly good of you, Sloley, but we'll do nothing of the kind. I think a meeting on Sunday's not a bad notion, but if we're going to anyone's house we'll go to mine. A bachelor has a pretty big pull in those sort of things.'

'Can't go to you,' Sloley answered. 'Too far away for Ricardo.'

Ricardo lived near Ely and Norne at Guildford.

'Don't worry about me,' interposed Ricardo. 'I'll come up the night before and stay in Town.'

'No,' said Norne, 'I can think of something worth two of that. You'll all come down and spend the weekend with me. I'd like to show you the new billiard room. We can have a game on Saturday evening, then on Sunday we'll have a clear day, free from interruption. We can get at this business early and stick at it till we're agreed. What about it?'

After a further short discussion this was agreed to. Norne was a comparatively wealthy man and his house was large and expensively run. He liked to fill it, and his weekend parties of sometimes as many as a dozen were well known. Each of the others present had been his guest on more than one previous occasion.

'Next Saturday, then?' said Sloley when the matter was decided.

'I can't go next Saturday,' Sir Ralph pointed out. 'I shall be in Paris. But that doesn't matter. You can get on all right without me.'

'No,' said Norne, 'we can't do without you. What about Saturday week?'

This also was agreed to and then Sloley made another proposal.

'I seem to be monopolising the conversation, but there is one other thing I should like to put up. It's not for me to suggest who your guests might be, you know, old man,' he glanced at Norne, 'but what about asking Minter and Sheen to attend? They're pretty good men, both of them, and they know the facts. It's just that when we're at this deadlock two fresh points of view might be a help.'

'If you all think so, I shall be delighted to have them,' said Norne.

The two men referred to were highly-placed officials of the Company. Charles Minter was the accountant, and Henry Sheen the secretary. In saying they were both good men, Sloley had kept strictly within the truth; indeed, in the case of Minter he was understating it. If Sheen was a sound, though not outstanding man, Minter was a genius in his own line. Had his constitution been good, he would have been a very exceptional man, but unhappily for himself, he was troubled by chronically poor health. However, even with this handicap his services were invaluable to the Company.

'I dare say Sloley's right,' Sir Ralph said after a short pause. 'We consult them at our regular board meetings. I

13

don't see why we shouldn't do the same at our private discussions.'

'You agree, Ricardo?' asked Norne.

'Oh, I agree, yes,' the little man returned. 'I'd like it.'

It was finally settled that all were to meet at Norne's house near Guildford in time for dinner on the following Saturday week, Norne undertaking to see Minter and Sheen and get them to join the party. The meeting then came to an end, Norne resuming work in his office and the other three leaving the building.

2

Enter Death

Sir Ralph Osenden duly went to Paris in an Imperial Airways liner, and was greatly delighted with his experience. He stayed there a week, partly on business and partly on pleasure, returning on the Thursday to his home near Ryde with the consciousness not only of duty well done, but of leisure happily spent.

Having rung up Norne and been assured that the weekend arrangement stood, he took the train from Portsmouth on Saturday afternoon. At Guildford he was met by Norne's elderly chauffeur, Whatman, whom he had known for years, and was driven through the fringe of the pleasant old town up to Guildown, where Norne had built his house. Though it was now dark, Osenden knew from previous visits the fine situation of the little estate. While comparatively close to the town, it was perched high on the side of the hill, and looked out over a charming and characteristic stretch of the woods and ridges and valleys of that entirely delightful part of Surrey.

The door was opened by a strange butler, and instead

of receiving the respectful greeting to which he was accustomed, Sir Ralph had to explain himself. The man immediately led the way to the library. Norne and Ricardo were buried in deep chairs before the fire.

'Ah, Osenden, glad to see you,' the former exclaimed, heaving himself up and wheeling over a third chair. 'Ricardo's just turned up. Sit down and have a spot?'

'And how's the gay city?' Ricardo asked, when the newcomer was settled.

Osenden said that the gay city was where it always was, and added that he had met Ricardo's friend, Dupont, in the foyer of the Opera House. The talk thereupon became personal and intimate.

'We're going to be a small party this evening,' Norne went on. 'Just the three of us for dinner.'

'How's that?' Sir Ralph asked. 'Aren't the others coming down?'

'Not till later. Sheen's youthful hope, it seems, is having a birthday, and there's some matter of a long-standing promise to take her to her first theatre. Sheen and Sloley are neighbours, and it appears the wives got together and Sloley has had to join the party with his youngsters. That's the man who wanted to invite us all to lunch without consulting his wife.'

'Ever met Mrs Sloley?' put in Ricardo.

'Never.'

'I have. Nice little woman. Too nice for Sloley, if you ask me.'

'I can imagine it,' Norne returned dryly.

'Then aren't those two coming down?' Sir Ralph asked again.

'They are: after their show. Sloley wanted to put it off

16

till tomorrow, but I said to come tonight. They should be here by twelve-thirty, and I don't suppose any of us will be in bed before that.'

'And what about Minter? Is he joining the happy throng also?'

'Minter has cried off so far as dinner is concerned, but he'll be here about nine. He rang up some time ago to say that he had one of his attacks and that he wanted to stay quiet for an hour or two. He said it was nothing, but that he'd wait and come down by the 8.15, instead of the five-something he'd intended.'

'Delicate chap, Minter,' Ricardo observed. 'A great pity. If he had ordinary health he'd be a pretty outstanding man.'

'He's an outstanding man as it is,' Norne declared. 'I don't know where you'd get a better accountant.'

'You know what I mean,' Ricardo insisted. 'If he's as good as he is with that handicap, what would he not be if he were physically strong?'

'Might be too good for us,' Norne commented. 'If he was such a genius as you suggest, he mightn't find the Company gave him enough scope.'

'It seems to me,' Sir Ralph said dryly, 'that as things are at present, the Company is giving him all the scope he could want.'

'You're right,' Ricardo admitted. 'Anyone who can pull us out of our present difficulties won't be short of something to think about. No developments, I suppose, Norne, since our last meeting?'

Norne shrugged. 'Only what you're seen for yourselves in the press—that our stock has dropped another two points.'

'Yes: very unfortunate that.' Sir Ralph shook his head dejectedly. 'It won't help us if we want to raise more capital.'

'It won't.' Norne agreed.

'Talking of that drop,' Ricardo observed, 'the sensitiveness of the market has always been a marvel to me. There have been some whispers as to our condition and at once there's a drop in our stock, exactly proportional to the strength of the rumours and the amount of doubt aroused.'

Norne nodded. 'That's true. On the Stock Exchange you can put an exact money value on fear: about the only way in the world it can be done.'

Gradually Ricardo and Norne became involved in a philosophical argument on the sociological reactions of fear, while Sir Ralph, who was more interested in art, dipped into a copy of *The Connoisseur*. Presently the dressing-bell rang and all three drifted upstairs to their rooms.

Dinner passed without incident and after coffee Norne took his guests to inspect the billiard room. It was a fine room and their obvious admiration pleased him. It was his new toy, and he was like a child showing it off.

Soon the question of a game arose. Norne wanted to sit out and watch his guests play, but Ricardo disclaimed the necessary skill, and presently Norne and Sir Ralph took each other on for a hundred up. Ricardo sat and smoked and joined in the desultory conversation.

Norne easily winning the first game, and Ricardo still wishing to stand out, Sir Ralph asked for his revenge and they played a second. Luck fell once more to Norne, though this time with a smaller lead. When they had finished, Norne glanced at the clock.

'By Jove!' he said, 'there's ten o'clock. Minter should have been here before this. I hope to goodness he's coming. I've come to agree with Sloley that he might be very helpful to us tomorrow.'

'He hasn't sent any further message?' Ricardo suggested.

'I haven't heard of any,' Norne returned, 'but we'll make sure.' He pressed one of the many buttons which occurred at intervals round the walls.

'Oh, Jeffries,' he went on when the man appeared, 'no sign of Mr Minter?'

'Yes, sir, he's come. He came about quarter-past nine.'

'Oh, he's come, has he? Why didn't you show him in?'

'He said he wasn't feeling very well, sir, and that he'd like to go quietly up to his room and lie down. I took him up and saw that he had everything he required.'

'You might have told me.'

'If you'll excuse me, sir, he said he'd like half an hour to quiet down first, and then I was to ask you if you'd go up and see him. I had decided to tell you at ten o'clock.'

'Oh, all right. He's in the pink room, isn't he?'

'Yes, sir.'

'Too bad that he should be laid up,' Norne went on when the man had withdrawn. 'I hope to goodness he'll be about tomorrow. I'll go up and see him now. Will you two take each other on till I come back?'

Five minutes later Norne returned. He had a folded paper in his hand and looked rather grave. 'I've seen the chap,' he said, 'and he certainly looks pretty bad. He's lying there in the semi-dark: says the light hurts his eyes. But he says it's an ordinary attack that he gets regularly, and that it just runs its course and passes.'

'What is it exactly that's wrong?'

19

'He said it was simply a common bilious attack with sickness and headache, and that this bad bout was his own fault for coming down tonight. He said he felt better when he was leaving home, but the train made him worse again.'

'So it would,' Ricardo said with feeling. 'I've suffered from the same thing and I know.'

'I wanted to send for a doctor, but he wouldn't hear of it. Said he only wanted a sleep, so I've told Jeffries not to call him in the morning. He evidently didn't want to talk, so I didn't stay.'

Norne held up the paper he was carrying. 'Here's a statement from Sheen,' he went on. 'I'm not sure that I've got the idea correctly, but it seems Sheen thought it might help us tomorrow if we had a list of our shareholders with a forecast of how they might take up additional stock. It appears that all previous issues were taken up by our own shareholders. Sheen suggests that those connected with the motor or shoe industries, for example, which are prosperous, should be more likely to support us than those in coal or shipping, which aren't. You see the idea?'

'I think so,' Sir Ralph said doubtfully, 'but I don't know that there's much in it.'

'I don't know that there is,' Norne agreed. 'It's probably a case of nothing like leather. Our worthy secretary deals with lists of shareholders, so a list of shareholders is what strikes him as the proper contribution to our discussion.'

'Of course we do normally use information of that kind,' Ricardo pointed out, 'though in a more general form. We judge the probable response to an issue by the state of the market.'

'That's so,' Norne admitted. 'Well, at all events, it seems

Sheen persuaded Sloley to go back with him to the office this evening and look over the list. They rang up Minter to ask him to call for it on his way down, so that he could check over their conclusions in the train. Minter said it seemed all right at a casual glance, but he was too seedy to consider it properly. He's passed the document on to me. What about looking over it now, or shall we leave it till tomorrow?'

Sir Ralph thought that as Sheen had taken so much trouble about it, the least they could do would be to look at it. Ricardo agreed, and their resolution to forswear business for the evening was rescinded, and they settled down to go into the document.

After study they had to agree that the figures were suggestive and even reassuring.

'It's all pretty problematic,' Ricardo declared, 'but it's ingenious, and it does seem to indicate that if we wanted capital, we'd get it. And after all, that's an important point for tomorrow.'

'I think so too,' Sir Ralph added. 'Whether we reconstruct or not, the question of raising capital will probably arise, and I think these figures are useful enough.'

Norne shrugged. 'Well, we've read the blessed paper and I vote we drop the subject for tonight. You two didn't have a game?'

Neither Sir Ralph nor Ricardo were enthusiastic about playing. Norne presently gave it up as a bad job, and the three men went back to the deep armchairs before the library fire. Ricardo possessed a seemingly unending fund of stories, most of which were new to the others. So entertaining was he, that time was forgotten till, with a start, Sir Ralph looked at the clock.

21

'Bless my soul, almost one o'clock!' he exclaimed. 'I had no idea it was so late. D'you know, Norne, if you don't mind, I'll turn in. I must get my proper sleep or I'll be no good tomorrow.'

'If you feel like it, of course. You know your way. Those two should be here by now.' He paused and listened. 'There they are, by Jove! Steps approaching: steps of Fate!'

As he spoke the door opened and Jeffries announced: 'Mr Sloley. Mr Sheen.'

'Hullo, you two,' Norne greeted them. 'I was just speaking of the devil, and see what happens. You must be cold. Pull in and have a spot.'

He busied himself with the decanter and glasses. Sir Ralph postponed his departure and the five men grouped themselves round the fire.

'Had a good run down?' went on Norne, as he handed round drinks.

'Quite good,' said Sheen, 'if not spectacular in the way of speed. We were held up by traffic leaving Town. Astonishing how full the streets are at theatre time.'

Norne nodded. 'I hate driving down. I always go by train.'

They chatted for a moment and then Sloley asked if Minter had arrived.

'He's in bed,' Norne answered. 'He came shortly after nine and went straight up. He seemed to me pretty bad, but he declared he only wanted a rest to be all right. You saw him earlier?'

'Yes, Sheen wanted him to have a look over his statement. You got that all right?'

22

'Rather. We studied it most carefully. Jolly good, if you ask me.'

Sheen looked pleased. 'I'll be glad if it's of use,' he said deprecatingly.

Norne nodded. 'Sure to be. Well, Sheen, I hear you've been celebrating. How did the birthday party go?'

Sheen waxed enthusiastic as he dilated on what had evidently been the greatest day in his daughter's life. Then for a few minutes the conversation became general, until Sir Ralph's departure for bed broke the party up.

In spite of his protestations about a long night's sleep, Sir Ralph was first down next morning. It was a brilliant autumn day. There had been a frost and every twig and branch and blade of grass was sparkling in the sun's rays. Sir Ralph, who was fond of a short walk before breakfast, put on a coat and stumped off along the top of the ridge. The air was sharp and as invigorating as wine. It reminded him of the fresh clear thinness of the Swiss uplands, where even elderly men feel overflowing with energy and ready for any adventure or exertion. Once again he allowed his gaze to rest appreciatively on the charming succession of wooded ridges which stretched away before him, and once again he felt a twinge of envy of Norne, whose lot was cast amid these delightful surroundings.

Norne and Sloley were down when he returned. Norne was bending over the dishes on the side table and Sloley fingering the *Sunday Times*.

'Hullo, Early Bird,' cried Sloley. 'Whence all this energy?'

'I always do it,' Sir Ralph replied mildly. 'Makes you feel good inside.'

'That's where you're wrong,' Sloley returned. 'What makes

me feel good inside is some of Norne's bacon and eggs. Steady on, Norne, I'm not a shark.'

'Sorry,' murmured Norne; 'my mistake. Morning, Osenden. Kippers, sole, bacon and eggs?'

'Sole, please. Been admiring your view again, Norne. I wonder if you appreciate your luck, living here?'

'Well, considering I came here and built because of it, I suppose I do. Tea beside you and coffee at the other end.'

They settled down to breakfast and were presently joined first by Sheen and then by Ricardo. Talk for a time was general, then Sloley made a reference to business. 'When are we to start this blessed conference, Norne?'

'Whenever you good people like,' Norne answered. 'The only thing is that we must give Minter a chance. There's plenty of time in any case.'

'How is Minter this morning?' Sir Ralph asked.

'Don't know. I told Jeffries he wasn't to be called, but I suppose it's not too early to do it now.'

As Norne spoke he pressed on a bell-push which lay on the table beside his plate.

'You might go up and see how Mr Minter is,' he told Jeffries. 'Ask him if he's coming down for breakfast or if he'd like it sent up.'

With his customary 'Very good, sir,' Jeffries disappeared.

'Not much news this morning,' Ricardo remarked, turning over the pages of the *Observer*.

'I see Mansfield was knocked out in the sixth round last night,' said Sloley. 'My eyes, I should like to have seen that.'

Sheen chuckled. 'What are you grousing about? You saw "The Lilac Butterfly," didn't you?'

'Lilac Grandmother,' Sloley repeated in accents of biting

scorn. 'Next time you want to throw a party, Sheen, I'll have hydrophobia.'

'I should never be surprised to hear of it,' Sheen returned gravely.

'Must have been a good show—while it lasted,' Norne commented, 'though six rounds is hardly your money's worth.'

Sloley replied and they went on to discuss the fight in detail.

Presently Jeffries returned. Sir Ralph happened to glance at him and looked again more curiously. The man's ineffable calm had evidently been disturbed. He approached Norne, bent down, and whispered in his ear.

Norne looked startled. He rose to his feet.

'Apparently Minter's not so well,' he said. 'If you'll excuse me, I'll go and see him.'

He went out and the conversation reverted to the accountant. Sir Ralph told the others about his going straight to bed on his arrival on the previous evening, and of Norne's visit to him and subsequent comments thereon. Sloley and Sheen gave their versions of the accountant's appearance and remarks during their interview at the office, and Ricardo again remarked what an outstanding man Minter would have been had his health been normal.

Norne did not immediately return and presently the topic was dropped. One after another finished breakfast, and moving to the library, busied themselves with tobacco and newspapers. It was obvious that there was going to be some delay about starting the conference.

Then Norne came in. He looked a good deal disturbed.

'I'm very sorry to tell you fellows,' he said gravely, 'that Minter died during the night. He has evidently been dead for some time. I've sent for the doctor, of course, but only as a matter of form. He can do nothing.'

There was a moment of hushed silence while his hearers looked blankly at each other. Then a chorus broke out of surprise, dismay and regret.

3

Enter Crime

Sir Ralph Osenden was genuinely distressed about Minter's death. He had known the accountant for a long time, indeed, ever since he had become connected with Nornes Limited, more than ten years earlier. And never during the whole of those years had the man's health been other than poor. Always he had looked ill and always he had been subject to distressing internal attacks. Sometimes these involved an absence from business of as much as two or three days. However, in all those years he had not grown appreciably worse, and Sir Ralph had come to accept him and his ailments as a permanent part of the Company's establishment. The shock of his sudden death was, therefore, all the greater.

Judging from their hushed voices, the other members of the party were experiencing similar emotions. Minter had not been exactly popular—he was too quiet and retiring for that—but he had been liked in a mild way by everyone with whom he had come in contact. There was no one,

Sir Ralph was sure, who would not be sorry to hear of what had happened.

It was not long before the sound of a motor announced the doctor's arrival. Norne hurried out to meet him and took him upstairs. But comparatively speaking, a considerable time passed before there was any further move. Then Norne came down alone. He was looking graver and more than a little worried.

'I'm afraid this affair's going to be worse even than we thought,' he announced. 'Hawthorn says he can't give a certificate.'

This time his hearers stared even more blankly than before.

'What does that mean?' Ricardo asked. 'He can't tell the cause of death?'

'Apparently not. He says there must be an inquest and probably a p.m. He's still up there looking about and he has 'phoned for the police.'

'The police! Bless my soul! What does he suspect?'

'I don't know a thing more than I've told you,' Norne answered. 'Hawthorn's a decent fellow, but he's close. He's been looking at a bottle of aspirins that was beside the bed, and asking whether Minter was depressed last night. I don't know whether you can take anything out of that.'

'Good God!' Sloley muttered, 'so that's the idea, is it? I don't believe it: not for a minute.'

'If you mean suicide,' Ricardo said more bluntly, 'neither do I. Minter was not that kind of man.'

Sir Ralph strongly agreed. 'If the death was not from natural causes, it was an accident. Minter might take an overdose by mistake, but never intentionally.'

'I entirely agree,' Norne nodded. 'We're probably jumping

to conclusions, but if things do look suspicious, accident would be the only possible explanation.'

'An accident wouldn't be so hard to explain either,' Ricardo observed. 'When a man's half-blind with a bilious headache he might take anything.'

Norne made a gesture of disapproval. 'We're jumping to conclusions,' he repeated. 'Let's wait till we know more about it.'

'We'll all agree with that,' Sheen declared. 'But there's something else that won't wait. What about telling Mrs Minter, Norne?'

'I know,' Norne said quickly; 'I've been thinking about that and rather funking it. I don't know that I oughtn't to run up and see her. It would be rather ghastly to do it over the telephone.'

'You know her?'

'I've met her. A fine looking woman: younger than Minter, I should think.'

'Sloley and I know her,' said Sheen. 'She was at our party yesterday. A rotten job, having to tell her.'

'Yes, but I'm afraid as his host it's mine. I'll go as soon as the police have come. They may want to see me.'

'It's very good of you, Norne,' Ricardo declared, 'but I'm sure you're doing the right thing!'

Sloley moved uneasily. 'It seems a bit heartless,' he said with an air of unusual deprecation, 'to introduce business at such a time. But after all, we're here for a purpose. The business which has brought us together is urgent. Tragedy or no tragedy, it won't wait. What are we going to do about it?'

The others nodded their agreement, but only Norne answered.

'There's no doubt in my mind what we should do,' he declared. 'As soon as I start, you fellows get going. Do the best you can to reach agreement. I'll not be more than three hours at the most and we can have a second session after lunch. If you can agree, I'll fall in with your views.'

As he spoke there came the sound of a second car, followed by a ring and then deep voices in the hall.

'The police,' Norne said and went out quickly.

'I felt rotten butting in like that,' said Sloley when the door had closed, 'but what could we do? We must get this blessed thing fixed up before the board.'

'You were quite right,' Ricardo assured him. 'If you hadn't spoken, I should. I suggest we get to work at once.'

This seemed good advice and they got out their papers and settled themselves round the library table. But they had scarcely got under way when Norne looked in.

'That's good,' he approved, glancing round the group. 'I shall not be longer than I can help. I've rung up Mrs Minter to prepare her for my call and I'm starting at once. I should say also that Sergeant Roxton is taking statements, and he'll want to see Sloley and Sheen about their interview with Minter last night.'

Norne nodded and withdrew and the others settled down to work. After a short time Jeffries came in to say the sergeant sent his compliments and could he see Mr Sloley? Sloley vanished for ten minutes, and was followed by Sheen. Interruptions then ceased, until shortly before lunch Norne again put in an appearance.

'I've seen that poor lady,' he said: 'a perfectly rotten job. She took it wonderfully well on the whole. When I'd told her I went for her sister, who lives at Finchley. She's looking after her for the present.'

There were murmurs of concern and sympathy and then Norne asked how the others had got on. For a moment no one replied, and then Sloley took upon himself the rôle of spokesman.

'Not so badly, I think,' he explained. 'We've rather agreed on a compromise—provisionally of course—and we're anxious to hear what you think of it. Shall I tell him?' He looked round.

The others nodded and Sloley went on. 'We incline to a reconstruction—a reconstruction in which no secret shall be made of our present unsatisfactory position; no glossing it over. At the same time we suggest a fresh issue, which would bring us in enough our way to pay and carry us on for some years. We think that if trade goes on improving, we should eventually make good. We're agreed so far, but we're not agreed as to the amount of the issue. However, our differences are getting narrower, and unless,' he grinned, 'you come in and upset the apple-cart, I think we'll reach a figure.'

Norne was evidently as pleased as he was surprised. 'I'm all for compromise, as you know,' he declared, 'and on the face of it, that sounds good. Of course, the other directors may insist on selling and closing down. However, suppose we chuck it for the moment and have lunch. Then we might have a short further go and settle the thing finally.'

Though at lunch they avoided the topic which most fully occupied their minds, there was a constraint over the meal. All, consciously or unconsciously, wished to finish their work and get away. The idea of staying on over Sunday night, as had been intended, was tacitly abandoned. Norne indeed assumed that it would be.

It was not till after lunch that Sir Ralph found himself

alone with Norne. 'Tell me,' he said, seizing the opportunity, 'what is happening? Is there going to be an inquest?'

'I don't know any more than you do,' Norne replied. 'Dr Hawthorn seemed to have no doubt that it would be necessary, but the sergeant said nothing about it.'

'Then what will you do—with the body?'

'I can't do anything till I hear. I propose when our conference is finished to get in touch with the police and find out. Either the body should be taken up to Minter's house, or Mrs Minter and her sister should come down here.'

Sir Ralph nodded. 'I'm sorry for that woman,' he declared, and then: 'There are no children?'

'No, and fortunately she'll be all right financially. I happen to know Minter had saved. Besides there'll be a pension from our fund.'

'Much?'

'No, not much. But enough to be comfortable on.'

Sir Ralph lowered his voice. 'I suppose, Norne, this affair won't affect our attitude at the board? I mean,' he hesitated, 'suppose this turns out to be suicide, do you think it would affect our issue? It couldn't be argued, could it, that the suicide was due to our unsatisfactory position?'

'I thought of that,' Norne admitted, 'but I don't believe there's anything in it. Granting our position does look bad: why should Minter be upset by it to that extent? If there was any question of fraud it might be different. But no one could suggest that.'

'Of course not,' Sir Ralph said hastily. 'The idea simply occurred to me.'

'If the issue wasn't taken up we might have to sell after all. However, that's the worst that could happen to us. By the way, Osenden, I've been wanting to talk to you about another matter.'

'Go on, Norne.'

'Well, it's the question of who's going to take Minter's place. I don't mean who's going to be our new accountant, but who's going to act temporarily. There's the opening of the big safe, for instance. As you know, I have one key and Minter had the other. We had both to be present with our keys before the door could be unlocked. And that door has to be opened every day.'

Sir Ralph waited without speaking.

'You, Osenden, are the vice-chairman, and it seems to me that you should step into the breach. I suggest that in the presence of the others Minter's key shall be handed over to you, and that you agree to keep it until the new accountant is appointed. I suggest further that you don't pretend to be anything but a figurehead, and let Pendlebury, Minter's chief clerk, do the work. He's a good chap, is Pendlebury, level headed and knows what he's about. In fact, I should think he'd have a good chance of getting the job.'

'Then why not give him the key?'

Norne shook his head. 'I don't think I dare do that. At present he's only a clerk. The directors don't even know him officially. On the other hand, you're not only a director, but you've been chosen vice-chairman.' Norne smiled slightly. 'If you do a bit of levanting, I can't be blamed: if he did, I could.'

'Neither of us could do that without your connivance. However, I'll agree to whatever you think best. What will it mean?'

'It'll mean turning up every day till the appointment's

33

made. It's a bit hard lines, I know, but I don't see what else we can do.'

'That's all right. What time will you want me to be there in the morning?'

Norne hesitated. 'I generally get busy about ten, but I dare say we could wait for a bit if that's too early.'

'Not a bit of it. I'll be there at ten, or earlier if you like.'

'How will you do it? It would mean a pretty early start from Ryde.'

'I won't go to Ryde. Something will probably be settled at Wednesday's board, and till then I'll stay at the club.'

'Well, it's good of you. That's a weight off my mind.'

At their adjourned conference the proposals made earlier were duly ratified, and a clear understanding was reached as to the policy to be recommended to the full board. Then Norne explained his idea in connection with Minter's key, which was approved by everyone present. The keys had been taken charge of by the police, but Norne rang them up and the transfer was effected.

This brought the business of the visit to an end, and soon all four guests left for Town in Sloley's car. Sir Ralph was dropped at his club in Pall Mall and Ricardo at Piccadilly Circus, both places being but little out of Sloley's and Sheen's way to their homes in Hampstead.

Sir Ralph was not too well pleased at having to assume the custody of the second key of the safe. In the first place, his having charge of it was a useless precaution, for he did not know enough about the business to check the papers or stones which might be taken out. In the second, he could not but feel the thing was a slap in Pendlebury's face. Pendlebury was the man who would actually do Minter's work, and he should have been given the key.

However, regrets were now useless. With a shrug Sir Ralph went to the club library for a book with which to while away the evening.

When he reached the office next morning it was obvious that the news was already common property. There was a kind of excited hush in the air. Faces wore a startled expression, and movements to and fro were just a little furtive. The prevailing feeling seemed to be eager interest, but here and there someone showed traces of genuine sorrow.

Norne had already arrived. Sir Ralph went to his room and sat reading the paper while the managing-director was going through his correspondence. Presently Norne looked up.

'Suppose we go over to Minter's office?' he suggested. 'You'll see better there what's to be done.'

Sir Ralph agreed and Norne led the way.

'You've met Pendlebury, haven't you?' Norne said as they walked down the corridor.

'I don't know that I have,' Sir Ralph answered. 'I don't remember doing so.'

'Then I'll introduce him. You'll find him a good chap to work with.'

Norne pushed open a door marked 'Private,' which led into a medium sized office containing three desks. At the desks men were working. They looked up as the others entered, and one of them, a smallish man with a square dependable face and a pleasant expression, rose to his feet. All three looked excited, but the man who rose was obviously anxious and upset as well.

'This is Pendlebury,' said Norne. 'I've told him just what has happened. Sir Ralph Osenden, Pendlebury.'

'How do you do?' said Osenden, holding out his hand.

The man came forward and shook hands. 'Very tragic affair this, Sir Ralph,' he said. 'We're all—' he included his companions with a glance—'very sorry indeed about Mr Minter.'

He spoke with such obvious sincerity that Sir Ralph warmed to him. 'So are we all,' he said sympathetically. 'Indeed, we were absolutely horrified yesterday morning when he didn't come down and we learnt what had happened.'

'Mr Minter was a pleasant man to work for,' Pendlebury went on. 'Always recognised anything that was done and stood up for his men when he could.'

Sir Ralph was sure of it. He could tell Pendlebury that he had always had the highest opinion of the late accountant, and that this was fully shared by all his colleagues.

Norne agreed politely, then went on with the immediate business. 'I've explained to Pendlebury that you will be taking Minter's place temporarily. I'm sure he'll give you all the help he can.'

'I shall be only too glad, sir.'

'Thank you,' said Sir Ralph, 'but I'm afraid you'll have to do most of the work yourself. However, between us we'll keep things going till something permanent is settled.'

'Well, it's you two for it,' Norne answered and with a short nod left the room.

'Will you come into the private office, Sir Ralph?' said Pendlebury when he had gone.

'Certainly,' Sir Ralph agreed. 'But first, won't you introduce me?' He pointed to the other two. 'Are these men not in the department?'

All three of the clerks were gratified and showed it. A few kindly remarks, and Sir Ralph felt he had made three friends. This important business over, he allowed Pendlebury to convoy him next door to what had been Minter's private office.

It was small and comfortably, though not elaborately, furnished, in which Sir Ralph thought it reflected the character of its late occupant. There was a table-desk, a small bookcase of technical works, a letter filing cabinet painted green, a couple of armchairs and a small built-in safe.

'The first thing is to get the books out of the safe,' Pendlebury began. 'I suppose, sir, you have Mr Minter's keys?'

Sir Ralph produced the keys and opened the safe. The ledgers were taken out and work began. As Sir Ralph had supposed, there was not a great deal that he was able to do, but he quickly saw that Pendlebury did not need his assistance.

They had not settled down for more than a few minutes when the desk telephone rang. It was Norne, and he said he wanted to open the large safe and would Sir Ralph go round and assist him? Sir Ralph accordingly left Pendlebury working and walked back to Norne's office.

This was a somewhat larger and more ornately furnished than that he had just left. The table-desk was similar in design, but was bigger and covered with a more expensive leather. The armchairs were deeper, the carpet softer, and there were more books, filling a greater number of sectional bookcases. The file cabinet was identical in each room, as were also the lamps, radiators and other fittings.

The great difference between the offices lay in the safes. While that in the accountant's was of moderate size,

Norne's was a veritable giant. It was built in so that its door projected only a few inches from the wall and was of modern design, and the work of a first-class firm.

In the office with Norne was an elderly man with a clean-shaven dependable face and an alert though rather bad-tempered expression. This was Miles, the foreman of the works department. Sir Ralph had met him before, but he did not know much about him except that he was supposed to be a good man at his job. Sir Ralph wished him good morning.

'Sorry for asking you to come along, Osenden,' Norne apologised, 'but Miles wants to get some stones for making up, and I therefore have to open the safe. Will you help me?'

The two directors inserted their keys and turned them, one after another. Each of these enabled the main handle to be rotated through a certain arc, releasing the door bolts. With a little effort Norne swung the great door open.

'Here are what you want, Miles,' he said; 'on Shelf B.'

Sir Ralph looked in as the door opened and was interested to see the array of little drawers and boxes, presumably containing stones, as well as the masses of papers and books, all stacked tidily and labelled with green card labels. What an accumulation of power was there! The power not only of sheer wealth, but the almost more potent force of knowledge! If the papers in that safe were published, what ruin might not follow; what skeletons in cupboards might not become revealed! How many old family jewels were there, which were believed by fond husbands to be in the jewel-cases of their wives! How many were there, believed by fond wives to be in the safes of their husbands! Sir Ralph was thrilled as he wondered how far the picture he had conjured up represented the facts—

A moment later, in stepping back to give place to Miles, he happened to glance at Norne's face. What he saw froze him stiff.

A very startling change had come over the managing-director's expression. For a moment it was slightly mystified, as if Norne were trying to account for some unusual and puzzling spectacle. But only for a moment. Mild mystification quickly gave place to amazement, amazement to consternation, and consternation to actual dread. It was evident that Miles was equally moved.

For some moments the three men stood transfixed. Then Norne suddenly became galvanised into furious life. Madly he seized drawer after drawer, pulled them out, glanced in, and slammed them shut again.

Sir Ralph moved as if coming out of a trance. 'For heaven's sake, Norne,' he gasped, 'what's the matter? What are you looking for?'

For some moments Norne continued his wild search. Then he stopped, and turning round, faced the others with an expression of positive horror. 'The stones!' he cried in a small voice, suddenly gone hoarse. 'The stones! Our entire stock! They're gone!'

Sir Ralph stared incredulously. 'Norne, do you know what you're saying?' he stammered, while Miles gave vent to a slow and lurid oath.

Norne for a moment seemed paralysed. Then slowly he regained some of his normal self-control. Looking white and scared, he once again took charge.

'Lock the door, will you, Miles, and then come and give me a hand. We'll go through all these drawers and make quite sure.'

'I can't believe it,' Sir Ralph declared helplessly.

'We'll soon know. Come on, Miles. I'll open them one by one and you look in with me. Osenden, will you take notes of anything we find?'

With grave faces the three men got to work and soon the entire safe had been gone over. Norne looked blankly at the others.

'All the stones are gone,' he said in a choked voice; 'all that are any good. The whole of that half million's worth! All gone!'

Looking already ten years older he returned to his desk and caught up the telephone. 'Whitehall, one two, one two,' he said urgently . . . 'Is that Scotland Yard? . . . I am the managing-director of Nornes Limited, the working jewellers, of Ronder Lane, Kingsway. There has been a very big robbery of precious stones here. Will you put me through to someone in authority!'

4

Enter the Yard

At the moment when Norne put through his call it happened that Chief-Inspector Joseph French was seated in his room in New Scotland Yard, trying to decide upon the means to be employed in the further pursuit of a particularly elusive burglar. The man had been traced from the Clifton house at which his crime was committed to Temple, Meads Station in Bristol and from there to Paddington. But at Paddington he had vanished, and French and those working under his orders were at a complete loss as to their next step.

It happened also that on this Monday morning it was French's turn to receive reports of fresh crimes and to allocate their preliminary investigation to such officers as were available. Therefore, when the local exchange received Norne's call, it was to him that it was put through.

He listened with close attention to the concise statement made by Norne. Here, it was evident, was the opening of what would almost certainly prove a very important case. He knew Nornes Limited by reputation, as one of the largest firms of working jewellers in London. If it were true that jewellery valued at the enormous sum of half a million sterling had been stolen, it would rank as one of the major thefts of the century.

In such cases of theft, time was usually of the first importance. The turning of the stolen jewels into money could not be carried out in a moment, and the sooner the usual sources of disposal were watched, the better. French decided that it would be quickest if he himself were to go to the firm's offices and get full particulars at first hand. He therefore replied accordingly, asking Norne to say nothing in the meantime of what had happened.

Norne rang off and French quickly made a number of other calls. Firstly he repeated the story in an even more condensed form to Sir Mortimer Ellison, the Assistant Commissioner under whose supervision he worked, and obtained his approval for his giving the case his personal attention. Next he instructed his assistant, Sergeant Carter, to be ready to accompany him. Two more calls secured the services of a finger-print expert and a photographer, while a fifth requisitioned a fast car. Then picking up his emergency case, which always stood packed with apparatus likely to be used in preliminary investigations, French hurried from his room. Within six minutes of the receipt of Norne's call, the little party turned out of the Yard gates on to the Embankment.

Joseph French had by this time quite got over the novelty of his promotion, and life as a chief-inspector had become to him the normal mode of existence. He had had a busy time since that case of the launch explosion off Cowes, in which the unhappy partners of the Chayle cement works had lost their lives. That case, though at first it had seemed one of the most unsatisfactory he had ever tackled, had in the end added considerably to his reputation. When at first failure had stared him in the face, he had imagined his superiors had regretted his promotion, but on his final success he was given to understand they were satisfied.

With two small exceptions, however, that case had represented the last occasion on which he had worked outside his room at the Yard. The first was that of a smash and grab raid in Nottingham. It was believed to be the work of a London gang, and he spent a couple of days in the Midland city co-ordinating the local efforts to find the men with those of his colleagues at the Yard. His part in the second case was also that of liaison officer between local and metropolitan workers. It was a murder case, the particularly brutal murder of a girl in a deserted bungalow near Dover. In this instance the combined efforts of the Dover police and the Yard were successful. A former lover was found, arrested, proved guilty, and hanged. But in the smash and grab case, to French's bitter disappointment, the raiders got clean away.

French, whose heart was in the country, wished constantly that he could get another out-of-Town job. His interest in this new robbery was, therefore, tinged with disappointment, in that he foresaw another period of Town working. What he longed for was green grass and trees, and better still, stretches of water. As far as the matter of surroundings went, the Southampton Water case had reached his ideal.

His mind was brought back to the present by a question from Carter. 'What is it this time, sir?' the sergeant asked, after an explorative glance at his superior's face.

'Safe robbery,' French returned. 'Nornes Limited, the jewellers. Half a million worth of stones gone over the weekend.'

Carter expressed his interest and surprise by an oath of judicious moderation. 'Half a million!' he repeated. 'Anything to go on?'

'Not so far. Guarded statement from Norne, the managing-director. Probably a son or nephew of the founder's.'

'Half a million's a tidy bit of money,' the photographer essayed. 'Was the stuff insured, sir?'

'I don't know,' said French, 'but I should think so; though probably not to its full value.'

As he spoke, the car turned from Kingsway into Ronder Lane and pulled up at the block containing the Norne premises. A moment later French and Carter had reached the public office, the other two men being told to wait in the car till called on.

'Mr French and Mr Carter to see Mr Norne,' French explained to the young man who came forward.

'Oh, yes,' the clerk answered, 'Mr Norne's expecting you. Will you come this way?'

French looked keenly at the youth. There was a certain excitement in his manner, and this same excitement was reflected in the bearing of such other employees as were to be seen along the corridors they traversed. French was slightly puzzled. It could scarcely be due to news of the robbery having leaked out, because he felt certain that such intelligence would have produced a much greater effect. Some other unusual event must also have taken place. French took a mental note to find it out.

His suspicions were strengthened when they came to Norne's anteroom and were handed over to Miss Barber, the pretty secretary. She also seemed upset, as if from some minor misfortune. However, she announced the visitors at once, and French had no chance of talking to her.

'Mr Norne?' French began, handing over his professional card. 'I took your message, and I thought in view of the seriousness of your statement I had better come along myself. This is my assistant, Sergeant Carter.'

Norne shook hands, then introduced Sir Ralph and Miles. 'We've only just made the discovery, chief-inspector, and we've done what you asked us about not mentioning it.'

'It's often wise in cases of this kind,' French returned. 'Now, sir, suppose you let me know the circumstances in your own words. I can ask questions later if I want to.'

The little party sat down, French and Carter opposite Norne at his desk and Sir Ralph and Miles in the armchairs. French and Carter laid open notebooks before them. It was Carter's business to take complete shorthand notes of the interview, while French made a practice of jotting down any points which struck him as suggestive.

'The facts,' began Norne, 'are very simple and very disastrous. You know, chief-inspector, what our business consists of? Perhaps I should tell you very generally?'

'If you please, sir.'

'We are not only manufacturing jewellers, but dealers in jewellery, both in cut and uncut single stones and in assembled pieces. We actually cut stones ourselves, and we mount them and build up complete articles of jewellery. We also buy made-up sets for resale or for breaking up and re-modelling. Finally we make temporary cash advances on the security of jewellery deposited with us. So that you will see that our business is many sided, and I may tell you that it is pretty large also: indeed, it is practically world wide.'

'I know it has that reputation, sir.'

'You will understand that to carry on such a business it is necessary for us to keep a large collection of stones and jewellery on the premises. We have been in the habit of storing it in that safe which you see. The safe was put in about twelve years ago, our former one being somewhat antiquated, and it was then the best that money could buy.'

French glanced round at the huge green door and nodded.

'It happened through a variety of causes that we have lately been carrying an unusually large quantity of stuff— approximately half a million pounds' worth. I had occasion to open the safe on Saturday morning and everything was then in order. While, of course, I didn't go through every drawer, I'm positive that nothing had been disturbed.

'This morning I again had to open the safe. I did it in the presence of these gentlemen. Instantly I saw that there had been a robbery. Several valuable made-up sets which had been stacked on trays were gone, and when I pulled open drawers at random I saw that they also had been emptied.

'I immediately got Mr Miles to help me to make an examination. We found that practically everything worth taking has gone. Instantly I telephoned to the Yard.'

'I follow. Was the stuff insured?'

Norne made a grimace. 'Only partially, I'm afraid.'

'I shall want details of that,' French declared. 'You are, of course, satisfied that the safe was securely locked when you left it on Saturday?'

'Absolutely. Both the accountant and I tried it, and besides the handle couldn't have been turned to the locked position until at least the first key was turned.'

'The first key? Then there are two?'

'Yes, two.'

'Just explain the method of opening, will you?'

'I'll show you.' Norne got up and went to the safe, followed by French and Sir Ralph. 'Now the handle is fastened.' He shook it to demonstrate. 'I put in and turn my key. That enables the handle to be moved through a certain arc. I take out my key and Sir Ralph puts in the second, into the same keyhole—as you see there is only one. When Sir Ralph turns his key, the locking is altered. The handle cannot now be put back through its first arc, but it can be moved on through a farther arc, and when it is so moved the door is unlocked.'

'That's clear, sir. And in locking?'

'In locking the process is reversed. The handle is moved to the middle position, and this enables Sir Ralph to turn his key. He turns it, and the handle cannot be put back to the "unlocked" position, but can be moved on the "locked" one. I then turn my key, which fastens it in the "locked" position.'

'I follow. Then you and Sir Ralph keep the keys?'

'I keep one and our accountant has always kept the other. Unfortunately the accountant has just died and Sir Ralph is temporarily keeping his key.'

'You can tell me about that later, sir. Now, when you came to open the safe this morning, did you see any sign of the lock having been tampered with?'

'None whatever.'

'Your keys worked all right?'

'Perfectly.'

'Then the thief had a pair of keys?'

'Obviously.'

'Quite so, sir.' French hesitated for a moment. 'Now I'm

making no accusation, but at first sight all that seems to point to someone inside the concern. Tell me, Mr Norne: speaking confidentially, is there anyone whom you can bring yourself to suspect? I'm not asking you to accuse anyone; only to give me a line for investigation.'

Norne shook his head. 'I can answer that at once, chief-inspector. I suspect no one, and I should be greatly surprised if any of our staff were mixed up in it. What do you say, Miles?'

The works foreman moved impulsively. 'I agree with you, Mr Norne,' he said earnestly. 'I don't know the clerical side so well, but I'm convinced the working fellows are all right.'

French made a deprecating gesture. 'That's all I want, gentlemen; I was bound to ask the question. And may I take it that none of you—' he glanced keenly from one to the other—'can give me any suggestion which might put me on the right track? You, Mr Norne?'

'I have already said not.'

'Sir Ralph?'

'I certainly cannot, chief-inspector.'

'I have to get an answer to the point-blank question, sir. You, Mr Miles?'

Miles could offer no help either.

'Are there any absentees among the staff this morning?'

'I couldn't answer that, chief-inspector. I'll inquire.'

Norne picked up his desk telephone and asked for a list of absentees.

'Very good,' said French, 'that's the first thing I want. The second is a detailed list of what is missing. I presume you can give me that?'

'I think so,' Norne answered. 'I should tell you about

48

that, chief-inspector. We card index everything that goes into the safe. The index is kept in the safe, and we are most careful to see that it is kept up to date. Now, all those cards have gone too.'

French whistled below his breath. 'Is that not another pointer, sir, to someone who knew your methods?'

'Not necessarily. It's a common practice, carding the contents.'

'Then you've no record of what you had?'

'I didn't say that. We should have. The index is dupli-cated, and we keep the duplicate in Mr Miles' office. That enables him to use the index without getting the safe opened. Unless the thief has taken the duplicate also, it'll be there. You didn't notice this morning, did you, Miles?'

Miles stood up. 'No, sir,' he answered. 'The cabinet is there all right, but I didn't open it this morning. I can see in a moment.'

'Is the duplicate record kept in a safe?'

'No, in a steel filing cabinet which is always kept locked.'

French also rose. 'I'd like to see just where and how it's kept,' he said. 'Perhaps, Mr Norne, I may go with Mr Miles? Carter, I don't want you.'

Miles led French to the floor below and through a heavy door into one of the workshops. Men were seated at desk-like benches, bending low over their fine work. Others were at diminutive lathes and grinding and polishing machines. Two things struck French in particular: the extreme cleanliness and the excellent lighting of every part of the room.

In one corner a small glass-walled office had been parti-tioned off. Miles walked across, and unlocking the door, threw it open.

49

It also was scrupulously clean. In one corner stood a vertical letter file of green-painted steel; on the top of which was a similarly finished card index cabinet. To this Miles pointed.

'Open it, please,' said French.

Miles produced his key and opened the four drawers. The index was complete.

'There,' said Norne when they had returned to his office, 'what did I tell you? That shows, doesn't it, that the thief was an outsider? If he'd known of its existence, he'd have taken Mr Miles' as well.'

'Not necessarily, I think, sir,' French returned. 'He probably took yours for his own convenience, rather than to impede the inquiry.'

'I wish you'd explain all that,' put in Sir Ralph. 'How does the index affect the matter?'

'Simply, sir, that it would let the thief immediately describe to his fences what he had to sell. I think I'm right in saying it takes a considerable time to make out a correct description of a stone?'

'Absolutely. The possession of the index would save an infinity of trouble.'

'Quite,' French agreed. 'Then with regard to impeding the inquiry. He may have forgotten that the first thing we should want would be a description of the stones for circulation, and that if he had delayed us getting that, it might have been a lot in his interest. However, whether by his oversight or not, we have the duplicate. Perhaps, sir, you could get a list made from those cards?'

'Certainly,' Norne agreed. 'But I'm afraid it will take some time. There's a lot to be done. I could of course divide the cards and put all our typists on to it.'

'I should be obliged if you would do so, sir. And they might make three or four carbon copies. Perhaps, sir, while you're arranging the matter I might use your telephone?'

French rang up the Yard and got through to Sir Mortimer Ellison. He gave him a brief report of what he had learned and asked him to have the steps taken usual in such cases. It was agreed that the premises of known fences should be watched, and that the Dutch police should be advised of the robbery, so that the same precautions might be taken in Amsterdam. The records of burglary by obtaining the keys of safes were to be looked up, and the movements of all thieves who favoured that method were to be checked up. Finally French asked that the police at the cross Channel ports should be asked to keep their eyes open for possible suspects.

There was not, of course, much chance that such vague methods would produce results. However, it was all that could be done for the moment. Further information would be sent out to the searchers as it was obtained.

'Now, sir,' French went on when Norne returned, 'about those keys. Were there no duplicates of those held by yourself and your accountant?'

'There were,' Norne answered. 'Each key was duplicated, and the duplicates were held, one in the strong room of the Company's bank, and the other in that of my own private bank. Even if a miracle had happened, and the strong room of one of these banks were burgled, it is out of the question that that could happen to both.'

'I shall ask you, sir, to come round with me to both banks later. Someone may have got at those keys by means of some forged instructions.'

'I don't think so,' said Norne, 'but of course we can try.'

'We shall have to do so. Now, sir, about your own key. Where, or rather how, do you keep it?'

Norne put his hand in his trousers' pocket and brought out a small ring of keys. 'There it is,' he said, holding one of the keys up for inspection. 'You see, the ring is attached to this chain, and the other end passes through a special hole cut in my trousers, and is held by a short steel bar, same as watch-chains used to be held in a waistcoat button-hole. No one could get the keys away without my feeling it, and I could not leave them in the safe or elsewhere and go away without them. I think it's quite a safe scheme.'

French thought so too when he had examined the arrangement. The chain was riveted solidly to the ring, and the bar was long and could not possibly be pulled through the hole in the trousers. French thought a skilful man might have distracted Norne's attention and cut the chain, but this was ruled out for the simple reason that the chain had not been cut.

'You're positive that you have never allowed this chain to be unhooked from your trousers?'

'Never, except at night.'

'Have you ever lent the bunch to anyone to open the safe for you?'

'Never.'

'Or for any other purpose? Keys are often borrowed to try to open some lock of which the key has been lost. It's a common trick under such circumstances to divert the owner's attention and take a wax impression.'

'No,' said Norne firmly, 'you may give up that idea. I never lent the keys and they were never taken off the trousers.'

'Except, as you say, at night?'

'Except at night, and, of course, when I changed my clothes. But I'm equally certain that no one could have got at them on these occasions. At night I put them under my pillow as well as locking the chain to a ring fixed to the bed. When I was changing I never let the keys out of my sight.'

'That, sir, seems conclusive enough. And yet if the duplicates were not obtained from the bank, yours must have been got hold of, for the simple reason that there was no other key in existence from which a copy could have been made.'

Norne made a little gesture of weariness. 'That's exactly what has been worrying me,' he declared. 'I entirely agree, but . . . simply it didn't happen. The more I think of it, the less I can understand it.'

'I suppose, sir, you didn't fall asleep under circumstances which might have given someone an opportunity? What about a mild drug?'

'Nothing of the kind. No, chief-inspector, I wish I could explain it, but I can't.'

'That's all right, sir,' French returned, 'We'll get it in time. Now, we've been speaking about your key. Let us consider the second, which you tell me was held by your accountant. You say also that he has recently died and his key is in Sir Ralph's charge. Perhaps you would give me details of all this?'

'Certainly. It's an unhappy business, not yet entirely cleared up. The truth is that Mr Minter died suddenly yesterday, or rather on Saturday night, at my house near Guildford. He was found dead yesterday morning, and the doctor was unable to give a certificate, so the Guildford police have the matter in hand. Perhaps I'd better tell you from the beginning?'

French looked very searchingly at the managing-director and agreed in a slightly dry tone.

'I must tell you then something which is absolutely confidential,' Norne resumed. 'I take it that you will keep it to yourself?'

'Unless it proves to be essential for the purposes of justice, certainly, sir.'

'It won't. It's only required to explain Minter's presence at my house, and for that you can say "business." The fact is, however, that things have been going badly lately with our company,' and Norne described the condition of affairs, leading on to the meeting, Minter's arrival and death, and finally the calling in of the police.

'I think I follow all that, sir,' French said when he had finished. 'In the meantime I shall only ask what was done about Mr Minter's keys?'

'I confess that in the upset I forgot all about them. When I remembered I thought it would be best if Sir Ralph took them over. I suggested it to him and he agreed. I got the keys from the police, who had taken charge of them, and handed them to Sir Ralph.'

'Then you think they couldn't have been tampered with before Sir Ralph got them?'

'I should say it was quite impossible. But I take it that's a matter for you rather than me.'

'I shall have to look into it, of course,' French agreed. 'Now, sir, what about that list of today's absentees?'

Norne picked up a paper from his desk. 'Here it is. It came in while you were getting the card index.'

'W. E. Carfax, and R. L. Jones?' French read inquiringly.

'Carfax is a junior clerk, and Jones a stone cutter and polisher: both in my opinion absolutely beyond suspicion.'

French nodded. 'Thank you, sir, I think that's about all I want at present. I should like one or two lists made out at your early convenience. One is a complete note of your staff, with a word or two of explanation as to who everybody is. Another a private note of those who might be expected to know what would be in the safe. And, of course, that vital list of what is missing.'

Norne agreed to supply these as soon as possible and French went on. 'I shall want next to make an examination of the safe with one or two experts. It would be a convenience if we could have this room?'

'That's easily arranged,' Norne agreed. 'We'll move out now.'

'Thank you, sir,' French said again, then to Carter: 'Run down and tell those fellows in the car to come up.' Carter vanished and French went on: 'One other point, sir, and I have done. You and Sir Ralph opened the safe and Mr Miles fingered his card index. We shall find finger-prints, I hope, on both. I want to take your prints, so as to eliminate them from those we shall follow up.'

'I have no objection,' said Norne and the others also agreed.

A moment later Carter returned with the photographer and finger-print expert. The prints of the three men were taken and they left the room. So began the second phase of the inquiry.

5

Enter Routine

French's first care was to make an inspection of the safe.

The large green door bore a plate with the maker's name; 'Russell Bros., Barking, London.' French noted the address, as a call on Messrs Russell would be an early item on his programme. The safe projected about six inches from the wall, showing its massive hinges.

'Get what prints you can before we open it,' he directed, standing back to let Boyle, the expert, get to work.

Boyle took his insufflator and projected clouds of fine greyish powder on to the smooth green surface. Then, partly by blowing and partly with a fine camel's hair brush, he removed the surplus deposited. A mass of prints, smudges and irregular marks became revealed. All of them were carefully photographed by the second man, Cooper.

Against the wall to the left of the safe and about thirty inches away stood the green painted steel letter file already mentioned. It was a couple of feet deep and, therefore, projected a foot and a half in front of the safe, and its top was just a little higher than the keyhole. It was the only piece of furniture close to the safe. French looked at it thoughtfully.

'Better do that too,' he said. 'One of the thieves might have rested his hand on it while he worked.'

The file was covered with impressions, all of which were duly photographed. Then while the technical men went on with the remainder of the room, French opened the safe.

He looked curiously at the interior. It was divided into pigeon holes of various sizes, some of which were filled with books and papers, some were fitted with nests of small drawers, some contained shallow wooden trays, and some were empty.

'You may do all this before we touch it,' he told Boyle. 'But I don't suppose we'll get much. These incredible fools have pawed the whole thing over. Opened every drawer, Norne said. If he'd wanted the thief to get clear away, he could scarcely have done more.'

As Boyle set to work he expressed his opinion of Norne in suitably forcible language. The interior of the safe revealed the same multitude of marks as the outside. One thing, however, was obvious to all three men. Many of the smudges indicated gloved fingers. It seemed unlikely, therefore, that any useful result would come from all their work.

However, that did not permit the shelving of any of it. Boyle and Cooper dealt with the marks. Then they reverted to the furniture while French returned to the safe.

He began by searching each drawer and shelf in the hope of finding some small object which the thief might have dropped. But he found nothing. Then he went on to the papers. These he did not examine so carefully, but he made sure that nothing was concealed among them which might prove a help.

The safe completed, he turned his attention to the room generally. Had the thief dropped anything there or left other traces? French examined every inch of the floor, desk, chairs and other furniture, but entirely without result.

The question of how the thief had entered the room then occupied his attention, but at this point was soon settled. According to Norne's statement neither of the doors—from the corridor and from the anteroom—were locked at night. On the other hand the window looked out on to Ronder Lane, with a sheer drop of about a hundred feet. The window could only have been reached by means of ropes from the roof, the chances of which French thought negligible.

The examination of the room complete, French turned to his next item, for already he had a rough programme made out in his mind. He sat down at Norne's desk and put through a call to the superintendent of the Guildford police. Explaining what had occurred, he asked for any available particulars of the death of Minter.

There was not much to tell. Minter had died; the doctor had refused a certificate; a post-mortem had been ordered; an inquest would be held as soon as the result was known. The case looked like one of suicide, but the superintendent gave this opinion with all reserve. He would with pleasure keep French advised of all developments.

'Well, super, there's just one thing I want,' said French, 'and that is the deceased's finger-prints. Will you let me have them?'

The super said he would have them taken at once, and French rang off.

The question of how the thief had got hold of the keys of the safe still seemed the most promising line of investigation. French stood up.

'You fellows finish what you're at and then get back to the Yard. You might check up those prints then, Boyle. The accountant's prints, that's the man who died at Guildford, will be sent up as soon as possible and you might check them up too. That'll be all then for the present.'

Tapping at the door, French went into the anteroom. Norne was seated in an armchair, dictating to Miss Barber.

'I wonder, sir, if you could come round with me to the banks now? By the time that you're back my fellows will be finished and you can have your room.'

'Of course, chief-inspector; I'll come at once.'

French signalled a taxi and they were driven to the head office of the London and Northern Bank, in Threadneedle Street. There Norne's name proved an immediate passport to the manager's office. Mr Suffolk gave one glance at his client's face and his own lengthened. However, he simply wished Norne good morning and waited for what was coming.

'I've got some pretty bad news for you, Suffolk,' Norne began, 'but first let me introduce Chief-Inspector French of Scotland Yard.'

The manager was polite, but this opening did not make him look any more cheerful. Having greeted French, he again sat waiting.

'We've had a robbery,' and Norne, without attempting to soften the news, went on to describe what had happened.

Mr Suffolk was appalled. It appeared, what French had not known, that the Norne account was somewhat over-drawn, and in the face of this news the manager did not see his bank getting back its money. Eagerly he inquired from French as to the prospects of recovering the missing stuff.

'It's in connection with that we want your help, sir,' French answered. 'Mr Norne tells me you hold a duplicate of one of the keys of his safe. I should like to know if you have this in your possession at the present time, and if so, whether it has recently been taken out.'

Suffolk looked at Norne. 'I didn't know we had that, Norne?' he questioned.

'You wouldn't,' Norne answered. 'It was with some other things in a locked box. The chief-inspector would like the box turned up, and I have the key and will open it here.'

The manager with a slightly aggrieved expression gave the necessary instructions and in a few moments the box was produced. Norne opened it.

'There's the key,' he said, pointing into the box.

'That's all right,' French returned. 'Now, sir,' he went on to Suffolk, 'I want to know how long it is since that box has been taken out, and who took it out?'

A clerk was appealed to. His book, he declared, bore a record of every time it had been asked for. The last occasion was over two years previously.

'That's probably correct,' Norne put in. 'Only stuff that is seldom required is kept in that box.'

'I should like to ask this young gentleman a question,' French said. 'Suppose the owner of that box were to come and say, "I want to open the box for a moment—not to take it away," is there no chance that the usual formalities might be omitted?'

'None,' answered the youth after a glance at his chief. 'You see, the box is not allowed out of the strong room without the necessary authority, and the client is never taken to the strong room. If it is taken out and opened and returned, it goes back on a new receipt.'

'That's quite correct,' Suffolk added. 'Personally I believe our system is quite watertight.'

'I'm sure it is, sir,' French said smoothly, 'but as you know, rules are not always kept as completely as they should. How, for example, about getting it by a forged order?'

Both men declared that their precautions would entirely prevent such a thing. They pointed out further that in the present instance the question would not arise, as the box had not been taken out at all—order or no order.

'That seems pretty conclusive evidence, Mr Norne,' French said as they left the bank. 'Now, I'd like you to come to the second bank and inquire about the other key.'

They went on to Norne's bank, Lloyd's, in Grace-church Street. Here their interview followed much the same lines as that they had just completed, and French left satisfied that as far as human testimony could be relied upon, this key had not been used either.

Having got rid of Norne with polite thanks for his help, French turned into a restaurant for a cup of coffee, the best substitute for a belated lunch for which he could afford time. As he sat munching rolls and butter with his gaze fixed firmly on the blank wall which bounded his forward vision, he tried to sum up what he had already learnt.

The safe had not been damaged, but had been opened in the normal way by means of its two keys.

Of these keys there were only two sets in existence: one held by Norne and his accountant, the other in the strong-rooms of the banks. That in the banks had not been used. Therefore it looked as if Norne's and the accountant's must have been.

Norne, however, had declared most positively that he

had not allowed his key out of his possession on any single occasion whatever. Was Norne lying, or was he honest but mistaken, or was his statement correct?

French saw that in a way it scarcely mattered what Minter had done with his key, provided he got the truth about Norne's. The safe could not be opened without Norne's. The first question then was: Was Norne reliable?

French felt that he couldn't say. The man had seemed straightforward, but he, French, had not seen enough of him to come to a definite conclusion. But on the face of it, it was unlikely that Norne should be lying. If he were, so far as French could see, it could only be for one of two reasons. Either the man was himself guilty of the theft—a rather far-fetched theory—or he was not going to admit to a negligence which would have been not far removed from criminal. In this latter case, however, he would have known the person who had the handling of the key, and to keep back this evidence would have been to take a very serious responsibility. On the whole, it seemed to French that, provisionally at all events, he must accept Norne's statement.

If so, could his key have been '*borrowed*' without his knowledge?

At the moment French did not see how, but the matter was obviously one for investigation. So far as he had gone, it certainly looked as if none of the known keys had been used.

But there was another possibility—not perhaps a very likely one, but one which had been in his mind from the start.

Suppose there was a third set of keys? French knew that extra keys were sometimes made for safes. It was a very old trick, occasionally practised by dishonest locksmiths in safe works. In fitting the keys they would have an opportunity of taking secret impressions. These could be smuggled home and extra keys could there be cut. An accomplice in the clerical side of the business would find out to whom the various safes in question were sold, and presently still another member of the gang would obtain access to the house where one of them had been installed, as a servant or a man from the gas works or the electricity station. He would not be watched, because the safe, being locked, would be considered secure, but with the extra keys he could make a fine haul. To guard against this form of robbery some careful people used two safes from different makers, placed one inside the other, on the grounds that no workman could get a key for more than one of them.

It was with this possibility in mind that French had noted the makers of the safe in Norne's office, and he decided that his next business would be to call on them.

A few minutes later he was shown into the office of Mr Russell, Senr., a shrewd-looking man with pleasant manners.

Mr Russell intimated that he would be glad to help the chief-inspector in any way in his power. But when he grasped the fact that French's business involved a reflection on his firm and their way of doing business, he became less expansive.

'But, my dear sir,' he said shortly, 'that trick is as old as the hills. You're not very complimentary to assume that we don't guard against it.'

French was apologetic, and Russell, mollified, presently agreed to describe their practice. He thought the chief-inspector would agree that it was as efficient as any that could be devised. French tactfully said he was sure of it.

It appeared that the firm were fully alive to the possibility of fraud or theft on the part of their men. For this reason only old hands who had been with them for many years, and of whose honesty they were completely satisfied, were entrusted with the fitting of the keys. These men, moreover, were paid a high rate of wages, so as to reduce temptation as far as possible.

At the same time further precautions were used where possible. In the case of safes with two keys each was cut by a different man separately, and only the foreman handled both keys. In the case brought forward by the chief-inspector, therefore, both locksmiths would have to have conspired together to commit a crime, a not very likely assumption.

The chief safeguard, however, was that Messrs Russell never sold a safe direct to a client. They dealt through agents, and it would have been almost impossible for the locksmiths to have learned the destination of any given safe. In the case in question that had been the procedure. The safe had been delivered to their agents in Victoria Street, who in turn had redirected it to Messrs Norne. No one at the Barking Works had known, or could have known, where it had gone.

French, feeling he had learnt all he could learn from Messrs Russell, returned to the Norne offices. There the list of missing stones was just being completed, and in a few minutes he had received it and was driving in a taxi to the Yard.

It happened that Sir Mortimer Ellison had not yet gone home, and French went to his room and gave him a concise report of the affair.

'I agree with you, it looks like an inside job,' the Assistant

Commissioner declared when he had finished. 'What sort are the crowd that you've met?'

'They certainly seem all right, sir,' French returned, 'but, of course, you never know.'

'You'll have to find out if any of them are in low water, or anything of that sort. They told you the firm was not doing too well. How serious was that?'

'I can't answer that yet, sir,' French admitted. 'I have it in my notes as one of the first things to be gone into. I want tonight to get the list of missing stuff out. It's rather a document,' and French held up his sheaf of typewritten pages.

'My word, yes. What about handling the case yourself?'

'I was going to ask you about that, sir.'

'I think you'd better. It's a big case and we must get the stuff.'

'Very good, sir,' French said quietly. He was not unconscious of the implied compliment in the Assistant Commissioner's words, but he recognised also the measure of responsibility involved. To fail to get both thieves and booty would be exceedingly unpleasant for himself.

He took his sheets to the printer and drew up a list of those to whom the circulars were to be sent. These included not only the police generally in this country and Amsterdam and other places where precious stones were handled in large quantities, but also certain legitimate dealers, to whom it was hoped some of the stones might be offered.

French had told Norne that when the reporters called he should allow them any reasonable information about the robbery that they asked for. As late that night he reached home and sat down for a few moments by the fire before going to bed, he saw that the papers had not lost their opportunity. Flare headlines described the affair as the biggest jewel robbery of the century, and the paragraphs following were written up with great skill. They did not convey much information, but they appeared to do so, and were exceedingly entertaining reading.

French was pleased. The information given was just what the thief or thieves would expect to see, and nothing in the nature of a clue was hinted at.

For some little time French sat on puffing gently at his pipe, while he considered his plan of campaign for the next day or for that day, for it was already past twelve o'clock. Then at last, his mind made up, he went upstairs and in a few minutes was sleeping the sleep of the weary.

The first item on his programme for the following morning was a visit to the Yard finger-print department, and as soon as he had gone through his letters he went across.

'Morning, Boyle,' he said. 'Have you got that print of the late accountant's from Guildford?'

'Yes, sir, I've just been going into it,' the man answered. 'It's all over the place. Look here.'

He pointed to a sheaf of photographic enlargements, upon which he had been working. 'Here,' he picked up one, 'is the Guildford print. And here,' he pointed to the others, 'are prints from the inside of the safe. There's no doubt they're the same.'

French nodded.

'That applies to Norne's also,' went on Boyle, producing more photographs. 'Those two men have been pretty well over the whole safe, inside and out, though there are more of Norne's prints than of Minter's.'

'Any others inside?' French asked, going at once to the essential point.

'Some of Miles's and these.' Boyle produced still more photographs.

'These' were smudges of the shape and size of finger-prints which appeared in several places, sometimes cutting across and wiping out the other prints, same as had been found on the outside of the safe.

'Gloves?' said French.

'Yes, sir: gloves. Thin gloves.'

'Indicating a fourth party?'

Though French put the question, he was really only thinking aloud. Did the fact that there were gloves neces-sarily prove that a fourth party was involved? Boyle evidently thought so, as was shown by his ready 'Quite so, sir.' But French was not so sure. If Norne and Minter were the culprits, they would probably have worn gloves as a blind: to produce this very suggestion that someone else had been there. No, unless there were further details he could not build up a theory.

'Very well, that's the safe. What about the rest of the room?'

'I've got several prints that I've not yet checked up,' Boyle returned. 'But, sir, I wondered if it was necessary to check them all up? There would be callers going in and out all day, and in any case, even if we found someone's print, it wouldn't prove he was the thief.'

To French this seemed sound. Besides, if the thief had worn gloves while working at the safe, he had probably done so during the entire visit.

'Right,' he agreed, 'keep them for a last resource. You can't get anything from the glove marks?'

'Only a suggestion that the man had large hands. This photograph is actual size; see the spread between the thumb and the first two fingers. Of course, I know that's not very reliable.'

French fitted his own hand over the prints. To cover them he had to keep his fingers and thumb well spread out. It was true what Boyle had said, that deductions from such facts were apt to mislead; at the same time French thought that in this case the suggestion was probably sound.

'I'll bear it in mind,' he admitted. 'That all?'

'That's all, I'm afraid, sir.'

French walked slowly back to his room. Though the value of finger-prints had become almost negligible since criminals had become aware of the dangers which lurked in them, he was still disappointed that this line of inquiry had not yielded more. As the matter stood, it looked as if the thief must be a biggish man, but this was by no means certain. Not much help so far, though better than nothing.

Sitting down in his chair, French looked once again at his notes. 'Finger-prints' seemed to be worked out for the moment. His next item was 'General interviews with staff,' and to that he now turned.

It represented, he knew, a mass of uninteresting and tedious work, pushed forward probably against unwillingness and obstruction, and probably ninety-nine per cent of it leading nowhere. Everyone in the Norne firm, with perhaps a few minor exceptions, would have to be interviewed. There was just the chance that someone might have seen an unknown person in the building, or a known person at an unusual hour or performing some unusual action. Even so remote a possibility could not be neglected.

It was much too big a job for him to tackle single-handed. He therefore took half a dozen men with him to the Norne building and set them to work. Certain members of the staff he had noted as important, and these he undertook himself. The first was Miss Barber, Norne's secretary. With Carter in attendance he presently knocked at her door.

She was a decidedly good-looking young woman and was very conscious of the fact. Her manner was supercilious, and French felt that only his chief-inspectorship saved him from actual scorn. He could not, however, complain of her answers to his questions, which were full enough and concisely given. She had been, she said with some sense of grievance, in the office on Saturday up till close on two o'clock. Mr Norne had gone as usual about twelve, but he had left some urgent work which she had stayed to finish. Yes, she thought she was the last to leave the building. No, so far as she knew, the cleaning staff had not turned up when she left. She had noticed nothing unusual at any time, nor had she seen anyone other than the people she always saw. On Monday morning nothing appeared to have been moved in her office or in Mr Norne's. In fact, she could give no information of any kind about the affair. Had she been able to do so, she would have done it before that.

French then gently pumped her as to her impressions of her fellow workers. Norne she evidently respected and, French thought, feared slightly. She liked in a condescending way Sir Ralph and Ricardo, evidently disliked Sloley and thought Sheen a fool. On Sloley she was particularly severe. French's shrewd suspicions were confirmed by an admission that he 'would be a bit too fresh if you'd let him,' and the fact that once she had seen him, not drunk, but 'happy'.

'How did he show it?' French asked with amused curiosity.

'Singing in the chief's room,' she answered shortly.

French mildly suggested that a man might sing without deserving the stigma of 'happiness'. But she said pertly that everyone had his own opinion about decent conduct, and French let it go at that.

But though Miss Barber was superior about most of those she met, there was one exception. Minter she had evidently admired. Not only did she consider him 'a bit of a genius in his own line,' but she had obviously liked him personally, and appeared genuinely sorry for his death.

Sheen's was the next name on French's list. From him he hoped to learn more. There were not only the general questions about possible unusual happenings, but he wished to get the secretary's statement about his and Sloley's meeting with Minter on the Saturday evening, as well as his story of the events at Guildford on the Sunday. He spent a good deal of time with Sheen, but he didn't learn anything of importance which he had not already known. Sheen said that the idea of making use of the list of shareholders had occurred to him on that Saturday morning, but he was doubtful as to its utility and had not then mentioned it to anyone. He wanted first to work the thing out and see if the result seemed worth while. When he had finished he was agreeably surprised to find that the information it gave was really helpful. He would have then discussed it with the others, but by that time they had left the building. In the afternoon and evening he had social engagements, at which Sloley was also present. He had, however, taken an opportunity of mentioning the thing to Sloley, and, Sloley seeming impressed, he had rung up Minter to tell him his results, and to ask his opinion on one or two points about which he himself was not satisfied.

Minter had also seemed interested, and when he told Sheen that he was not going down to Guildford till the 8.15 train, Sheen asked him to call at the office on the way, where he would meet him and give him the actual papers. Minter had agreed, saying he would look over them in the train and report to the others.

This arrangement had been carried out. Between his engagements, he and Sloley had met Minter at the office, handed him the list, and discussed the points in question. Minter had then gone on to Waterloo, and Sheen and Sloley had walked across to the Aldwych Theatre.

French did not greatly take to Sheen. The man seemed self-opinionated and interested only in his own affairs, and French found himself sympathising with Miss Barber's view that he was a fool.

Sloley was not often to be found in the Norne offices, but the burglary had kept him hanging about in the hope of learning further details, and French seized the opportunity to get his statement also.

Sloley, however, had nothing fresh to tell. He confirmed in all essential points what Sheen had said—what, indeed, had been said by Norne at French's first interview. Sloley was willing enough to give his information, but French did not take to him either, believing him to be noisy and aggressive and a potential bully.

Mrs Rebecca Turbot, the head charwoman, interviewed at her home, said that she and her helpers usually cleaned the offices on Saturday afternoon. On the previous Saturday, however, she had an engagement in the early afternoon which made her late getting to work. Instead, therefore, of finishing about six, it was eight o'clock before she had done. Just before leaving she had seen the three men arrive; Minter first by himself, and then Sloley and Sheen together. She had left immediately after, and on her way out had noticed a taxi standing before the door.

This confirmed Sloley's and Sheen's statements, and French felt that he had obtained all the information he could hope for from these persons. Norne, Sir Ralph Osenden, and Miles, the foreman, he had already interrogated, and as he had now heard the most promising witnesses without obtaining any very clear lead towards a working theory, he began to feel a little baffled and uncertain as to what should be his next step.

However, as he was considering the matter, it was settled for him. A clerk came up to say that he was wanted on the telephone in Miss Barber's room.

6

Enter the Borough Force

The call was from Superintendent* Fenning of the Guildford Borough Police, sent through the Yard. It was Fenning with whom French had already been in communication about the death of Minter, and from whom he had obtained the deceased's finger-prints.

A couple of years previously he had met Fenning. That was when he had been in Guildford in connection with what had come to be known as the Hog's Back Mystery; the strange disappearance of Dr James Earle from his house not far from Seale. During that long drawn-out investigation French had got to know the triangle of country between Guildford, Farnham and Godalming like the palm of his own hand, and though he had not come a great deal in contact with the Guildford super, he had seen enough of him to form a high opinion of his merits.

---

* There is no Superintendent in the Guildford Borough Police. The rank is used to avoid referring to an existing officer.—F.W.C.

'There has been a development down here,' came Fenning's voice. 'I don't know that I care to discuss it over the 'phone. I wondered if you would care either to come down or to send a representative who could report to you?'

For French the suggestion came at just the right moment. He was feeling at a loose end, and it was obvious that if his presence were required at Guildford, no one could say that his activities in Town were lacking in energy.

'I'll go myself,' he replied promptly. 'You may expect me by the next train.'

Having satisfied himself that the men who were interviewing the Norne staff were getting on reasonably well, he set off for Waterloo. There he had time for a snack before his train. An hour later he was greeted by Superintendent Fenning at the Borough headquarters.

'Very pleased to see you again, chief-inspector,' said the super heartily. 'And very pleased to have to say "Chief." We were all very glad when we heard of that little addition to your title.'

He was a good fellow, Fenning. French found it pleasant to be greeted in so kindly a way.

'Very good of you, super,' he answered. 'I feel myself lucky, I meet with so much kindness. All the same I envy you people who live within reach of the country, particularly when it's country like yours here.'

For a time they chatted. Fenning had a nephew at the Yard and he begged for an unbiassed opinion of the young man. French asked after Superintendent Sheaf of Farnham and several other friends he had made at the time of the Hog's Back case. At last they came to business.

'It's about the death of this man Minter,' Fenning began. 'I don't know if you heard the details?'

'I heard what Norne and Sloley and Sheen and Ricardo had to say about it,' French answered. 'I don't know if their stories covered everything.'

'I should fancy not,' Fenning returned dryly. 'I'll tell you. As you know, Minter was unwell on the Saturday afternoon, but was able to come down to Norne's by the 8.15 from Waterloo. He had to go to bed on arrival and was seen only by the butler and Norne. Norne reported him looking ill to the other guests, and that,' Fenning made a gesture emphasising the point, 'was all.'

'I heard about that.'

'Quite: I needn't repeat it. In the morning Minter was found dead and the doctor wouldn't give a certificate. Everyone assumed natural causes, though one or two suggested suicide or accident as an alternative.'

'What sort of accident? Poison?'

'That was the suggestion: that the man had taken by mistake an overdose of some drug or sleeping draught. There were no facts to support the idea, except that the man was dead, and if it should prove not to be from natural causes, no other explanation could be put up.'

French nodded without speaking. 'Well, I had a chat with Dr Hawthorn, who examined him, but he's a secretive sort of chap and I didn't get a lot out of him. He said he couldn't say anything definite until he had made a postmortem, but he advised me not to banish the idea of foul play from my mind.'

French whistled. 'A broadish hint!'

'Yes. As a result, of course, I made a much more careful inquiry than I otherwise would. I found one or two interesting things about which I'll tell you in a moment. But I confess I didn't take the case very seriously till this morning.

Shortly before I rang you up I got the result of the autopsy. I think, chief-inspector, it will surprise you. Minter was murdered by suffocation.'

'Suffocation!'

'I thought you weren't expecting that. Dr Hawthorn says there's no doubt of it whatever. He gives the technical details. Shall I read them?'

'No good to me. The results are all I want.'

'He says it was done with great care and skill; there is scarcely an outward sign on the body. All the same its appearance suggested suffocation. But he was by no means sure. So when he could find no other cause of death, he refused the certificate. He wasn't going to say it was murder till he was certain, but neither was he was going to take any risks. He therefore rang us up and remained in the room till we arrived.'

'A good man.'

'One of the best, though as I said, secretive: he might have told me what was in his mind. He says the deceased had been tied up. Both wrists and ankles show bruises, but they are so extremely slight that the tying must have been done gently and with something soft. He suggests broad bands of silk or something of that kind. And he says that the appearances suggest to him, though he can't be sure of it, that the deceased did struggle, though in a very feeble way.'

'What about the mouth? Does that not show marks?'

'Quite right: he had been gagged. The mouth is bruised, but surprisingly little. Here again something soft must have been used.'

French moved uneasily. 'By heck, super, this is a surprising turn. And a nasty one. I'm always glad when a chap that murders by suffocation goes to the scaffold. Hanging's about too good for him.'

'I agree. In this case it was an easy job. The poor fellow couldn't put up any real resistance. Hadn't the strength.'

'That all the doctor says?'

'There was just one other point. The inside of the mouth was more bruised than the outside. The doctor suggests that a cloth must have been used and the mouth stuffed full, and then the nose held.'

'We'll have to get that fellow, super.'

'I don't know,' said Fenning slowly, 'that I haven't got him already. I have something more to tell you.'

French grinned. 'You're as bad as Dr Hawthorn,' he declared. 'What have you still got up your sleeve?'

'Perhaps a good deal: perhaps nothing,' the super rejoined. 'I don't know yet. I'll have to wait for the analyst's report before I can tell you.'

'What is that: the stomach and organs?'

'Yes, and something else as well. I'll tell you.'

The super paused to light a second cigarette, then went on. 'On the table at the head of the bed we found two objects. One was a small-sized bottle of aspirin, half-empty. The other was an ordinary glass or tumbler, containing a drop or two of what looked like water. The bottle had apparently belonged to the deceased, as no one admitted having seen it before. The glass was part of the room furniture and had been taken from the wash basin.

'Owing to the doctor's attitude we tested both for finger-prints, a precaution that I dare say we mightn't otherwise have troubled about. We got a rather curious result. I wish, chief-inspector, you could have seen the glass yourself. I'd be interested to hear your remarks. But it's with the analyst.'

'Tell me.'

'I can do a little better. Here are some fairly decent photographs.' Fenning opened a folder and passed over four full-plate prints. 'These are of the glass, showing it slightly enlarged. They're taken from north, east, south, and west, so that when placed in that order they give a record of the markings right round the glass. That thumb-print, for instance, that you see on the left of what I call the east print, is the same as that on the right of the north print. You follow?'

'Clearly. It's as good as having the glass.'

'Then what do you make of it?'

There were six prints on the glass, all clearly marked. But whereas five of them were reasonably complete, the sixth was partially wiped out. The top and bottom were gone as if the glass had been cleaned in those areas, leaving a narrow sharp-edged band across the centre of the print. The complete five represented the thumb and four fingers of a right hand.

'Are these Minter's?' French asked.

For answer Fenning passed over a set of cards. 'Those are Minter's,' he said.

It scarcely needed the lens Fenning also pushed across for French to identify them. The prints were Minter's; that is, the five complete ones. The portion of the sixth belonged to someone else. French looked up inquiringly.

'Something interesting about those prints, chief-inspector,' Fenning said, sitting back in his chair and rubbing his hands; 'unless I'm altogether barking up the wrong tree.'

French began whistling softly below his breath as he bent over the photographs. 'Do you mean the five?' he asked.

'The five, yes. But you may not be able to see what I'm trying to get at on the photographs. It's much clearer on the glass itself. In fact, it wasn't till I noticed it that I had the photos taken.' He paused, then continued. 'I should tell you that on the bottle of aspirins there were three prints, Minter's thumb and first and second fingers, very clear.'

'Only those?'

'Only those.'

'And except for that bit of a sixth print, only Minter's five on the glass. Is that what you mean, super? That there should be more?'

Fenning nodded. 'That's one thing, chief-inspector, though it's not the most important.'

'If the glass was taken from the washing-table, it must have been put there by someone, presumably the chambermaid. Should it bear her prints? She might have given it a final wipe with a cloth on setting it down and not handled it with her bare fingers.'

'Something else about the prints, chief-inspector. Have another look at them.'

French frowned as he concentrated on the problem. It would not do for a country policeman, not even the superintendent of an important borough like Guildford, to see anything that he, French, had missed. The prints seemed all right. They were clear and they were obviously genuine. And they were just where one would expect to find them if the glass had been lifted to drink from it.

Ah! but were they? French looked with even keener interest. The fingers seemed to be correctly placed and spaced. But what about the thumb?

'Have you another glass there?' French asked.

Fenning clapped his hands. 'Good for you, chief-inspector,' he exclaimed. 'I see you've got it.' He stepped out of the room, returning in a moment with a glass. French picked it up, placing his fingers as nearly as possible in the positions shown on the photographs. Then he stared at his thumb. The axis or centre-line lay at a different angle to that of Minter's: different by about thirty degrees.

Slowly he began to experiment. Holding the glass in his other hand, he tried to alter his grip so as to turn his thumb through that thirty degrees. But he could not do so. He looked at Fenning.

'They've been faked on,' he said.

Something like admiration showed in Fenning's eyes. 'Because of the thumb?' he asked.

'Yes, the thumb's, so to speak, out of drawing.'

'That's the phrase! As I see it, someone has wiped that glass and pressed the fingers on it. The fingers are right enough because they were all done together and they held their position. But the thumb was put on separately at the opposite side of the glass. In doing it the glass got twisted, and the thumb-print doesn't register up with the others.'

'I entirely agree,' said French. 'I had a case something like it before.'

'You had?'

'Yes: case of a solicitor found shot. He was supposed to have committed suicide, and we got his prints on the gun: his prints only. But we found the same thing there: the prints were badly put on. They were all there, but they didn't register the relative positions of the fingers of a hand.'

The admiration of the superintendent seemed to suffer a slight eclipse.

'Well, there it is,' he said with truth. 'But there's more in it than that, chief-inspector. Have another look.'

'I know,' said French, who had regained his self-assurance. 'You mean the other print? The print that was only partly wiped off?'

'The print that was missed when the glass was cleaned,' Fenning said grimly. 'Yes, we recognised the importance of that print. We sent a photograph up to your people to see if they could identify it.'

'And could they? I didn't hear about it.'

'They could. It was Norne's!'

French gave an ejaculation of surprise, partly because he really was surprised, and partly to indicate appreciation of the super's story. Then he sat silent, thinking over this unexpected development.

The more he did so, the more significant it seemed to become. It was true, of course, that he had recognised that the accountant might have been murdered and that any member of Norne's household might have murdered him. But he had looked on the matter as a mere academic possibility; something that should be noted if every contingency were to be covered, but not something which need be seriously considered. Now consideration of it had become vital.

But might there not be even more in it than that? French whistled below his breath as he followed up the thought. It was a habit his subordinates knew well, and and they also knew that when they heard the soft hissing sounds, it was more prudent to keep silence than to speak. Fenning heard them and took them as a tribute to his story.

French continued his mental groping. If Norne had murdered Minter, could it be that the crime was connected in some obscure way with the theft? Admittedly he didn't see how; and yet . . . If there were no connection, it would certainly be a strange coincidence that the two things should happen in the same surroundings.

'By Jove, super,' he said at last, 'that gives one something to think about.'

Fenning beamed. His story had gone better even than he had hoped. 'I thought it would probably interest you,' he admitted.

'Norne didn't mention the aspirin in his first statement,' went on French. 'What does he say now?'

'I've not asked him. I've only just got to know what I've told you.'

'Quite. Now, I'd like to be clear about your theory, super. From your sending the bottle and glass to the analyst, it looks as if you suspected poison. But if Minter was suffocated, how would that come in?'

'I didn't suspect poison: I suspected a large dose of aspirin. Something to keep the man quiet.'

French smote his thigh. 'That's the ticket,' he cried. 'That's the point I couldn't get. Frail and small as Minter was, it wouldn't be easy either to tie him up or to smother him without a struggle. A dose of aspirin might make all the difference. The man would be so drowsy the job could be done with ease.'

'That's what I thought. Well, chief-inspector, I rang you up before taking any step, because I wondered if you might be interested in connection with your own case.'

'You mean you think this is connected with the theft?'

'I wondered if you would think so.'

'I've been wondering it myself since you told me. Candidly, I don't know for the moment see how it could be, and yet I admit the thing is very suggestive.'

'I thought so, and that is really what I wanted to discuss with you. If there's any chance of a connection between this and the theft, it occurs to me that we ought to work together. Else we'll overlap and we might even spoil each other's inquiry.'

French was enthusiastic. He entirely agreed. Nothing would, indeed, give him greater pleasure than to work with the super. He had to admit that it was not often that he met with such a broad-minded outlook. Well, since the super had consulted him, he would like to make a suggestion. 'It seems to me, if you agree, that we should hold our hand for the present. You could get the inquest adjourned on some technical ground that wouldn't put the wind up Norne. Then let us keep what we know dark until the Minter affair is gone into thoroughly. I suggest that while you continue looking into the details of the crime here in Guildford, I go into the history of Minter and his dealings and health and all about him. That must be done in Town. Probably between the two of us we'd find a motive, or which at present I can see no suggestion.'

Fenning said he entirely approved this proposal, which, indeed, he was about to make himself. The talk then became more technical and some points of procedure were settled. In brief, these meant little more than that both officers would do their utmost in their respective spheres and pool results, helping each other in every way possible.

At the end of the discussion Fenning made an offer which French thought not only correct, but generous.

'You're going to work on Minter,' he said. 'It occurs to

me that you might like to see the body and the bedroom at Norne's and so on before you return to Town?'

Nothing could have suited French better. He had, indeed, decided to ask Fenning if he could do so, but he much preferred the offer to come from the super himself.

'Good,' Fenning returned. 'Then let's go right on at once.'

Fenning put away the photographs, slipped a notebook into his pocket, and rang for his car.

'We'll see the body first,' he explained, 'and then drive up to Norne's. Will you come along, chief-inspector?'

7

A Change of Scene

French and Fenning soon reached the mortuary. Fenning unlocked the door and they passed in.

The body lay on a slab, covered with a sheet. Fenning pulled this back and the two men stood gazing.

French was surprised by the natural appearance of the remains. All that he could see in any way out of the common was a faint suggestion of violet in the pallor of the face and neck, a slight congestion in the eyes, and just a trace of froth about the lips. The bruises were so slight that had it not been for the doctor's report he probably would not have noticed them at all. His opinion of Hawthorn rose sharply.

He was struck also by the deceased's small size and light build. Probably he was not more than five feet six or thereabouts, and French was sure he weighed less than ten stone. The face looked old and drawn. The hair, though still plentiful, was white, the cheeks sunken, and the hands thin and claw-like.

'Mrs Minter has been down here and seen him,' said

Fenning. 'I wanted her not to, but she insisted. Of course, it's been a help in a way. It settles the question of formal identification.'

'When is the body to be handed over?'

'After the inquest tomorrow morning: if the doctor's ready, as I expect he will be. I had already decided to do what you suggest, and the inquest will be adjourned after the minimum formal evidence. What about going on, chief-inspector?'

Leaving the mortuary, they got into Fenning's car and drove out for a short distance along the Godalming road. Then turning to the right, they ascended the hill to Guildown. First they passed through a residential area of good houses, each in its well-planted grounds, then came out on the open slopes of the hill. Guildown was really the northern end of the Hog's Back; indeed, the ancient Farnham road, which ran from Guildford straight on to the Hog's Back, passed immediately behind the higher houses. Severno, Norne's villa, was one of these, but it stood alone, about quarter of a mile farther from the town than the rest, its drive forming the continuation of the made road. French was delighted with the view, and when they reached the gate he stopped for a moment to enjoy it.

The house was built in the form of an L, with the sides pointing south and east respectively and the hall door in the angle between the two. To the north was the projection of the new billiard room, which changed the L into a rather clumsy T. To the south and east lay the view, and on these sides there were only flower beds and low shrubs. The old track to Farnham ran behind the house to the west, and Norne had planted most of the intervening space with trees, some of which had already grown to a fair size. To the north, behind the new billiard room wing, lay the garage and kitchen garden.

The two men walked round the grounds to get a general view of the layout, then approaching the door, Fenning rang. Immediately it was opened by Jeffries.

'Good afternoon,' said Fenning pleasantly. 'I want to show my colleague the room where Mr Minter died, and then I think we should like to ask you another question or two.'

French looked with approval at the butler. He thought he knew his type. Old-fashioned, careful, loyal and straight-forward: that was how at first sight he would have described him. He imagined his statement would be accur-ate and truthful, though, of course, this was only an opinion and, like other opinions, would have to be tested.

'You know your way, sir,' Jeffries said with a motion of his hand towards the stair. 'If you ring when you're ready, I shall be at your service.'

'Thank you, Jeffries. Come along, will you, chief-inspector?'

Minter's room, which had been sealed by Fenning, was situated in the back of the southern wing, facing the trees and the old Farnham road. It was not large, but was supplied with luxurious built-in furniture, electric heating, hidden lighting except for the bed reading-lamp, and an elaborately fitted private bathroom. Beside the bed was a hinged shelf bearing a few books.

'He was lying in bed when he was found,' Fenner explained, 'and there on that shelf at the head of the bed were the bottle and glass. The lights were all off except that in the bathroom. The bathroom door was open, and that made a reduced though sufficient light in here. Norne states that this arrangement obtained when he visited the room, and that Minter explained that when he had these bilious attacks he liked a little light, but that the full glare was too much for his eyes.'

'Reasonable enough.'

'Quite. I've had bilious headaches myself and I know how you feel. Except for these matters, the room was as you see it. And, of course, that Minter's clothes have been taken away.'

'There doesn't seem to be anything of interest in the room, other than what you've told me,' said French after a careful look round.

'As a matter of fact, there isn't,' Fenning agreed. 'Now, I've already taken a statement from Alice, the housemaid, but after our discovery with the glass we might ask her a few more questions.'

This again was exactly what French wished for. 'Right,' he said; 'suppose we take the butler first,' and clinched the affair by ringing the bell. In a moment Jeffries appeared.

'Come in and close the door, will you?' said Fenning. 'My friend would like to hear your statement from yourself. Doesn't believe I could repeat it correctly, you know.' There was the suspicion of a wink about Fenning's left eye as he spoke.

Jeffries bowed correctly, but his expression showed that he appreciated the super's friendliness.

'Sit down here and tell the story once again from the beginning,' Fenning went on, and thus adjured, Jeffries sat down and began.

'The first thing, gentlemen, was that Mr Norne told me he was having five gentlemen to stay over the weekend.

Three would be coming down in time for dinner on Saturday evening, and two late that night. He said he had arranged with Mrs Peacock about their rooms.'

'Mrs Peacock?' asked French.

'The housekeeper, sir. Well, the necessary preparations were made. Then on Saturday afternoon there came a telephone from Mr Minter, saying he was not feeling well and that he wouldn't come down till after dinner: at 9.08, he said. I replied that would be all right and that the car would meet him at the station.'

'Did he ask for Mr Norne?' Fenning inquired.

'No, sir. He asked who was speaking and I said Mr Norne's butler. Then he said, "You needn't disturb him now, but will you tell Mr Norne." I conveyed the message to Mr Norne at once.'

'And what did Mr Norne say?'

'He made no special comment.'

'Quite.'

'The other two guests—'

'Just a moment,' French interposed. 'Can you say at what time Mr Minter 'phoned?'

'You asked me that, sir,' Jeffries looked at Fenning, 'and I wasn't able to answer it exactly. But it was about half-past four.'

'About half-past four,' French repeated. 'Good enough.'

'I arranged with Whatman, that's the chauffeur, to meet Mr Minter at 9.08. He arrived as expected. I thought he certainly did look a sick man. He was hunched forward and was shivering. Of course, it was a cold night. I said, "Would you like to see Mr Norne at once or go to your room first?" He said, "Tell you the truth, I'm not feeling well and I'd like to go to bed. I'll be all right in the morning."

'I said, "Very good, sir. Come this way," and I carried his suitcase up here. I wanted to unpack and to help him to bed, but he wouldn't allow me. "I'm accustomed to do for myself," he said. "I can manage." I was going out, but he stopped me. "I'd like to see Mr Norne when I've settled down a bit," he said. "Would you ask him to look in, say, in half an hour?" I gave Mr Norne the message at ten o'clock and he went up.'

'You saw him go?'

'Yes, sir.'

'Did you see him come down again?'

'Yes, sir; in about five or six minutes.'

'Did anyone else visit Mr Minter that night?' French put in.

'No, sir.'

'I'm not doubting you, but how are you so sure of that?'

'I would have heard them and seen their shadow. I'll tell you. When Mr Norne went down I had finished for the night, excepting that I didn't go to bed in case I should be wanted when the two gentlemen came about one o'clock. As a matter of fact, I was wanted. I had to help Mr Sloley to put away his car, take up the gentlemen's suitcases, and help generally. I therefore lay down on my bed, but I opened the door of my room, so that I should hear if either of the gentlemen in the library should go to bed. I should have heard if anyone had gone to Mr Minter's room, and it happens that a light on the stairs throws a shadow of anyone passing into my room and I'd have seen that.'

'You didn't sleep at all?'

'No, sir.'

'Were you reading?'

90

For the first time Jeffries seemed slightly confused. 'I was doing a crossword puzzle, sir,' he admitted with hesitation.

French grinned. 'I sympathise with you there,' he said. 'Many a one I've done myself. I think, super, if Jeffries doesn't mind, we'd like to see his room and where the shadow falls.'

Fenning agreed and Jeffries led the way. Opposite the head of the stairs was a door, opening into a passage which led to the servants' quarters. In a few feet this passage turned at right angles, and at the turn was Jeffries' door. The head of his bed was opposite the door, and it was therefore obvious that with the two doors open he could lie on his bed and see the head of the stairs. Moreover, a light from halfway up the stairs shone directly in, and this light would necessarily be obscured if anyone passed from the stairs to the wing in which Minter was sleeping.

After considering all this, French found himself forced to the conclusion that no one had entered the deceased's room while Jeffries was on the watch. A word to Fenning showed that he was equally convinced.

'That takes us up to about one o'clock,' French went on. 'It was about one that Mr Sloley and Mr Sheen arrived?'

'Shortly before one, sir; about ten minutes to.'

'Very well, it takes us up to ten minutes to one. Did they go to bed soon?'

'Yes, they had drinks and went in about ten minutes.'

'I take it you also closed your door and went to sleep?'

'Yes, sir.'

'Then someone might have gone to Mr Minter's room after one o'clock?'

Jeffries seemed somewhat taken aback. 'I suppose they might,' he admitted slowly.

French nodded, exchanging glances with Fenning.

'Very well, what was the next thing?' the super went on.

'Mr Norne had told me on his way downstairs not to call Mr Minter in the morning. I therefore didn't do so. But when the others were at breakfast Mr Norne told me to ask him if he'd like his breakfast upstairs. I came up and knocked, two or three times. Then I opened the door and looked in. Mr Minter was in bed and when I called him he didn't move. I went closer and then'—Jeffries seemed even now upset at the thought of it— 'I saw he was dead. I went down and told Mr Norne and he came up. He sent me at once to ring up Dr Hawthorn, and then after a few minutes Dr Hawthorn sent me to ring up you, sir.'

'I follow. Now tell me this,' the super continued, 'did you hear any unusual sounds that night?'

Jeffries shook his head decidedly. 'No, sir; nothing of the kind.'

'And there's nothing else you can tell us that might bear on the subject?'

'Nothing, sir.'

'Well,' declared the super, 'we're both much obliged to you, Jeffries. I wish you'd send in Alice. Tell her we'll not keep her long: just a question or two.'

Jeffries allowed himself a faintly sardonic smile at this, but he bowed politely and said he would give the message.

'That all works in,' French said with some eagerness when they were alone. 'Minter asks for Norne to give him Sheen's list. Norne had intended to go up to see him, but this request makes things all the easier. Norne realises that he cannot murder him then, for though ill, Minter is still in possession of all his faculties and would struggle. But he persuades him to take one or two aspirins. Actually he gives him a number, broken up. Then after one o'clock, when Minter is drugged and everyone else is in bed, he slips back and smothers him.'

''Pon my soul, chief-inspector, it's like enough.'

'I think,' went on French, 'we can see a step farther. Norne did the smothering so carefully that he believed he had left no traces. If there was nothing to suggest smothering, Minter could only have died from the overdose of the drug. And if there were no prints on the glass but Minter's, there was proof that Minter had taken the stuff himself; that is, that the affair was either accident or suicide.'

'I'll bet you're right. Norne never believed suspicion would arise.'

'And still doesn't.'

'And still doesn't. And that's the way to keep him.'

French's reply was interrupted by the entrance of Alice, a pretty girl in housemaid's uniform. 'You sent for me, sir?' she said to Fenning.

'Thank you, Alice; we just wanted to ask one or two questions. Sit down for a moment, won't you?'

The girl sat down. She was evidently nervous, but Fenning's manner was pleasant and she soon pulled herself together.

'It was about the glass that we found on that table at the head of the bed. Do you remember?'

Alice didn't remember. She was struck all of a heap when the thing had happened and hadn't paid any attention to glasses. She had, however, seen that there was a carafe and glass on the washstand, and on looking over she now saw that the glass was missing. Fenning asked her to bring in a glass of the same kind, and she produced one identical with that of the photograph.

93

'Did you clean the glass when you were preparing the room for Mr Minter?' the super went on.

This question, it was soon apparent, lacked in tact. It was a personal reflection on the perfect housemaid. French stepped into the breach.

'What the super means is, just how did you clean it?' he explained. 'Was it done outside and brought in finished, or did you do it here?'

In this inquiry French was allowed to perceive that he was skating on thin ice. However, by dint of assurances that her excellent technique was not being called in question, he at last discovered what he wanted to know.

The glass had been washed and polished in the room. It had not been handled in a cloth, but Alice had placed it upon the washstand with her bare hand. It should therefore have borne her finger-prints.

Alice could give no further help. She had heard nothing in the night nor had she noticed anything unusual at any time during the weekend. Thanking her again, Fenning dismissed her.

'My compliments to Mrs Peacock,' he said as she was moving out, 'and if she could spare me a few minutes here, I should be obliged.'

'I'll tell her,' said Alice, and vanished.

The housekeeper proved to be an elderly, dried-up and very official type of woman. She had attended during the weekend strictly to her business and to nothing else. On receiving information from Mr Norne that a weekend party was expected, she had with his advice allocated and prepared the rooms and given the necessary instructions to the servants. She had not personally seen Mr Minter, and beyond the facts that he had come and gone to bed at once, and next morning had been found dead, she knew nothing of the circumstances. No, she had seen nothing in any way unusual, nor had she heard anything in the night.

'That seems to cover the obvious inquiries in the house,' Fenning said when she had gone. 'Anything else you'd like to do before we go?'

'I'd like a word with the chauffeur,' French returned. 'If I'm to follow up Minter's day, as I probably shall have to, I might as well get the journey checked over at first hand.'

'I hadn't forgotten Whatman. We'll see him on the way out. Then that's all here.'

They went downstairs and round to the garage. Whatman was shining up the bright parts of Norne's big car. He was an elderly man of superior type and French felt at once that his evidence would be reliable.

He had, however, little to say that was new. As instructed, he met Mr Minter off the 9.08 train. He knew Mr Minter slightly, having driven him to and from the station on one or two previous occasions.

When he saw him he thought he looked ill. He was bent forward and his collar was turned up high round his neck as if he were cold. He seemed feeble, and he, Whatman, had helped him into the car at the station and out again at the house. Jeffries had taken his suitcase in and he had put away the car, and that was all he could tell them.

It seemed to French all they could expect to hear. After a question or two, Whatman was dismissed.

'Well, super,' said French as they returned to the police station, 'I'm glad I came down and I'm obliged for all you've done for me. The idea is then that we work on quietly for the present, and don't say what we've discovered to anyone. Norne in particular is not to be put on his guard. We'll not ask him for an explanation till we know better where we are. Is that right?'

'I agree. But don't you think he should be kept under supervision?'

French thought that constant supervision was unnecessary, on the grounds that so striking looking a man would be immediately taken if he did make a break. But he agreed that he should be watched going home and to the station each night and morning, so that any attempt at a getaway should be known at once. For the same reason French undertook to see that his arrival at his office in the morning and after lunch was duly reported.

On his way back to Town, French experienced some qualms as to whether his advice about the arrest of Norne was sound. But as he again considered the circumstances, he saw that to make an arrest without any idea of the suspect's motive would only be asking for trouble. No, he had been correct. A stronger case was necessary before any such drastic step was taken.

And it was probably up to him to make the necessary advance. The motive—if Norne were guilty—lay for certain in Town, possibly even in the theft. If so, Fenning could scarcely get on to it.

French determined that if the case depended on himself, he would not be found wanting.

8

Enter Theory

That night as he sat smoking before going to bed, French continued wrestling with his problem. He had evolved a fairly satisfactory theory of the murder of Minter, but so far he had been unable to find the motive. Was there really nothing to indicate it?

Very little thought, however, showed him that there might well be a motive. Suppose there were a connection between the murder and the theft and that these two, Norne and Minter, were the thieves? Suppose that, seeing their livelihood threatened, they had decided on desperate measures to retrieve their fortunes? Suppose that Norne had lent Minter his key, that Minter had burgled the safe, divided the spoils, and brought Norne down his share? Suppose that either they had quarrelled about the division, or that Norne had decided that a shared secret was too dangerous for his peace of mind, and had silenced Minter's tongue? Or suppose that Norne had wanted the whole of the swag?

Here was all the motive any investigating officer could want. But was it the truth?

97

If it were, French ought not only to be able to get his man, but to recover the booty as well. Neither Norne nor Minter, if they were guilty, could have in so short a time got rid of so great a haul. French rather timorously congratulated himself. All the same he had misgivings. To have reached a solution so soon seemed just a bit too good to be true.

There were, moreover, some difficulties in the theory. When, for example, could Minter have rifled the safe? If it were full on Saturday morning, it could only have been done on that afternoon. Here, then, was an obvious line of research. Could the whole of the man's time be accounted for?

Again, if Minter had rifled the safe, where was the booty? It was surely unlikely that he had brought it down in his suitcase. If not, where was it? Another matter to be looked into.

When he reached the Yard next morning French found a note from Sir Mortimer Ellison saying he would be glad to have his personal report on the case. After hurriedly looking through a disappointing collection of reports, he went into the presence.

'I think you did the right thing in going to Guildford,' Sir Mortimer approved when French had made his statement. 'Have you any theory?'

'Only in a tentative way, sir,' French answered. 'I thought that possibly—' and he indicated the lines on which his mind had been travelling.

'There's motive there, certainly,' Sir Mortimer agreed. 'Those fellows must have felt pretty sick about their business. What would you or I feel like, French, if we knew the Yard was going to be discontinued, and that not only would our salaries go, but that our other possessions would be taken to pay arrears of rent. And the more comfortable we were here, the worse we'd feel. That's the position of those fellows. They had practically everything to lose if their firm went under, and they might very well have agreed that whoever else went down, they weren't going to.'

'That's what I thought, sir.'

'And, of course, there was ample opportunity also,' Sir Mortimer went on as if he had not heard. 'Then, as you suggest, Minter was got out of the way so that Norne might feel safe, or that he might get more of the swag. Yes, I think that's reasonable enough. Any alternatives?'

French hesitated. 'I'm afraid not so far, sir. I've not done as much thinking about the thing as I hope to.'

Sir Mortimer gazed unseeingly before him from beneath his heavy eyelids. Absently his fingers crept to a box, opened it, and drew out a cigarette. He lighted it as if in a dream, and began slowly smoking.

'I suppose,' he said presently, 'that Norne couldn't have done it to get Minter's key? I mean, that Minter himself was innocent? Let's see how that would work out. Norne wants the stuff, but he can't get Minter's key. He could borrow it, of course, but Minter's a sharp chap, and when the burglary came off, he would tumble to what had happened. How would that do—that Norne did the killing to get Minter's key and silence Minter?'

French hesitated. 'Could he have got it, sir? The key was presumably with Minter as long as he was conscious. Otherwise he'd have made a fuss about it. Then it was taken charge of by the Guildford sergeant early in the morning. Norne couldn't have taken it to Town.'

'Obviously. But he could have taken a pressing of it and

an accomplice could have made it during Sunday, and that night either Norne or the accomplice or both of them could have gone to London and done the job. I don't put this forward as inspired. But think it over also.'

French said he would certainly do so, and that he was grateful for the hint. He was not, however, impressed. If Norne were capable of working out the scheme that he apparently had, he was surely capable of obtaining an impression of Minter's key without having to murder him for it. However, that was what he, French, had to think over.

'I agree with you,' Sir Mortimer went on, 'that you will have to go into Minter's movements on the Saturday. Though whether you will be solving the Guildford superintendent's case or your own, I don't know. How about the other inquiries?'

'Nothing valuable has come in, sir. None of the stolen stuff has been put on the market, and we've got nothing helpful from the Norne staff.'

Sir Mortimer made a languid gesture of dismissal. 'Well,' he said, 'we must just stick to it. That's life, French! Just sticking to it, eh?'

'It's about the size of it, sir,' French returned rather grimly. It *was* about the size of it! The phrase described just about ninety-nine per cent of French's waking life. For the other one per cent there might be luck or inspiration, success or failure, triumph or tears. But 'just sticking to it' covered practically all his normal existence.

As he returned to his room he saw that for the next day at least his programme was settled. If Minter were a confederate of Norne's he must have stolen the stuff between the closing of the office on Saturday and eight o'clock that night. That Saturday afternoon of Minter's must be checked up before an advance could be hoped for.

Then suddenly French wondered if he hadn't made a mistake. Was there any evidence that the jewels were in the safe on Saturday morning?

He remembered another jewel robbery in which it was found the thief had actually disposed of his haul *before* the discovery of the theft. Could that have been done in this case? Could Minter and Norne have been selling stones for some time, gradually clearing out the safe, perhaps replacing those which would be seen by other members of the staff by paste copies? If anything of this kind had been done, the most promising clue, the coming of the stones on to the market, had probably gone west.

It was therefore not to Minter's house that French presently headed, but back to the Norne Company's offices. If evidence existed as to the contents of the safe on Saturday morning, he must get hold of it.

With Sergeant Carter in attendance he asked to see Miles, the foreman of the Works Department. Miles was the man who had the duplicate card index, so that he might know just what stones were available for making up his sets. Next to Norne and Minter, Miles used the safe most.

French found it a little difficult to frame his question without giving away his suspicion of Norne. Norne had said the stuff was there on Saturday morning. Therefore, theoretically there could be no doubt of this. After some thought, however, French devised a plan. He consulted his list of the stolen property and fixed on a group of four large diamonds of outstanding beauty and value.

'I want your help on a small point, Mr Miles,' he began.

'It's about those four large stones you called the "Raggamond Four." Those.' His finger slid down the list.

'I know them well,' Miles returned. 'They were to be used in a pendant we were making for the Duchess of Skye. Worth a fortune, those four alone.'

'So I understand. Now, Mr Miles, I'm interested in those four stones. I don't say we're on the track of them, but I'd like to be quite sure when they were in the safe. We know from Mr Norne that the contents appeared to be intact on Saturday morning, but it has occurred to me that perhaps these four stones might have been abstracted before that time. Can you settle the point for me?'

Miles looked a little puzzled. 'Have you asked Mr Norne?' he said doubtfully.

'No,' said French, 'I didn't want to disturb him till he'd finished his correspondence. I shall ask him though, if you can't tell me.'

Miles made a slightly deprecating gesture. 'I can't and that's a fact,' he answered. 'Those four stones were in one of the drawers, but I hadn't that drawer open on Saturday, nor indeed for several days before that.'

'You had the safe open on Saturday then?'

'Oh, yes, I had the safe open. I wanted stones for different jobs we were working on.'

'Quite. Well, so far as you could see, was everything there?'

'Certainly it was. If I had missed anything, do you think I wouldn't have mentioned it?'

'I didn't mean that, Mr Miles. What I wanted to get at was how much of the contents you saw? How many drawers you opened, for instance?'

Miles nodded. 'I could hardly say. A dozen at least;

probably more. But besides that a lot of the stuff was in trays that I could see. I don't mean that I examined it over tray by tray, but I had a look round and if any quantity was missing I should have noticed it.'

French thought he might accept this evidence. If so, his first point was settled. The theft had not taken place before Saturday afternoon.

'By the way,' he said as he rose to his feet, 'could you tell me what time you saw the safe open?'

'About eleven.'

'The work in hand was not put away in the safe when the shop closed?'

'Not in that safe. We have a smaller one here for that.'

The next man to be interviewed was obviously Pendlebury, Minter's chief clerk, and French found him in his late chief's room. Pendlebury looked a man of the highest type, and the more French talked to him, the more convinced of this he became. Pendlebury had already been interrogated, but he made no difficulty about answering further questions.

When testing theories French usually inquired about irrelevant matters as well as the vital one, in order to keep his objective secret. He did so in this instance, but the only points which really interested him were the hours at which Minter had reached and left the office on the fateful day.

Of both these times Pendlebury was able to speak with decision. Minter had arrived on the stroke of half-past nine. He was a man of very regular habits, and was seldom more than a minute or two before or after his time. He had been in his office during the whole morning, except for about ten minutes during which he went to

103

see Norne. That was about eleven. He had left as usual at twelve forty-five.

'What sort of humour was Mr Minter in that day?' French went on.

'Much as usual,' Pendlebury returned; 'I didn't notice anything one way or another.'

'He was a man of—eh—even temper?'

'He was a man of good temper. Only when he was ill he was a bit irritable, and there was some excuse for that.'

'I agree. He didn't complain of his health on Saturday?'

'No. Of course, you couldn't count that as anything. He never did complain unless he was really bad.'

'Bilious, wasn't he?'

Pendlebury became more confidential. 'I don't know,' he said in a lower tone. 'He called it biliousness, but I always suspected something more serious. Ulcer or something of that sort, I imagined. But, of course, I don't know any more than you do.'

'Did it come on suddenly?'

'It did. Often he would seem well enough in the morning and in the afternoon he would have to go home. And it cleared up in the same way. Often he would come in looking like a rag and able to do very little, and by lunch time he was all right.'

'So the fact that he seemed well enough on Saturday morning wouldn't conflict with the statement that he was ill in the evening?'

'Not in any way at all.'

From 11 a.m., then, when the contents of the safe were still intact, till 12.45, when Minter left the building, the man had been in his office, under the observation of Pendlebury. French had already taken preliminary statements from Sheen and Sloley, in which both men had declared that Minter had met them in the office shortly before eight o'clock on the Saturday evening. This had been confirmed by Mrs Turbot, the charwoman, who had seen the three men arrive.

Unless Sloley and Sheen were also in the affair—and a conspiracy of four seemed unthinkable—Minter could not have cleared out the safe during that late visit. From that visit until his death every moment of his time was accounted for. Therefore, the only period still remaining doubtful was that from 12.45 to 8 p.m.

After lunch French set off with Carter for Rapallo, as Minter had named his house in Peacehaven Avenue, St John's Wood. The house was small and unpretentious, standing in what might by courtesy be called its own grounds; thirty feet in front and forty behind, with about five at each side. But such ground as there was had been made the most of. The windows were screened from the road by evergreens, kept low to prevent interference with the light. The entrance path, edged with flower-beds, was at one side of the tiny property, while at the other was a miniature but beautifully arranged rock garden. At the back French glimpsed grass edged with shrubs. The Minters had evidently not kept a car, or at least, there was no garage on the premises.

The door was opened by an elderly and very respectable looking maid, a type which was formerly common enough, but which for many years has seemed extinct. She looked at the visitors questioningly. French explained himself and asked for Mrs Minter.

'Come in, gentlemen,' the woman replied, opening the door. 'I'll see if Mrs Minter can receive you. You understand that she has not been well.'

'Tell her,' said French, 'that only urgent business forces me to intrude on her at such a time. I can understand how she must be feeling.'

The maid vanished, reappeared, and invited them to enter.

Mrs Minter was a surprise to French. Comparatively young, she was tall, stately, and extremely good-looking, though with a rather hard face. Handsome rather than pretty, he thought. Though dressed simply in some dark material, he would have bet long odds that her clothes had cost a lot of money. She did not speak, but looked from French's card to himself with an air of slightly insolent inquiry.

He began by apologising for his visit and stating the regret he felt in asking her to discuss her husband's death. She answered coldly that she understood that this was unavoidable, and that she would answer any reasonable questions. French thanked her briefly and began.

First he asked her about her husband's health. She confirmed what Pendlebury had told him, saying that Dr Fotherby-Wentworth, who had attended him, had called his attacks indigestion, and adding that if the chief-inspector were interested, she would suggest his calling on the doctor.

'Thank you, madam, I'll do so,' French answered, and turned to the fatal Saturday's attack. But here Mrs Minter could not help him. She had left home for the Sheen's party immediately after lunch. At lunch her husband had seemed much as usual, though he was undoubtedly depressed. He had been depressed for some time, and she believed it was due to the precarious position of his firm, about which he had told her. He had certainly not

106

complained of a headache, but she agreed with the chief-inspector that this was no reason to suppose he might not have been ill at five o'clock. After lunch, she had never seen him again—until she had identified his remains at Guildford.

'What time did you get home, madam?' French inquired.

'About half-past eleven. I had supper with the Sheens and went with them to the theatre.'

'Mr Minter was here when you left for your party?'

'Oh, yes, I left him in here. He was lying on the sofa, smoking and reading.'

'You live alone here, madam? I mean there was just yourself and Mr Minter and the servant in the house?'

'That was all. We had no family.'

French paused. This seemed to be all the information he could expect from Mrs Minter. He ran his eye quickly down his notes, then stod up.

'I'm much obliged, madam,' he said. 'That's all I require at present. Now, if you please, I should like a word with your maid.'

Mrs Minter rang the bell. 'Take these gentlemen into the dining room, Martha,' she said, 'and answer their questions.'

The interview had been easier than French had anticipated. Mrs Minter had been unexpectedly philosophic about her husband's death. Her manner, while correct, had remained cold and slightly contemptuous, and if she felt grief, she had certainly been successful in hiding it.

The dining room faced towards the back of the house, and through its window French could see the little back garden. Once again he was struck with the ingenuity which had been shown in developing the tiny area. With its centre of grass, its summer-house and its background of shrubs, it might have been in the heart of the country.

The maid said her name was Martha Belden, and that she had been with the Minters for five years. She described Minter's state of health, much as Mrs Minter had done. She had evidently liked him, and was sorry for his death.

On Saturday afternoon, she went on, Mrs Minter had gone out about half-past two. Mr Minter was on the sofa in the drawing room when she left. When Martha had washed up the lunch things she went up to her room and started some sewing. She stayed up there for perhaps an hour, then feeling cold, she brought her sewing down to the kitchen.

'Was Mr Minter still in the drawing room?' French interposed.

'Yes, he was there all the time.'

'Now just tell me how you know that?'

'If he had come out of the drawing room I should have heard him. It's a small house and I've got good ears. As a matter of fact, I did hear him come out and go back.'

French smiled. 'That's pretty conclusive,' he admitted. 'What did he come for?'

'To answer the telephone.'

'Better and better. What time was that?'

Martha paused. 'About three. I was upstairs and was on my way down to answer it, but Mr Minter came out of the drawing room and did it himself.'

'And he went back there when he had spoken?'

'Yes, immediately.'

French nodded. 'Now, we've got to about three o'clock, with Mr Minter in the drawing room. Do you happen to know what that message was about?'

Martha shook her head. 'I've no idea,' she declared, then after a moment's pause she went on: 'Mr Minter changed his plans that afternoon. He was going to leave before five, and then he didn't go till after seven. I wondered if he had got a message then or later which made him do so. Of course, I don't know that; it's merely an idea I got that it might be.'

'I'm glad you mentioned it. Now you said, "then or later." Did Mr Minter get some other communication that afternoon?'

'Yes, there was a second telephone message about half-past four. I was coming to that.'

'Right. Go ahead in your own way. What happened after three o'clock?'

'Well, as I said I stayed in my room till I began to feel cold and then came down to the kitchen. I suppose I came down about,' she paused again, 'half-past three or quarter to four. Mr Minter remained in the drawing room. About four the bell rang for tea and I brought it in. That was about quarter-past four. Mr Minter was still lying reading on the sofa.'

'How did he seem?'

'I didn't notice anything one way or another. He seemed as usual.'

'Would he have had tea if he was feeling ill?'

'Oh, yes, he might. In fact, it was generally a cup of tea he asked for when he was feeling seedy.'

'Very well. About quarter-past four you left it in for him. What happened next?'

'About half-past four the telephone rang again. He came out and spoke. Then he—'

'A moment. Did you hear what he said?'

The woman looked slightly indignant. 'No,' she said shortly, 'I didn't.'

'I'm not,' said French, with a disarming gesture, 'questioning your statement, but I noticed the telephone was in the hall, and the kitchen, I take it, is close by, and it would be natural for you to overhear some words. I'm not suggesting you would listen, you know.'

Martha seemed mollified. 'I didn't hear,' she repeated. 'When he began to speak I pushed the door to, as I always do. I heard the murmur of his voice, but I couldn't make out the words.'

French nodded. 'Very good,' he said, 'if you didn't, you didn't. Did he speak for any time?'

'No, not very long. Well, he stayed on in the drawing room till about five, and then he went up to his room. I heard him moving about, and I think he was packing his things for the weekend, because he came down about ten minutes later with his suitcase. He left it in the hall and went back to the drawing room.'

'That would bring it to about ten minutes past five?'

'About that'

'Very good. When did you see him next?'

'When he was going away.' Martha stopped suddenly and made a slight gesture of negation. 'No, I'm wrong. I saw him for a moment before that. A man called, an out of work, asking for help. I don't hold with giving to people at the door, but Mr Minter was very kindly that way, and he always had to be told when anyone called. So I went into the drawing room and told him. He gave me a shilling for the man.'

'About what time was that?'

'About six.'

'And did Mr Minter stay in the drawing room till he left?'

'Yes, except for going up to his room again before starting, he was in the drawing room all the time.'

'Then what time did he leave?'

'About half-past seven.'

'How?'

'How?'

'Did he walk or go by taxi?'

'By taxi.'

'Did you call it for him?'

'No, it must have been arranged. It came to the door and the man rang.'

French paused. 'Who ordered the taxi?'

'He must have done it himself, I suppose. I never thought. Or perhaps Mrs Minter did it?'

French did not reply. It was unlikely Mrs Minter had done it, as unknown to her, Minter had changed the hour of his start.

For the first time Carter spoke. 'Perhaps, sir, that was one of the 'phones? Maybe he was ringing up a garage?'

'But I understood you to say,' French turned again towards Martha, 'that the telephone bell rang and called him out of the drawing room on both occasions? Are you sure he didn't come out and ring up either of those times?'

'No, I'm quite sure the bell rang first each time.'

'Well, we'll have to get that cleared up: not that it matters much. Where do you generally get taxis?'

'We ring Nuttall's Garage at the foot of the hill.'

'You saw Mr Minter off?'

'Yes, I put the suitcase in the taxi.'

'Did you hear the address he gave?'

'Yes, his office at the bottom of Kingsway.'

In a way French felt disappointed in this interview. Martha's manner was so convincing that he felt he must accept her statement. And if so, Minter's day was now fully accounted for. It was impossible that he could at any time have had private access to the safe, and therefore, he must be acquitted of any connection with the robbery. However, before coming to a final conclusion French decided he would check up on the taximan who drove Minter. If his testimony supported the rest, he would have to realise that his first theory of the crime had gone west.

9

Enter Chemical Analysis

'Now,' said French, coming to a halt on the footpath, 'Let's see what we've to do still. We've got to see Minter's doctor and we've got to find that blessed taxi. Which shall we do first?'

'The doctor lives in this street, sir,' Carter answered. 'I asked the maid.'

'Good!' French approved. 'Let's get the doctor off our hands.'

A hundred yards farther on a brass plate gleamed across the road. They went over and read: 'J. Mortimer Fotherby-Wentworth, M.D.' Another five minutes and they were in the doctor's consulting room, asking for information as to the state of the late Minter's health.

Dr Fotherby-Wentworth, however, had little new to tell them, beyond the technical name for the deceased's malady. He confirmed the statements already made to French about the attacks, their severity, symptoms, and duration.

'Can you tell me whether the deceased was accustomed to use aspirin?' French went on.

The doctor shook his head. 'If you mean, did I order it to him, I did not. But you know as well as I do, chief-inspector, that many people use it without asking their doctor. Whether he did or not, I don't know.'

This being all they seemed likely to learn, they took their leave. 'Let's get on to that garage,' French said. 'Where is the place?'

Inquiries from a passing postman and a five minutes walk brought them to Nuttall's garage, and a short further delay ran Mr Nuttall, the proprietor, to earth. French showed him his official card and was promptly invited into the office.

'I'm anxious, Mr Nuttall,' he began, 'to trace a taxi which took the late Mr Minter of "Rapallo," Peacehaven Avenue to Waterloo on last Saturday evening. I understand Mr Minter dealt with you, and I have called to ask if you did the job?'

Nuttall looked up uneasily. 'Yes, we did it. Nothing wrong, I hope?'

'Not a thing,' French assured him. 'The matter concerns the late Mr Minter only. We want to know if he made any calls on his way to the station.'

Nuttall nodded, opened a book, and began to turn over the pages.

'What time on Saturday was the car ordered for?' went on French.

The man's finger stopped on its way down the page. 'This is it, I reckon,' he said. 'Rapallo, Peacehaven Avenue, 4.45 changed to 7.30 prompt.'

'That's the ticket,' French returned. 'Can you tell me how the change of time was sent?'

'By 'phone.'

'At what time?'

'It happens that just by chance I can tell you that. We don't note the time of the order, you understand, but only when the taxi's wanted.'

'Lucky for me, Mr Nuttall. What was the time?'

Nuttall looked reminiscent. 'It must have been just about three,' he explained. 'I took the call myself. I remember thinking the boy was away a long time on a message I'd sent him, and I looked at the clock.'

This did not quite clear up the situation. Martha Belden had said that the ringing of the telephone had called Minter out of the drawing room both at 3 and at 4.30.

'You didn't by any chance ring Mr Minter up in the first instance, I suppose?' French asked. 'We were told he was rung up for that call, not that he rang up himself.'

'He rang me up all right.'

It looked then as if Minter had received some other call at the time, and had taken advantage of his being at the instrument to ring up the garage. The same explanation probably obtained in the case of the 4.30 call, when Minter had spoken to Norne's butler. All the same French was mildly surprised that this call had not been made at 3 with the other.

'Thank you, Mr Nuttall, that's all I want from you,' he said. 'But I should like a word with the driver of the taxi.'

French was having a run of luck. It appeared the man was in the garage. Nuttall sent for him.

Joseph Weekes was an elderly man with brusque manners and a surly appearance. However, he seemed reliable, and when once he was made to understand that the interview was not a prelude to trouble for himself, told his story willingly enough.

115

He had been instructed, he said, to call at Rapallo at 7.30 prompt, and he had done so: four or five minutes before his time in fact. Mr Minter had been waiting for him and came out at once and they started before time. The servant put a suitcase into the taxi and saw Mr Minter off.

He had driven Mr Minter on different occasions, and knew his appearance. Mr Minter had told him to drive to Norne's Limited, in Ronder Lane at the bottom of Kingsway. He had done so. Mr Minter had got out, had told him to wait, and had gone into the building. He had used a key.

He, Weekes, had waited about quarter of an hour, and then Mr Minter had come out again with another man. The man was tall and he, Weekes, would know him if he saw him again. The tall man put Mr Minter into the taxi and told him, Weekes, to go on to Waterloo. He had done so. At Waterloo Mr Minter had paid him, adding a tip. Mr Minter had disappeared into the station and he, Weekes, had driven back to the garage.

This testimony seemed to French finally to clinch that he had already received. Minter was innocent! The proof was complete and conclusive. And now it was borne in on French that at bottom he had never really suspected Minter. Theft of this kind was not in the man's character, as he judged it.

French felt as if he were completing a chapter of the inquiry as he marked Minter's name off his list of suspects, and turned to consider the next which figured there.

Norne! From the discovery of Norne's finger-print on the glass in Minter's room, with the suggestion this carried that he was the murderer, Norne had been the likely man.

French saw that he must now concentrate on Norne as he had already done on Minter. An inquiry on similar lines should give him his result.

Before going home that night he rang up Fenning at Guildford to report progress. He was guarded in the way he spoke, mentioning no names, and the super took the same precaution in his reply. It was clear from his investigations, French said, that the deceased was innocent of the robbery, and he was now considering whether the man they had suspected of murder couldn't also be the thief. He was about to start checking up this man's movements during the critical period.

To this Fenning replied that in his own investigation he had already checked up the whole of the time spent by the man in question while at his home. This included two periods. The first was from his arrival about two o'clock on the Saturday afternoon up till his departure for Town about 10.15 on the Sunday morning. The second was from his return from Town about 1.30 on the Sunday, up till his leaving for the office on Monday morning. This left only the Sunday visit to Town to be inquired into.

'What about the two nights?' French asked.

'I think you may take it the nights are all right,' Fenning returned. 'The car was definitely not taken out, and I don't think he would have been fool enough to use anyone else's.'

To French this sounded reasonable, though he took a note to discuss the point with Fenning on their next meeting.

To decide Norne's innocence or guilt of the theft, French had then only to find out what the man did during Sunday morning. Had he paid his visit to Mrs Minter and then cleared out the safe before returning to Guildford? He could, French reminded himself, have cut a key from Minter's during the night.

French struck an apologetic note when next morning he called for the second time on Mrs Minter. He was exceedingly sorry to trouble her again, but as she would understand, in an inquiry of the kind fresh points kept on arising. He would keep her only a moment.

Martha, who opened the door and listened to all this, seemed somehow taken aback. She said she thought Mrs Minter was engaged, but she would make inquiries. In the meantime would the chief-inspector wait in the dining room?

French was by nature observant, and by use he had still further developed this faculty. He, therefore, noted when passing through the hall that a man's coat, bowler hat and gloves were lying on a side table. He saw, further, that the hat, which was upside down with the gloves across it, bore upon its band the initials A.R. It was obvious that Mr A.R., whoever he might be, was madam's guest in the drawing room.

Now, French had many times noted the laying down of bowler hats. Most men place them as they are worn, crown uppermost. But a few invariably do the opposite and keep the brim up. Some, moreover, put their gloves into or on to the hat, and some lay them beside it.

French gave no more than an automatic passing attention to the matter, which indeed did not interest him. He settled down to wait, but in less than five minutes there were masculine steps in the hall, the growl of a man's voice, Martha's 'Good afternoon, sir,' and the closing of the hall door. At once the maid came to the dining room and asked French if he would go to her mistress.

On seeing Mrs Minter, French repeated his apology, adding that he hoped he had not come at an inopportune time.

'Don't apologise, chief-inspector,' the lady answered in the same coldly contemptuous way as before. 'It was only my cousin. What can I do for you?'

French said he was grateful. He wanted, if Mrs Minter would kindly give it to him, a more detailed account of what happened on the previous Sunday morning in connection with Mr Norne's visit. When he came, when he went, and things of that kind.

Mrs Minter raised her eyebrows. 'Surely Mr Norne would have told you that if you had asked him?' she replied. 'I don't see why you have come to me.'

'It's because our business is handled in a less pleasant way than we should like ourselves, madam,' French answered. 'Mr Norne has told me what happened, but I am required by our regulations never to take a statement without getting all the confirmation I can. I shall have next to ask the same questions of your maid. I assure you that that doesn't mean that I doubt what either you or Mr Norne say. It is purely routine and if I didn't do it I should lose my job.'

'Rather unpleasant that, isn't it?'

'I don't think so, madam. Most of our cases get to court sooner or later, and such information is required for court.'

Mrs Minter nodded. 'I see. I didn't appreciate that at first. In any case, I suppose if you ask questions, we have to answer?'

'Not necessarily: you can refuse if you wish to. But that's unwise because it arouses unnecessary suspicions. When you see that my questions are merely routine, I don't see why you should object to them.'

119

She shrugged with a bored air. 'Well, what do you want to know?'

'About Mr Norne's visit, principally from the point of view of time. When did he arrive, Mrs Minter?'

'I can tell you that. His call was so unusual that I looked at the clock. It was just half-past eleven.'

'And when did he leave?'

Mrs Minter was not so sure of this. She had been upset by the news and not paid much attention to anything else. After thought, however, she was able to give approximate times, not only of when Norne left for the last time, but also of when he went for her sister and brought her back.

'What is your sister's name and address, please, madam?'

'Have you to see her too?'

'I'm afraid so. Our rule is, get every check possible.'

'What a ghastly job!' Skilfully she managed to convey that it was he, rather than the job, that she thought objectionable. 'Very well, my sister's name is Kershaw, Mrs Milly Kershaw, St Neot's, 25 Upper Broad Walk, Golders Green.'

French completed the afternoon with the detailed inquiries on which he had dilated to Mrs Minter. On leaving the presence he once again interviewed Martha Belden. She, interested in the matter of the approaching lunch, had kept a wary eye on the clock, and she was able to reply more convincingly, if not more accurately, to French's questions. As a matter of fact, however, both women agreed fairly closely in their recollections. When he left St John's Wood he was pretty well satisfied that Norne had arrived at 11.30, had left for Golders Green at 11.45, and had returned at 12.15. On this second call he had not gone in, leaving immediately for Guildford.

This seemed to be tending towards the conclusion that

Norne had not deviated from the path of rectitude on that Sunday morning, but French deliberately forbore to reach a conclusion until he had seen Mrs Kershaw.

'Get a taxi,' he said to Carter, and when he had given the Golders Green address, he went on: 'We want to time this run, Carter. Make a schedule, will you, noting traffic delays.'

Their driver was a smart fellow and they didn't lose much time. On Sunday morning, of course, the streets would be clearer of traffic, but even so, French did not think that Norne could have gone much quicker. The run took sixteen minutes, including four minutes delay at crossings. French decided to drop a couple more minutes, and take ten minutes as the minimum time Norne could have taken.

'Ten and ten makes twenty, and twenty from thirty leaves ten. Now, if we find that Norne was ten minutes at this place, he couldn't have visited the office on his way.'

Indeed, French already knew that he couldn't have done so in any case. The whole ten minutes would scarcely have allowed it, even if he had made no call at 'St Neot's.'

Mrs Kershaw, however, fully substantiated the call and her statement was confirmed by her servant. As both women seemed reasonably reliable, French had no doubt as to its truth.

Here then was Norne's complete Sunday morning. He had left his home at 10.15 and reached Mrs Minter's at 11.30. An hour and a quarter was obviously a reasonable time to have taken. He could not have called at the office during his stay in Town, and as he had taken about the same time to return to Guildford as he had to come up, this period was equally covered.

There was then no escaping the conclusion that Norne had not personally robbed the safe. Unless, therefore, he had an accomplice, he was innocent of theft.

As French returned to the Yard he kept turning the affair over in his mind. What was there against Norne in this matter of the robbery? Why was he a suspect at all?

There was nothing against him—nothing whatever—except the one thing, the suspicion that he had murdered Minter. If he were proved innocent of that, suspicion of the theft would collapse immediately.

Was he guilty of the murder? Here again the idea hinged on one thing and one thing only. The fingerprints. If Norne could explain those prints, there would be nothing against him on any count.

Could he explain them? French wondered if the time had not arrived to ask him.

When he reached the Yard he rang up Fenning and put the question to him. Fenning, it appeared, had been about to ring up French. The analyst's report had just come in, together with a further statement from Dr Hawthorn, and as these seemed important to the superintendent, he wondered whether French would care to go down to discuss them. 'We could then consider interrogating our friend,' he added.

'I'll be with you about three,' replied French and rang off.

Fenning was ready for them when a couple of hours later French and Carter were shown into his office.

'Good of you to come down, chief-inspector,' he began. 'I hope you won't be disappointed. But it's much more satisfactory to discuss these things directly than over the 'phone. Here's the analyst's report. I suggest we take it first.'

The document was couched in technical language most of which, in spite of French's long experience, was beyond him. But the essential fact was as clear and unmistakable as it was unexpected. A short time before his death Minter had had a fairly large dose of a butyl-chloral hydrate sleeping draught.

'So that's what Norne was giving him,' French exclaimed. 'My word, he's no fool! He has the aspirin bottle and pretends to shake out the tablets from it, and Minter, therefore, takes them without hesitation. But really Norne drops in this powerful hypnotic instead.'

Fenning glanced at him curiously. 'That was what I thought when I first read it,' he said slowly.

'And that explains Minter's not struggling,' went on French, not noticing the other's manner. 'Before he was suffocated, he was doped.'

'Why, then, should he be tied?'

'Precaution. He was asleep, but he might awake. Norne was taking no chances.'

'The gag?'

French stared. 'Hang it all,' he said presently, 'I had forgotten the gag. I don't know. Or, yes, I do,' he went on in a moment. 'Norne would gag him before he tied him up, lest he might wake and cry out. Then he would tie him up, lest he might wake and struggle. What about that, super?'

'It's neat, chief-inspector. It's very neat, I admit.' He paused, then added, 'But I'm afraid it's not the truth.'

'Not the truth?'

'Well: if it were, it would mean that Minter was murdered after one o'clock, wouldn't it?'

'After two: for Norne would scarcely act till the house had settled down. Norne doped him at ten, then when the house was quiet by two o'clock, he slipped back into the room and smothered him. What's wrong with that?'

'Only that it won't work.' Fenning made a gesture of apology. 'It was a shame not to tell you at first, chief, but there's a further statement from the doctor—in answer to a question from me. The doctor estimates Minter was murdered about ten.'

For a moment French looked annoyed, then he began to laugh. 'Now, that was too bad, super,' he exclaimed, 'to lead me up the path like that! I said already you were as bad as your doctor, and so you are.'

Fenning laughed deprecatingly. 'I didn't mean to pull your leg,' he declared. 'I wanted to see if you'd get into the same difficulty as I have. This opinion of the doctor doesn't seem to work in with anything.'

'They can't tell the time of a death, these doctors. He may be hours wrong. Is he a good man?'

'He's the police doctor and as good as they're made. He seemed pretty sure of it. I was going to ask you to come over and hear what he has to say.'

'I'd like to, but he'll not convince me.'

Fenning nodded. 'You see, if he's right, it means that Minter must have taken the stuff himself: which would be almost too lucky for Norne.'

'He never did,' French returned. 'Minter asked Jeffries to send Norne in about ten o'clock. He wouldn't have done that if he'd kown he'd be asleep.'

124

'That's so. Suppose he took it when Norne was in?'

'Then that gets us back to the difficulty of carrying out the murder without dope.'

'You're right.' There was silence for a moment and then Fenning went on. 'It would look almost as if Jeffries was in it and had given him the dope ready for Norne.'

French shook his head. 'I don't believe that,' he declared, 'though, of course, I've no proof. Norne may have tricked Jeffries by pretending the butyl-chloral hydrate was aspirin. But I can't imagine Jeffries party to the affair.'

'I agree. But it's a bit puzzling.'

There was silence for a moment, then French spoke.

'Did you have the matter in the glass analysed?'

'Yes: pure water only. But that would obtain whichever tablets were taken, unless they were broken up for quicker action.'

'Were the remaining tablets examined?'

'They were aspirin.'

French got up and began to pace the room. 'I don't think it's such a puzzle after all,' he said. 'The doctor's mistaken as to the time of death. That's my belief at all events.'

'What about coming along and seeing him?'

'I'm ready.'

Fenning got up, but French stopped him with a gesture.

'But look here, super. We're forgetting the fingerprints on the glass. Norne *must* have given Minter the dope. Else why the business of the prints?'

'I know, but that only makes it worse. If Norne committed the murder at ten o'clock, why did he bother with the dope, which wouldn't have had time to act?'

'Oh, damn,' said French, 'I don't know. Let's go on and see the doctor.'

Fenning laughed. 'That's pretty much the way I feel too,' he declared. 'And I don't know that a dose of Dr Hawthorn is going to cure either of us.'

'The nastier the medicine, the better the cure,' French grunted. Fenning said nothing, but rang for his car.

10

Enter Medical Jurisprudence

Dr Hawthorn lived in a large detached house on the Epsom Road. He was a tall man with a quiet manner and French took to him instantly. His greeting was curt, but adequate. French felt his statements would be cautious, but reliable.

He was ready to discuss the case from any angle, but he had little to tell them that they had not already known. Fenning then asked him about the time of death. He was very frank in his reply.

'It's not a matter about which a medical man can be dogmatic,' he explained. 'There are a good many factors to be taken into consideration, but not a single one of them is absolute. What I mean is that everyone of the factors is liable to mislead; exceptions have been noted to every conclusion. I don't want to go into purely technical details, but I may say that this case is similar to most in that the results arrived at are a compromise of slightly conflicting factors. Briefly speaking, the conclusion I reached from the degree of rigor mortis and hypostasis—body staining, you know—and other indications present, showed death to have taken place slightly later than the approximate time I put in my report. On the other hand, the amount of cooling which had taken place pointed to a considerably earlier hour. Neither indication, as I said before, was necessarily accurate, so what I did was to compromise and give a time mean to the two results.'

'That's interesting, sir,' French said. 'Might I ask you what variation these different sets of indications represented?'

'That I can, of course, only answer approximately, chief-inspector. Had I left the cooling out of account, I should probably have placed the time of death at from ten to twelve. Had I gone by the cooling only, I should have said seven to ten, or earlier. It's possible, though unlikely, that a death at seven o'clock might have produced the rigor mortis and staining found, but I think it's scarcely possible that with death at mid-night the body could have cooled as much as it did. It seemed to me reasonable to give a qualified opinion that death occurred between nine and eleven, or say, more or less about ten.'

'One other question, sir. Which set of indications, the rigor mortis lot, or the cooling, would you consider the more reliable?'

Dr Hawthorn smiled slightly. 'Another rather difficult question, I'm afraid. On the whole I should say that the cooling was the more reliable. Allowances have to be made, of course, for various factors even here. The temperature of the atmosphere, the amount of clothing or other covering over the body, the build, the health, the cause of death: allowance must be made for these and other matters. For instance, death from asphyxia, as we have here, tends to slow up the cooling, and so on.'

French shrugged. 'A bit chancy work, if I may say so, sir,' he suggested. 'But there's one thing we're very anxious to know. I may ask this, super?'

'Of course, chief. The more we can get to know, the better.'

'Well, we want to know whether the murder was definitely committed before, say, two o'clock?'

'Two? Oh, yes, definitely. When I said it wasn't possible to be dogmatic about such matters, I meant within reasonable limits. But when it comes to periods of several hours, it's a different thing. I give it as my deliberate opinion that it was committed before twelve at the very latest. Between ourselves and not to be put into writing, I may say I haven't the slightest doubt in my own mind.'

French and Fenning exchanged glances. 'We couldn't ask more than that, sir. There is just one other point. Those bruises you mentioned, the wrists and ankles and mouth: were they incurred before or after death?'

'Before death most certainly.'

This being all they could expect to get from Hawthorn, the two officers returned to the police station. There they turned to the question of whether Norne should be asked to explain the finger-prints. The matter was really one for Fenning, but French felt that anything that he could learn about the members of the Norne firm might help him with his own case, and he was keen to be present.

'What about staying down here this evening, chief-inspector?' the super ended up. 'If you can, we'll go out and see what he has to say.'

'If you're not satisfied it means an arrest,' French pointed out.

'I know it does,' Fenning agreed. 'I must risk that.'

129

It was getting on towards nine o'clock that night when the two officers drove up the Guildown hill to Severno. Fenning had provided himself with the necessary warrant, in case they decided that an arrest was advisable. But both were of the opinion that if Norne could put up any reasonable kind of explanation, they would appear to accept it and try to calm any fears which their visit might have aroused.

Fenning seemed worried. 'I'm not happy about this business and that's a fact,' he declared with an anxious look. 'If I arrest this man and don't get a conviction, it'll not do me much good: nor you either, chief-inspector, because we can't hide the fact that we're working more or less together in the case. Norne's a pretty influential man. If I make a mistake now, there'll be the hell of a row.'

'Are you not satisfied he's your man?'

'I don't see how it could have been anybody else. But I've no motive: that's what makes me think. If I had a motive I wouldn't care: I'd be justified. But I haven't a case that I could bring into court and I may as well admit it.'

'Let's hear what he has to say. If he's guilty we'll know from his manner, if not from his words.'

'I hope so,' Fenning agreed dismally.

Just then they reached Severno and climbed heavily out of the car to put the matter to the test.

They were shown into the library, where Norne was sitting at the fire. With the curtains drawn and the lights on, hidden lights which filled the room with radiance, though softly and without glare, the room gave an impression of extraordinary peace and comfort. The colour scheme was brown, light almost to biscuit colour on the upper walls, dark almost to jet on the polished mahogany furniture. There were no reflections save from the curved legs of chairs and other woodwork near the blazing log fire. Books covered one complete wall, and had overflowed on to occasional tables and even to the massive desk which stood in the middle of the room. Norne sat reading in a brown leather armchair. He got up on seeing his visitors.

'Good evening, superintendent. Good evening, chief-inspector,' he greeted them. 'Won't you pull forward chairs and sit down? Will you smoke?' He pushed forward a cigarette box of heavy chased silver.

'Thank you, sir, we don't smoke when we're on duty,' Fenning replied with a slight brusqueness which French put down to nervousness. 'We're both sorry to trouble you at this hour, but certain matters have to be cleared up, and we couldn't get you in the day time. It's about Mr Minter's death, of course.'

As he spoke Fenning took the armchair to which Norne had waved. French at the same time moved a high chair to the desk and opened his notebook. Norne, having taken and lit a cigarette, sat down again where he was before.

'Does this hunting in couples mean that you think his death was connected with the robbery?' he asked.

'We think so, sir.'

'Very good. Go ahead.'

'The matter is a little awkward,' Fenning went on. 'I think, chief-inspector, we'd better tell Mr Norne exactly what's in our minds?'

'It's the best way,' French approved, while Norne looked from one to the other with mild surprise, not wholly unmixed with apprehension.

'Well, sir, it's this,' Fenning went on as Norne remained

131

silent; 'there are certain points about this case which, as I say, have got to be explained, and which only you can explain. These points—there's no use in beating about the bush: I may as well tell you—these points suggest that you know more about the affair than you've told us. They suggest—well, I needn't put that into words. Now, sir, I'm sure that there's a good explanation for everything, but I'm afraid I'll have to ask you to make it.'

The super paused as if unwilling to go on, and French could feel his anxiety lest he should commit himself to a wrong course. French came to his aid.

'Not to put too fine a point on it, sir,' he said, 'these points of which the super is speaking seem at first sight to incriminate yourself. The super would like you to make a more complete statement than you have done.'

'That's it, Mr Norne,' Fenning added, 'though before you speak I must give the formal warning that you needn't reply unless you like, and that if you do so, what you say may be used in evidence. At the same time, I hope you will see your way to give us the satisfaction which it's our duty to ask.'

French could have smiled to see how thoroughly Fenning was covering himself for a retreat in good order, should such become desirable. And then he suddenly grew more interested. Norne was beginning to exhibit all the traces of a bad conscience, with which French was so familiar. The man moved uneasily, then spoke with an attempt at a joke which fell flat as it was made.

'This sounds very alarming, superintendent.' He smiled unsteadily. 'I hope you don't mean to arrest me?'

'Now, sir, I've said nothing about arrest. What we would like would be a fuller account of what took place in

Mr Minter's bedroom when you visited him on the Saturday night.'

'I think I told you everything,' Norne was beginning, but Fenning interrupted him.

'No, sir, you have not. There was a matter of a glass.'

Norne did not reply. He was evidently thinking deeply. Then as if coming to a decision, he said: 'Well, and what if there was?'

'Only, sir, that you should have told us about it. Have you any objection to doing so now?'

'None,' Norne said shortly, 'though I don't see what matter it makes. What happened about the glass was this. Minter was lying there groaning a little and evidently very sick. I said to him, "I'll call the doctor," as I've already told you. He said not to do so, as he had often been in that state before and it would shortly pass. "I'd like an aspirin," he said then, and he went on to tell me to look in his waistcoat pocket for a bottle. I found it and then he said he would take two. "Shake out two and give them to me with some water," he said. I did so. I shook out two and poured some water into the glass on the wash-stand and gave it to him. But he said on second thoughts he wouldn't take it just then and to leave it beside him. This I did. I left it on the little table at the head of the bed. What about it all?'

'Why did you not tell us that before?' Fenning asked.

'Why should I have? What did it matter?' He paused, then with a gesture of throwing everything to the winds went on: 'No, superintendent, I'll tell you why I didn't. When Minter was found dead I became panic-stricken that perhaps I had given him the wrong medicine by mistake and that unwittingly I might have poisoned him. I've been terribly upset in case that may have happened, and I am still.'

'But you actually gave him nothing?'

'No, but I put out what I thought were two aspirin tablets for him to take.'

'Do you know if he took them?'

'He must have. They were gone in the morning and the water was drunk.'

'Did you touch the glass when you were in the room on the Sunday morning?'

'No. I saw it there with the bottle. I didn't touch either.'

Fenning hesitated a moment. 'I think I'd better tell you, sir, that Mr Minter was not poisoned.'

Norne sat up with surprise and relief printed on every feature. 'Not poisoned?' he exclaimed. 'That's good news. Then what did he die of?'

'That remains to be seen,' Fenning said darkly. 'Now your own statement's not quite complete. You say that because you thought the deceased had died from poison, and that you might in error have given him that poison or put it in his way; because you thought this you wanted to keep it dark that you had handled the glass? Is that right?'

Norne wiped the little drops of sweat off his brow. 'Yes, that's correct.'

'But, sir, you must have known that your fingerprints were on the glass?'

'Oh, was that how you got on to it? I didn't think of it till the doctor was there, and then it was too late to do anything.'

'But you didn't know then that the death was not natural?'

Norne shrugged. 'I saw the doctor looking at the bottle and glass with a very grave expression, and when he said that he couldn't give a certificate and that the police would have to be advised, I guessed something was wrong.'

'You state positively that you didn't wipe the glass?'

'Most certainly I did not. I almost wish I had.'

Fenning moved uneasily. 'Now, I would like you to reconsider that point, Mr Norne. Let us all forget what you've said and go back to it afresh. I suggest your memory has been slightly at fault. Think now: did you not at any time wipe that glass? Remember, Mr Minter was not poisoned: it can't injure you. But we want the truth.'

Norne looked more puzzled than ever. 'I assure you most solemnly I did nothing of the kind. I can't think what you're trying to get at.'

'Then that's all right,' Fenning said easily. 'I'm sorry for having troubled you about it, but you must admit it was your own fault. You should have told us about that business of the glass and not let us find your prints on it and wonder how they got there?'

Norne passed his hand over his forehead. 'I suppose I should,' he admitted. 'Well, I'm glad you're satisfied at all events. But why did you ask me about the wiping?'

'Because, sir, the glass had been wiped.'

'It had?' Norne shook his head helplessly. 'That's beyond me. It could only have been done by Minter, I suppose, but why he should have done it, I can't see.'

'Well, we'll let that matter pass. Now, there's another point. I understand from you that you and Sir Ralph Osenden and Mr Ricardo were here in this room before ten o'clock until Messrs Sloley and Sheen turned up about one. Is that so?'

'Yes, that's so, certainly.'

'Were you here absolutely all the time without any exception?'

Norne hesitated. 'I don't think I said that none of us left the room at all. As a matter of fact, I went to the morning-room for an old print that I had been describing. But that was only for a few minutes.'

French and Fenning exchanged glances. 'How long would you say you were out of the room?'

'Ten or twelve minutes. I couldn't find the print at once and had to look through a couple of biggish folios.'

'What time was that, sir?'

'About half-past ten, I should think. I didn't look.'

'And was that the only time you left the room?'

'The only time.'

'I follow. And the other two gentlemen? Did they leave the room between ten and one?'

'Not unless it was during this period when I was getting the print.'

Fenning sat silent for a few moments, then he spoke to French. 'That's all, I think, chief-inspector, that we want to ask Mr Norne?'

French agreed. He and Fenning then set themselves to reassure the managing-director. Before they left they thought they had succeeded in doing so.

'Guilty or not guilty,' Fenning said as they drove down the hill from Guildown, 'we've no case against him—not to take into court anyhow.'

'Do you think there's anything in his leaving the room?'

'I thought there might be at first, but I'm not so sure now. We've Jeffries' corroboration that he didn't go upstairs.'

'Quite.'

'I may as well admit,' Fenning went on in a sudden burst of confidence, 'that I'm not at all sure he's our man.'

'He came out of the interview better than I expected,' French returned. 'I agree with you, super, you haven't enough to go on. I watched him while you were questioning him, and it was my opinion that he was speaking the truth.'

'Mine too, chief. Well, if we're right, it leaves us in the soup.'

'Yes, if Norne's not guilty, we've got to start right at the beginning again.'

'What time's your train? Can you come back to the station for a minute or two?'

'Of course. Any train'll do me.'

'If we're to believe Norne,' Fenning went on when they had settled down with their pipes in his room, 'the wiping of the glass becomes fundamental. If Norne didn't do it, who did? Minter didn't: we may bank on that. Even if for some unknown reason he had wiped it, he would never have grasped it in that particular way. So it means that some third person was in the room during the night.'

'That's also proved by the disappearance of the two aspirin tablets—unless Minter put them back in the bottle. According to the analyst's report, he hadn't taken them.'

'That's so.'

'What's sticking me,' French observed, 'is this. According to Jeffries *no one* went into the room between ten o'clock and one. According to the doctor, Minter was suffocated before twelve. We seem to have got to a deadlock.'

Fenning nodded. 'I know, damn it all. It's a confounded puzzle, chief. I don't see light anywhere.'

'Nor I. No light about the murder. No light about the theft. It's not looking too well for either of us, super.'

For some little time silence reigned, as both men sat puffing gloomily at their pipes and gazing before them into empty space. Then Fenning shook himself.

'What's the next move?' he said as he got up and knocked out his pipe on the grate. 'Have you a programme ready?'

French took out his notebook and slowly turned the pages. 'Considering the robbery, not the murder,' he returned, 'what I had in my mind was this: Norne and Minter were the men with the keys. Between us we've now gone into their movements during the critical period, and I'm satisfied neither of them opened the safe—for the simple reason that neither had the opportunity.' French paused and added: 'Except on one occasion.'

Fenning looked up more hopefully. 'It's not my way to talk about mere unsupported ideas,' French went on, 'but as we're discussing the thing I'll break my rule. That one occasion, as I see it, was when Minter called at the office on the Saturday evening. What went on during that call? That's going to be my next line.'

The super's hopeful look changed to one of disappointment. 'H'm,' he grunted, 'do you think there's much to be got there?'

'I don't,' French said frankly, 'but it's a straw and I'm drowning. That's the best I can say of it.'

'Just what's your idea?'

'Well, if the firm went down, Sloley and Sheen were going to sink with the others. They had a motive for the robbery, and if they somehow diddled Minter, they would have a motive for the murder: they wouldn't want him to put two and two together when he learned the stones were gone.'

'You mean they might have got Minter's key?'

'Something of that kind.'

'What about Norne's?'

French shrugged. 'I realise that difficulty. But if I get anything about that meeting in the office, it'll be time enough to consider Norne.'

'Of course,' Fenning went on, 'even if Sloley and Sheen had a motive for the murder, they couldn't have committed it.'

'You mean that they hadn't the opportunity?'

'I mean that they were in a theatre in London when Minter was suffocated in Guildford. I suppose, by the way, there's no doubt of that?'

'Next item on my list,' said French. 'I'll make sure.'

'Well, you've got something to go on with. I'm hanged if I have.'

'I expect to be in the same position shortly,' French rejoined. 'What time is that blessed train, super?'

On the way up to Town French's thoughts remained concentrated on his problem. Sloley and Sheen! Could one or both of them be guilty?'

The case against them which he had outlined to Fenning was plausible enough. They might have on some previous occasion taken an impression of Norne's key, and so required only Minter's to commit the theft, and they might have devised some plan to get Minter's on that Saturday evening. Of course, they couldn't have committed the robbery while Minter was in the office—unless Minter was party to it. Nor could they have stolen Minter's key: he had it with him at Guildford. At most they could only have taken an impression of it. But could they not then have made a second key on Sunday evening and robbed the safe that night?

This seemed possible, though French could not pretend it was extremely likely. All the same, he continued reviewing the probabilities of their guilt.

In the first place, there was the question of motive. If the firm went down it would be as serious for Sloley and Sheen as for the others, and it might well be that they were not prepared to face such a disastrous prospect. Then further, they had arranged for Minter to call at the office. They wanted to discuss, or said they wanted to discuss, that return of Sheen's about the probable response existing shareholders might make to a new issue. French was not a business man, but to him that return didn't seem to be of a very valuable character. Was it a genuine contribution to the problem the directors had to solve, or was it devised simply as an excuse to get Minter to the office?

So much supported the theory of their guilt. But there was the weighty argument against it pointed out by Fenning: the question of the murder. French didn't see how either Sloley or Sheen could be guilty of the murder. If they weren't, did it not mean that they were innocent of the theft also?

Curse it all, the thing was very puzzling. However, his analysis had confirmed his decision. Sloley and Sheen were his only suspects. He must come to a definite conclusion as to their innocence or guilt. Before going to sleep he resolved that next morning he would start work on this new phase of the inquiry.

11

Enter Two Alibis

The reports with which French began the next day proved dismal reading. Most careful watch was being kept by diamond merchants, jewellers, superior pawnbrokers, and those who dealt in gems, not only in England, but over most of the world, and not a single stone of the hundreds stolen had yet come to light. Whether the thieves had so far been unable to get rid of any of them, which French hoped; or whether their methods of doing so were so good as to leave no trace, which he feared; the result was the same. The line of inquiry which in such cases usually gave the best results, was proving barren.

French sighed as he put the papers away and turned to the day's programme. In accordance with his decision of the previous evening, he was to settle the question of Sloley and Sheen: if he could.

With Carter, therefore, he presently went to the Norne offices and asked to see Sheen.

He had already taken Sheen's preliminary statement, and he began by expressing his regret at troubling him again so soon. Sheen said he was sure the chief-inspector's was a most difficult job, and that so far as he was concerned, all he wanted was to help. 'I'm as anxious as anyone that you should get hold of that stuff,' he added. 'If it's not recovered the firm will go down, and if it goes down, there's good-bye to my job. It's a serious matter for people like myself, who are dependent on what they earn for their livelihood.'

'I can understand it must be an anxious time, sir,' French admitted, and their relations being thus established on an amicable basis, French turned to business.

'I wish, sir, that you'd kindly repeat what you've already told me about that Saturday, only please give me this time the most complete detail. You were at work here that morning?'

'Yes, I was here for my usual time: from about half-past nine till a few minutes before one.'

'Quite. And then?'

'Well,' Sheen went on with a smile, 'I told you that Saturday was an important day in my family. My little girl—my only child—was celebrating her tenth birthday. She was to have a children's party in the afternoon, and was to be taken to her first theatre in the evening. It wasn't actually her birthday, but it was the nearest day to it we could arrange. I needn't go into that—it had to be a Saturday to suit me, and so on.'

'That's all right, sir. I can understand.'

'Well, I had got the hint in the morning that it would ease preparations for the party if I were to get lunch down Town. If you're a family man, I dare say you can understand that, too?'

'I can, sir,' French rejoined in heartfelt tones.

142

'Quite. I take a light lunch, and I slipped into a café for some coffee, afterwards going on home. I got there, I suppose, about two. I think I already explained that I had spent the morning getting out my list of shareholders, but I don't remember telling you why I was so anxious about that. It was to show my keenness and my desire to help. This was the first time I had been asked to join one of the directors' conferences, and I wanted to justify the compliment which had been paid me. I'm being very open with you, chief-inspector, and I expect you not to give me away.'

'That's all right, sir. You may be satisfied I'll use nothing that is not essential.'

'Very well, it happened that at the party a question of the interpretation of some of the figures arose in my mind, and I thought I should like to consult Minter on the point. Minter, I knew, was going down to Norne's in time for dinner. So I slipped away and rang him up then and there. He told me he was not feeling very well, and was not going down to Norne's till after dinner. Well, I didn't want to worry him with business if he wasn't well, so it occurred to me that we might meet before he started in the evening instead. I put this up to him, telling him what I had in mind, and in the end it was decided he would call at the office about seven-fifty, on his way to the eight-fifteen train.

'I should explain to you, perhaps, why that suited me? Or are you not interested in that?'

French shrugged. 'I can't pretend it's very vital, sir, but when you're telling the story, you might as well make it complete.'

'Well, we were going to the Aldwych Theatre, which, as you know, is just beside the office. Our play was at 8.30. This would give me time to meet Minter, see him off about

143

8.05 to catch the 8.15 at Waterloo, put my papers away, walk to the theatre and be in plenty of time to meet my wife and her friends at the theatre. Of course I'd have to leave home .before them, but as I expected the same suggestion would be made about dinner as about lunch, I'd probably have had to do this in any case. You follow?'

'Yes, sir, it's very clear.'

'The party dragged out its weary length. My brother-in-law, Lyde, who, I think I told you, is an actor unhappily temporarily out of a job, did a sort of one-man variety show for the children that wasn't so bad. But otherwise it was a ghastly business.' Sheen smiled crookedly. 'But the kiddies liked it. That decent fellow Sloley and his wife had come, also Mrs Minter. The rest you wouldn't know. Well, I happened to tell Sloley what I had arranged with Minter, and he said at once that he'd come to the office with me. "Look here," he said, "we'll slip away and have a bit of dinner in Town and go on there. We'd only be a nuisance here anyway." He didn't say it, but I knew very well what he wanted—to get away from my party at the earliest possible moment, and I did what I could to make it easy for him. Besides, I was glad to have his company.

'He went home and changed—we live close to one another—and then we went and had some dinner at the Holborn and then on down to the office. We got there about quarter to eight. In about five minutes Minter joined us. The three of us discussed the figures, and Minter cleared up the point that had been worrying me. Then I suggested that he should take the figures with him and show them to Norne and the others so that they could think over them before the meeting, to which he agreed.

'Minter then left; I suppose that would be about two or

144

three minutes past eight. Sloley and I followed him and walked to the Aldwych, where we met the others and where the child saw her first play.'

'I understand, sir. Then after the theatre you went down to Guildford?'

'Yes. Sloley had parked his car in Ronder Lane. As soon as we had seen our people into taxis we set off. I don't know if I said that Mrs Sloley and Mrs Minter and the two Sloley children had joined us.'

'I think you told me that before. You got down to Guildford without incident?'

'Yes.'

'Quite,' said French absently. This statement was certainly pretty complete. There was not much still to inquire into. He thought for a moment and asked: 'And then on Sunday?'

'On Sunday afternoon I came back to Town with Sloley, Osenden and Ricardo.'

'And went home?'

'Yes.'

'You remained at home till Monday morning?'

'I did,' Sheen answered grimly. 'I was glad to get the chance. I hadn't had much of a weekend.'

'There's just one other point, Mr Sheen. You said you 'phoned Mr Minter, asking him to call at the office. What time was that?'

'I told you: seven-fifty.'

'Sorry, sir. I mean what time did you 'phone?'

'Oh. Getting on to half-past four, I think. I'm not positive.'

This, then, accounted for the second call Minter had received. French decided to put a man on to try to trace the first one. He got up.

'Well, sir, I'm much obliged to you. That's all I want.

Some little point may arise afterwards, and if so, you won't mind my coming back to you. Now I've to see Mr Sloley. Do you happen to know if he's here today?'

For answer Sheen took up his desk telephone. 'Oh, Norne, is Sloley about?' There was a silence. 'Oh, he is, is he? The chief-inspector's here, and would like to see him.' Another silence and Sheen put down the telephone.

'He's with Mr Norne. If you go along to Miss Barber's room, she'll fix you up.'

'Come along, Carter,' French said. 'We've wasted too much of Mr Sheen's time as it is,' and with a brief word of thanks, the two police officers left the room.

Miss Barber was in a much more agreeable mood than on the occasion of French's previous interview. She smiled and answered pleasantly when he greeted her and seemed to have forgotten her own importance and superiority.

'We were looking for Mr Sloley,' French explained presently, 'and were told you could produce him on demand. Would you kindly work the miracle for us?'

'I can,' she answered graciously, 'and I will. Come this way.'

She led them out of the office and along the passage to a small waiting room furnished with a table and three or four easy-chairs. 'If you wait there for a couple of minutes,' she went on, 'I'll send him in.' Her air of scornful super-iority was superb, but there was a smile in her eye to which French responded.

'She doesn't half own the office, does she, sir?' Carter grinned.

'Conceited young idiot,' French agreed.

'I heard her,' went on Carter reminiscently, 'slanging the

146

porter the other day. He'd forgotten a letter of something and she told him off about it proper. I wondered the man took it from her.'

'A girl like that has the ear of the boss,' said French, 'and so she doesn't know her own size.'

'They're all the same,' Carter said darkly. 'My daughter thinks she's the Lord Almighty about the house.'

'And I bet she gets off with it,' French returned.

Carter shook his head a trifle sheepishly, but his denial was interrupted by the entrance of Sloley.

'Good morning, gentlemen,' he said breezily. 'I hear you want to see me, chief-inspector? Well, here I am.'

'Thank you, sir,' French returned. 'I've just been getting a statement from Mr Sheen about the events of last weekend, and I should be glad if you would kindly let me have your account of the same period.'

'Of course, chief-inspector. But I think I told you that already.'

'You did, sir; you gave me a short preliminary statement. Now I want the same thing, only in full detail.'

Sloley didn't see why his former statement wasn't good enough: he certainly had taken trouble enough to make it complete. But eventually he supposed that French knew his own business, and agreed in a resigned way to answer questions.

As a matter of fact, however, he had nothing new to tell. On all the essential points he confirmed what Sheen had said. It appeared that on Saturday he wasn't in the office till the evening, as he only attended if there was a directors' meeting. He had spent the afternoon at Sheen's party, and had jumped at the chance of leaving it which dining with Sheen and going to the office presented. Minter certainly appeared ill when he turned up, though he, Sloley, had seen him looking worse. But he had taken the precaution to go down to the office door and see the man into his taxi. After the theatre he and Sheen had driven down to Guildford.

Believing that he had obtained from Sloley as much as he could possibly expect, French thanked him and with Carter returned to the Yard. There he put a man on to try to trace the telephone call which Minter had received about 3 p.m. on the Saturday afternoon. Then he sat down to consider what he had learnt and plan his next step.

He soon saw that he was not so much further on from Sloley's and Sheen's evidence as he had hoped he would be. What he had learnt did not definitely answer the question of whether or not these two men were guilty of the robbery. It was true that their story was reasonable and hung together, and if it were true, they were undoubtedly innocent. But French knew that if they were guilty their story would still be reasonable and hang together. They would see to that.

He got up and began to pace the room. Mentally he worried the problem as a dog worries a bone. How was he to learn the truth? Was the answer buried in what they had told him, if only he could disinter it? Or must he think out further tests?

Then his thoughts reverted to what he had already seen was the fundamental issue in the affair. Everything hinged on the question of whether Sloley and Sheen had or had not murdered Minter. If they had somehow obtained his key, and feared that when he learned of the robbery he would suspect this and give them away, their only safeguard would have been murder. Conversely, if they had not murdered him, would it not show they had nothing to fear from him?

French then went to the vital point. If they had nothing to fear from him, did it mean that they had not robbed the safe?

The answer to this was not so obvious, and yet as he thought over it, French became increasingly convinced that it did mean this. They couldn't, he felt sure, have played *any* trick with the key, which Minter would not have suspected as soon as he heard of the robbery. And they couldn't have risked his suspicion.

The more French thought over it, the more convinced he became that his conclusion was correct: the guilt or innocence of these men of the murder was the essential point. They were guilty of both crimes or of neither.

If he were right, and he was sure that he was, his next investigation resolved itself into one simple inquiry. Were Sloley and Sheen really in Town at eleven o'clock on that Saturday night, as they said? If they were, it was utterly impossible that they could have committed the murder.

Glad to be up against a definite issue, French decided to put the matter to the test forthwith. With Carter he set off, therefore, for Sheen's house in Hampstead. He chose Sheen's rather than Sloley's because he knew that Sheen would be at the office, whereas Sloley might be at home, and he wanted independent evidence.

The house turned out to be a small one in a rather poor street, and it looked shabby and uncared for. The door was opened by Mrs Sheen herself, and from her appearance French saw that she was engaged in housework. She was a small washed-out woman who had once probably been pretty, but who had now very definitely lost her good looks. She looked doubtfully from French to Carter. French raised his hat.

'Good afternoon, madam. You are Mrs Sheen, aren't you?'

She nodded, waiting with her hand on the door.

French introduced himself, and she moved back, making way for the two men to enter the narrow, poorly furnished hall. 'Come in,' she invited, though obviously unwillingly. 'My brother's here, but you won't mind.'

She threw open a door and French and Carter passed into a small dining room, giving on to the garden in the back. French caught a glimpse of a grass plot with shrubs stretching back to a brick wall of the richest and most mellow shade, of a small shed through the open door of which appeared a bench and rack of tools, and of a wooden bird table on which was stretched in an attitude of replete satisfaction a huge black cat.

In the room the furniture was like that in the hall, of poor quality and shabby, and not a great deal of it at that. There was, however, a cheerful fire in the grate, and the two armchairs, though their leatherette coverings were worn into holes, were deep and comfortable looking. In one of them a man was lounging. He was small and slight like his sister, with a thin clean-shaven intelligent face. He got up as the others entered.

'This is Chief-Inspector French, Lambert,' said Mrs Sheen. 'My brother, Mr Lyde.' She paused for a moment while the men nodded to each other, then went on. 'Perhaps my brother could answer some of your questions, chief-inspector. I'm engaged for a few minutes. Tell the chief-inspector what you can, Lambert, and I'll be back presently.'

She disappeared and Lyde pointed to the second armchair, pulling out one of the smaller chairs for Carter.

'Won't you sit down, gentlemen. I've heard about you from the brother-in-law, chief-inspector.'

'I suppose so, Mr Lyde.' French had forgotten the existence of this individual, but he now remembered that both Sloley and Sheen had spoken of him. This was the actor, temporarily out of a job, who had given a turn at the children's party.

'I rather doubt that you can give me the information I require,' French went on. 'It's about the Saturday of the robbery. I'm trying to make a sort of timetable of what everyone did during that weekend; a matter of routine which we always have to do. It concerns the late Mr Minter, but we have to check his movements up by everyone else's. Now, Mr Sheen has told me a great deal, but he wasn't sure of some of the times and I'd like to get them checked.'

'I'm afraid I can't help you then. I didn't come across Mr Minter at all. In fact, I scarcely knew him.'

'Quite so, but perhaps about Saturday afternoon you could tell me something? You were here that afternoon?'

'As a matter of fact I wasn't, except for a few minutes. The Sheens were giving a children's party, and as this house was too small, they had it in the Blue Tiger in the next street. I was there.' He smiled sardonically. 'Couldn't get out of it, you know.'

'I heard about that, sir. You were good enough to give some kind of entertainment?'

'Yes; couldn't get out of that either. I'm on the stage, you know; or rather off it at present. It's been the devil of a time for our profession.'

151

'I've heard so, sir.' French was sympathetic. 'Mr Sheen and Mr Sloley were at the party, I understand?'

'Yes; they couldn't get out of it either.'

'My first question then is, can you tell me what time they left?'

'About six, I think, but I really am not certain. I left about half-past six—I was crossing by the 8.20 to Paris—and they had gone some little time before that.'

'Then you didn't see Mr Sheen again that night?'

'No, I dined alone on my way to Victoria.'

This being all the information French could hope for from Lyde, the two men drifted into conversation about France and Channel crossings and flights. Lyde had, it appeared, gone to Fontainebleau for the Sunday. He had old associations with the place, and in spite of, or perhaps because of, the fact that it was rather cold, he had enjoyed a long tramp through the forest. His business engagement didn't take place till that evening.

In the middle of reminiscences of Continental travel, Mrs Sheen came in. Lyde thereupon made his excuses and vanished.

French went through his usual preamble as to the need for checking certain times of which Mr Sheen was not quite sure. Then he asked about the time of everything from the afternoon on, as he had begun to do in the case of Lyde. He only, of course, wanted the one figure, but he didn't wish that attention should be called to that.

In the end he obtained a quite definite answer to his question. The show had been over at five minutes before eleven; Mrs Sheen had looked at her watch and was quite sure. They had gone out at once and after a little delay Sheen had got taxis. She and Mrs Sloley and the children had taken one, and Mrs Minter, who lived in a different direction, the other. They had left the theatre at three or four minutes past eleven, arriving home at twenty-five minutes past. She was sure of this because she had again looked at her watch, being concerned about the children being kept up so late. Sheen and Sloley had remained behind at the theatre, as they were driving down to Guildford.

This in itself seemed conclusive proof of the innocence of the two men. Minter must have been dead before the party left the theatre, or if not, long before Sloley and Sheen could have reached Guildford. French was tempted to leave it at that, but after all Mrs Sheen was Sheen's wife, and would therefore be biased in her evidence. Rather grudgingly French continued to get all the available confirmation.

First he saw Mrs Sloley and Mrs Minter, and learned that their testimony agreed with Mrs Sheen's. He went to the Aldwych Theatre, and ascertained that the show in question always ended about or before eleven. Lastly, he found the taxi which had conveyed the Sheen party home, and was assured by the driver that he had not started till the show was over.

Sloley and Sheen were therefore definitely innocent of the murder. And unless French's ideas were wrong from beginning to end, if they were innocent of the murder, they were innocent of the theft.

It was in a depressed state of mind that French rang up Superintendent Fenning and told him the result of his inquiries. The four most likely suspects were now out of it, and infinitely worse than that, French could not visualise any other promising line of research. Fenning was equally despondent. He had learnt nothing fresh about the murder, and didn't see how he was going to. Fortunately for both of them, the next day was Sunday, and both decided they would take a complete holiday, so as to attack their respective problems with a fresh mind on Monday morning.

12

Enter Intrigue

French spent a rather unhappy Monday in going through his notes and trying for the hundredth time to find some indication, if not of the truth, at least of a fresh line of inquiry. But he seemed to have covered all the possibilities. Nowhere could he see a glimmering of light.

On Tuesday he had to attend court in connection with another case, but on Wednesday morning he went down to the Norne offices with the intention of having another chat with Miss Barber. He wished to get from her a note of any unusual visitors to Norne, or of anyone who had waited alone in Norne's room, or who had seen Norne there after ordinary office hours. He was not hopeful of the result, but for the moment he could think of nothing more promising.

He reached the office to find that a board meeting was in progress. On the table outside Norne's door were the hats and coats and umbrellas of the assembled directors. 'Something important on?' he asked.

'Well,' Miss Barber answered with a slight return to her

usual scornful manner, 'I don't know whether you would call it important. They're deciding whether or not we're to announce our bankruptcy.'

'I thought that was dealt with a week ago,' French returned. 'Mr Norne gave me to understand that the weekend meeting at his house when Mr Minter died, was to settle that point for the following Wednesday.'

'So it was. But on account of the theft they postponed the decision for a week. There's a special meeting today.'

French nodded and pursued the even tenor of his inquiries. But from Miss Barber he received no help. He had asked her these questions before, she had answered them to the best of her ability, and she didn't see why she should have to put up with them all over again. Presently he gave it up in despair.

In moving towards the door, he passed close to the table on which were lying the directors' hats and coats. Automatically he noted, as he always did, which hats were placed right side up and which upside down. As he glanced at one in the latter position, he felt a sudden quickening of interest.

It was a black bowler, and across it lay a pair of yellow wash-leather gloves. There was something familiar about that combination. French moved over and glanced into the hat. On the band were stuck the letters A. R. It was the same hat, so he could have sworn, that he had seen in Minter's hall on the occasion of his last visit.

'Who is A. R.?' he asked, pointing to the hat.

'A. R. would stand for Claude Willington Norne or Ralph Osenden, wouldn't it?' said the lady scornfully.

'I don't know all your directors' names,' French returned mildly. 'Are you trying to tell me it's Mr Ricardo?'

'A. R. stands for Anthony Ricardo, I suppose. He's the only one whose name begins with R.'

'I see. Cousin of Mrs Minter's, isn't he?'

The girl snorted. 'Not likely. What put that in your head?'

'But seriously I thought he was. Are you sure?'

'Well, I'm not related to either of 'em, so I don't know. But I should have thought that anyone with half an eye would have known they weren't the same class.'

'This is very interesting,' French assured her. 'Which do you mean is too good for the other?'

She grew a little sulky, thinking he was pulling her leg. 'I thought you were finding out about all the people concerned,' she said pertly. 'Why, Ricardo, he's a gentleman; he's got a fine place out near Ely; member of a club in the West End, and so on. What did you think Minter was? Little more than a clerk, he was.'

'So you don't believe that handsome is that handsome does?' French grinned.

'Never heard of it.'

'I don't suppose you did,' said French, which didn't please her either. 'Were Mr Ricardo and Mr Minter not friends, then?'

'They weren't enemies, if that's what you mean. But they weren't friends either. Why, Mr Ricardo never came across Minter. He never went to his office or anything like that.'

'I see. Well, it doesn't matter to me if they were brothers.'

'I suppose that's why you were asking so interestedly.'

'That's the reason. Well, Miss Barber, if you think of anything that might help me, don't fail to give me a ring.'

That the girl was wrong as to the 'class' of Mrs Minter was obvious to French. Both she and Ricardo unquestionably belonged to the so-called 'upper' classes. There was nothing improbable in the idea that they were cousins.

Then French remembered the curious air of embarrassment which Martha Belden had shown on the occasion of French's call. The way in which she had said that Mrs Minter was engaged, and had asked him to wait, carefully shutting him in to the back of the house so that he could not see the departing guest. Why should she have been embarrassed? If Ricardo was Mrs Minter's cousin, why should not he, French, have been shown up at once?

It was probably all nonsense, but French's calling had made him suspicious. Could there, he wondered, be another explanation of that call, that embarrassment, that immediate disappearance?

It might, he thought, be interesting to find out whether Ricardo was indeed Mrs Minter's cousin. If he were not, and if the bond between the two were of a different kind, might he not be on to something valuable, even vital? Could it be that he was going to find another possible motive for Minter's murder, not connected with the robbery?

To French it didn't seem likely. At the same time he knew that he would have no peace of mind until he had settled the question. For a moment he hesitated, wondering if the affair were Fenning's job rather than his own. Then he decided to ignore the possibility.

Turning into a street booth, he put through a call to Mrs Minter. He was (of course) sorry to trouble her again, but he had to admit that he had not yet solved the problem of Mr Minter's death, and in the hope of getting a line on some possible enemy, he wondered if he might look through Mr Minter's private desk and papers?

158

The lady was evidently unwilling, but apparently she liked still less to refuse, and she presently gave a rather grudging consent. In half an hour French was at the house.

Martha evidently had her orders. She greeted him sourly, showed him into the deceased's study, and withdrew, closing the door.

French hadn't expected such a *carte blanche* as this. With a feeling of surprised thankfulness, he settled down to go through the desk.

He worked hard, for he did not know how soon he might be interrupted. Quickly, but thoroughly, he ran through the papers and books. They were mostly connected in one way or another with finance—bills, receipts, bank and cheque-books, notices about rent, taxes, gas and the like. There were some bundles of letters on various subjects, and a set of diaries going back over several years. But none of them seemed of the slightest use.

Presently leaving the desk, he began to look over the remaining furniture. There were several book-cases, one an old-fashioned affair with a lower cupboard. The key of the latter was in the lock, and going down on his knees, French opened it and began a search through its contents.

Almost at once he came on what he had been hoping to find—a relic of a by-gone age—a scrap-book into which letters, pictures, newspaper articles and such like had been pasted. Taking it to the desk, he rapidly turned over the pages.

He felt he could scarcely hope to find what he desired in the first book he picked up, and he was therefore the more pleased when, within a dozen pages of the beginning, he came on the very thing. Some luck!

It was a newspaper paragraph and under the date of

159

July, 1910, it described the wedding of Charles Minter, of Droitwich, in the County of Worcester, with Clara Florence Crabbe, of Ombersley, in the same county. The report was very complete, but the name of Ricardo did not appear among the donors of presents.

This, of course, meant very little. There were a dozen reasons why the man might not have given a present. At the same time it was suggestive.

Leaving the house, French went to the nearest police station and rang up the officer in charge at Ely. Would he please find out for him how long Mr Anthony Ricardo had been living at Garth House, Cambridge Road, and also, if possible, whether he had been there during July, 1910?

Late that evening the reply came back. Garth Cottage had belonged to the late Colonel Ricardo, Anthony's father, and Anthony had lived there all his life. He had been there in May of 1910, for local records showed that he had been a speaker at a political meeting in that month. The officer, however, could not tell whether he had been there in July without asking him, which he presumed French didn't wish done.

This information was sufficiently suggestive to make French wish for more. He thought he might risk a direct question.

Accordingly, next morning he rang up Miss Barber and asked when she thought he could see Ricardo. She answered that he was then in the office. A decision had not been reached on the bankruptcy question on the previous day, and the board was sitting again.

When it ended French was waiting at the office. If not engaged, could Mr Ricardo spare him a few minutes?

He wanted to check up a few times mentioned in his former statement.

Ricardo seemed rather bored at the idea, but he said he was not busy and what did the chief-inspector want to know?

French took him through the whole of his original statement, asking for an estimate of the hour at which everything had happened and trying to get more complete details of the happenings at Norne's. This was not exactly lost time, as if Ricardo did come under suspicion, it would have to be done in any case. Ricardo grew more and more exasperated as the interrogation proceeded, repeatedly stating that he had already answered the questions, but French took no notice of his protests, plodding on to the bitter end.

When this was reached, he closed his notebook, stood up, and thanked his victim courteously for his patience. This mollified Ricardo, and he chatted in a friendly enough way.

French had opened the door and was withdrawing when he suddenly drew back. 'By the way, Mr Ricardo, talking of another matter altogether, can you tell me whether Mrs Robert Soames of Hellifield is still alive?'

Mrs Robert Soames of Hellifield, he had learned from the Worcester newspaper, was the aunt of Clara Crabbe. She had been at the wedding and had given a present. French knew that he was taking a risk in asking the question. If Ricardo had heard Mrs Minter speak of her aunt, he might answer it in such a way that French would be no further on.

Ricardo, however, reacted in the most satisfactory manner. He stared and said, 'Never heard of her. Who is she when she's at home?'

'Mr Leonard Crabbe's sister,' said French, feeling that he would be sure of his ground if he mentioned Mrs Minter's father.

'And who the devil might Mr Leonard Crabbe be?' Ricardo retorted testily.

'An old friend of mine who used to live at Ely,' French answered smoothly. 'I thought perhaps you might have known him.'

Ricardo shook his head and French could not but think that there was an implication in the gesture that French's friends were not likely to be his. 'Never heard of him,' he repeated in a final voice as if dismissing the subject, and French was very willing to relinquish it.

From all this it followed that Ricardo and Mrs Minter were not connected. If they had been cousins the man would have known the names. There was something then between them. Were they mere acquaintances or was it something more intimate?

French continued turning the matter over in his mind. If he, supposing himself in Ricardo's place, were anxious to carry on an intrigue with Clara Minter, how would he arrange their meetings?

Not, he was positive, at either of their houses. While he might occasionally call at Minter's, some safer *rendezvous* would be an essential. Where might such be found?

Obviously only in London: more than likely a flat in some quiet and discreet neighbourhood: probably not too far from St John's Wood . . .

French wondered how he could find such a flat, assuming it existed. Then he thought that perhaps Ricardo himself might show it to him. On the chance he would put a couple of men on to shadow Ricardo.

Then French took a sudden decision. Instead of 'phoning for men, he would do the shadowing himself. It was a long time since he had done such work and it would be a novelty. But this was not his real reason. In his heart of hearts he knew that he was doing it because he had nothing else to go on with.

Ricardo was still in the building. He was chatting with some of the other directors in the central hall. French passed out into Ronder Lane, and slipping round into Kingsway, hailed a passing taxi.

'Scotland Yard,' he said, showing the driver his card. 'I want you to follow a man. Pull in to the pavement and I'll point him out.'

As he spoke, Ricardo and Osenden emerged into Kingsway. They stood talking on the footpath for a moment, then separated. Sir Ralph hailed a taxi, while Ricardo walked slowly south and turned west into Aldwych.

'Can't go that way, guv'ner,' the driver called with a grin. 'One way street.'

French returned the grin. Then he jumped out and followed his man on foot.

Ricardo walked to the nearest telephone booth and put through a call. Then he went down to the Strand. He did not look round, and French had no difficulty in keeping him in sight.

For a short time the chase continued westwards and then the quarry turned south—into the Savoy Hotel. French watched him enter the doors, then turned back. A line of taxis stood on the hotel approach road, and he made for the hindmost. There he explained the circumstances to the driver, climbed in, and sat watching the hotel door through the rear window.

It was just quarter to one, and French wondered if his luck was in. For half an hour he crouched in his hiding-place, and then with something of a thrill he saw that it was. A taxi drove up and Mrs Minter left it and entered the building.

There ensued a tedious period of waiting. For over an hour French hung about, killing time in the least ostentatious way he could. Then his patience was rewarded. Ricardo and Mrs Minter appeared, a taxi was called, and they stepped in and were driven off.

French followed in another taxi. His driver proved a good man and kept so close to the other that they avoided separation by traffic signals. The chase led along the Strand, and through Trafalgar Square, Piccadilly Circus, Oxford Circus, Marble Arch and Edgware Road to Maida Vale. There it turned down Clifton Gardens, and so to Rennington Street. At No. 573 it stopped. In accordance with instructions, French's driver continued on past the other taxi, and turning into the first side street, also stopped.

Shadowing was not now so easy. The street was a quiet one, and a loafer would soon become conspicuous. French decided to call in professional aid. He soon found two constables, and promising to make it right with their superior officers, enlisted their help. They were to patrol the two ends of Rennington Street, and watch for the emergence of the couple. He, French, would remain in the district, relieving the constables in turn, so that their continued presence should not attract attention.

It proved a long vigil. Not till nearly eight was there a sign of the pair, and during this time the constables had been changed and French had got himself some food. About ten minutes to eight a taxi drove to the door and the two got in and were driven away.

French allowed a little time to elapse, then went to the house and knocked.

The door was opened by a small, wizened old woman, who examined French critically out of a pair of very sharp eyes.

'Good evening,' he said. 'Are you the owner or the care-taker of the house?'

She gave him a further prolonged stare. 'And what is it to you?' she retorted presently.

'I'll tell you, madam,' French said in an official tone. 'I'm a chief-inspector of police from Scotland Yard, and if you'll let me come in for a moment I'll explain my business.'

Once again there was a keen scrutiny, but the lady was by this time apparently satisfied, for she opened the door and motioned him into the hall.

'Come in here,' she said, leading the way downstairs into a small basement sitting room.

'Sit down,' she said pointing to a chair, and seating herself at a tiny desk. 'Now what is it?'

French thanked her briefly and sat down. 'I'm engaged in an inquiry,' he began, 'which has nothing whatever to do with you. I have simply come for a little information. For various reasons I want to find out how long the lady and gentleman who have just gone out have been using your house.'

'There's nothing wrong about their using the house,' she said combatively.

'I know there's not,' French agreed. 'I told you my inquiry had nothing to do with you. It's the gentleman that I'm really interested in. You needn't be afraid to tell me.'

She winked her small and rather evil eye. 'Oh, it's one of these divorce cases, is it?' she went on, then without waiting for an answer, added: 'Well, what's it going to be worth to me to come over with what I know?'

'If your evidence should be required in court, you'll get your expenses,' French declared, 'but we official police daren't pay for it beforehand.'

She demurred, but he frightened her with vague threats and she answered his questions.

It appeared that 'Mr Parkinson' had rented a small flat on the first floor, her best flat, some ten months previously. Since that date he had been a fairly frequent visitor, occasionally alone, but usually with 'Mrs Parkinson.' Nearly always the visits had been paid in the afternoon, though sometimes the parties came before lunch. On these occasions they brought lunch with them. It was part of her bargain that she should keep the rooms clean, and she had removed partially consumed chickens and grouse, and partially emptied bottles of superlatively excellent wine. On two occasions only had the couple remained all night.

Having warned Mrs Mickleham to be silent as to his visit, French went wearily home. He had had a long and boring day, but it had been worth it. He was pleased to find that his hand had not lost its cunning in the practical work of a detective officer. He had obtained his information with, he felt, all the skill and speed of the most efficient of the younger men of the service. Of course, he had had luck: he would be the last to deny it. Still, it had been a good bit of work and he was well satisfied with himself.

But when he came to consider the information he had

gained, he became a good deal less triumphant. Was he on to the real motive of the murder, or was the whole thing a mare's nest?

He banished the problem from his mind that night, settling down in his chair with a novel. But next morning in the office he tackled it seriously.

A little consideration convinced him as to the adequacy of the motive. If these two persons were really deeply in love, their present way of living would be unendurable. Of course, it might be said, why keep it secret? Why not go away together and be done with it? But this might not have suited Ricardo. He was a man of some standing and had lived all his life in his place at Ely, as had his father before him. He might not have been willing to give up his position and circle of friends as, even in these days, he would have had to do if he had gone off with another man's wife. Yes, there was certainly motive on Ricardo's part, and probably on Mrs Minter's as well.

But had either of them opportunity? French writhed as he thought of this difficult point. Mrs Minter was at the theatre with the Sloleys and Sheens and was therefore out of it. But Ricardo, he supposed, had as much opportunity as anyone else at Guildford; though that, as far as he could see, was none at all.

That really was the puzzle in a nutshell: *no one* had any opportunity!

The fact, then, that he, French, couldn't see how Ricardo could be guilty of the murder, didn't prove him innocent, because French couldn't see how anyone could be guilty. Quite definitely, there was some factor about the murder which he, French, had overlooked, and this factor might show Ricardo as guilty as anyone else.

But this question of guilt of the murder was, after all, not his, French's, job. He really must confine himself to the robbery, and here he couldn't see that his new discovery was any help at all. The fact that Ricardo and Clara Minter were in love didn't explain why Ricardo, a man apparently with plenty of money, should burgle the safe. Still less did it explain how he could have done it.

French put through another call to the police at Ely. He would like a secret report on Ricardo, with special regard to his finances and domestic affairs. Could this be managed?

The officer said he would put it in hand at once and French rang off.

His thoughts went back from his own case to Fenning's. Both he and Fenning had made some hideous oversight. It *must* be so, because the evidence, as at present understood, was contradictory. Where such conditions obtained, experience had told him that the fault was his own. He was misreading some of the apparent facts.

For the hundredth time he considered that Saturday night in Norne's house. Norne had visited Minter about ten; the only visitor for hours. The doctor said Minter had been murdered about ten. How could there be any doubt of Norne's guilt?

There couldn't be; and yet French wasn't sure. His instincts told him to believe Norne's denials. Of course, instincts were not infallible, but still . . .

Then an idea recurred to him which had already entered his mind, but which he had not seriously considered. If no one other than Norne had entered Minter's room by the door, what about the window? Had someone paid a secret visit to the deceased shortly after ten?

If this could be proved, the whole case, as far as the murder was concerned, would fall into line and become intelligible.

But this would not help the robbery. Well, damn the robbery for the moment. French felt he must consult with Fenning about that window idea. He rang him up and said he was going down to Guildford by the next train.

13

Enter a Rope

Superintendent Fenning listened with politeness but no great enthusiasm to French's new idea.

'Yes,' he said when he had heard it to the end, 'I agree that if someone had used the window, that would explain a good deal. Who have you in mind? Norne?'

'Norne admits he left the others for ten or twelve minutes about half-past ten. Ricardo and Osenden may also have left the room. If so, any one of them could have carried out any trick, unknown to the other two.'

Fenning nodded expectantly.

'Suppose,' continued French, 'Norne threw out a rope ladder when he was up at ten. Or if you like, suppose Ricardo or Osenden found out that Minter was to have that room and threw out a rope ladder before ever Minter arrived. Couldn't whoever did that have climbed up, killed Minter, climbed down again, and gone back into the library, without anyone being a bit the wiser?'

'And conveniently closed the window from the inside and removed the ladder from the ground.'

'H'm,' said French, 'that's a nasty one. My point is simply this: Minter was probably murdered about ten. If Norne didn't do it during his known visit and if Jeffries' statement is true, entrance through the window is the only possibility left.'

Fenning saw that French was keen on his idea and evidently wished to humour him, for he said: 'Let's go up and have another look at the room.'

This was what French had really wanted and he agreed with alacrity. Fenning rang for his car, and a few minutes later the two men reached Severno.

Norne had not required the room Minter had occupied, and as the adjourned inquest had not yet been held, Fenning had kept the door sealed. He now broke the seals and they entered. French crossed the room to the window.

It was an ordinary four-sectioned window with lead lights and steel frames. Three vertical wooden bars divided it into the four sections. The whole of the two end sections opened outwards on side hinges, the hinges being at the extreme sides of the windows. The bottom portions of the two centre sections were fixed, but their upper two-fifths opened outwards, the hinges being along the tops. The wooden bars and surrounding casing were painted cream and the steel frames black.

'Now, let's see,' said French when he had assimilated these facts, 'you found the two side windows shut and latched, and the upper quadrants of the centre ones partly open?'

'That's correct.'

'Well, see, super. Suppose a man set a ladder up against the sill, he could put his arm in through one of the centre upper quadrants and reach down and unlatch the adjoining side window.'

'Those latches should always be put to the side of the frame away from the quadrant for that very reason.'

'Yes, but they very seldom are. They weren't here, at all events. Do you agree with that, super?'

'That a man standing on the sill could stretch in through the quadrant and open a side window? Yes, I suppose he could.'

'And if he could open a side window, he could enter by it?'

'Naturally.'

'And again, if he left the room by a side window, he could close it and latch it while standing on the sill?'

'Agreed.'

French slowly rubbed his hands. 'Well, you know,' he declared, 'I believe that's what was done.'

For a moment the super did not reply. Then he shook himself slightly. 'I'm blessed but it sounds likely enough,' he admitted. 'And, of course, if Norne had given Minter the dope at ten o'clock, Minter would have been asleep by half-past.'

French agreed as he moved close up to the window and looked down. 'A wooden ladder would have done the trick,' he went on. 'The gravel path down there is hard; the butts wouldn't show.' Really, this idea looked more and more likely the longer he thought over it.

Fenning was looking more impressed. 'As a matter of routine we tested the window hasps for prints,' he said, 'and there were none on any of them. It seemed not unreasonable, for the maid said they hadn't been touched for some time. But in the face of what you've been saying, we ought to know how much time.'

French nodded quickly. 'That's it, super,' he approved.

'We'll have her up now.' Fenning crossed the room and pressed the bell. Presently Jeffries entered.

'Send up Alice, will you, please.'

The maid was sure of her facts. The side windows had been opened and closed on the Thursday preceding Minter's death, when the room had had its usual turn out. The quadrants had been left open on that occasion and since then neither had been touched.

'Thursday to Sunday,' the super said when she had gone. 'Prints should have remained for that time, surely?'

'Was there anything else handled on that Thursday and not again till Sunday?' French asked. 'Get that girl back.'

Alice was not able to answer this question so readily. In fact, it took a deal of prompting before she thought of anything. At last, however, she said that on that same Thursday she had opened and closed the door of a built-in cupboard near the bed. This, she believed, had not been opened since.

'That's right,' Fenning agreed. 'I remember this girl's prints were on the door handle. And if so, chief-inspector, it looks as if you were right about the window.'

'I wish, Alice,' said French suddenly, 'you'd take us to another room with a window like this.'

'Next door?'

'The very thing.'

They went in next door and French resumed: 'Now, I want you to open that window just as you did the other one on that Thursday, and then close it again. Wait; let me clean the handles.'

When she had done so, French let her go. Then he got some powder from his emergency case in the car and dusted the handles. Clear prints came out.

173

The super nodded several times. 'That about fixes it, chief,' he declared with something approaching awe in his manner. 'You're on to a bull's eye this time. The absence of prints in the next room proves that somebody cleaned the handles.'

'It looks like a true bill right enough,' French agreed. Though this was not really his case and he kept on reminding himself of the fact, he was as nearly excited as his dignity would allow. 'I think we may take it someone has used a ladder, and that could only be for the one thing.'

Fenning agreed. 'And the man that used the ladder,' he concluded, 'is the man we want for the murder.'

As they spoke they had been walking slowly back to the room Minter had occupied. French crossed once again to the window.

'Let's have another squint at this window,' he suggested. 'If a ladder was used, it would have rested against the sill. With luck we might find dents, or perhaps a scratch from a shoe.'

They settled down to it, scrutinising every inch of the window, inside and out, as well as the floor adjoining.

For a time neither spoke, each being fully occupied. Then French gave a little exclamation. 'Look here, super,' he went on. 'What do you make of those?'

They were two slight scrapes on the centre mullion, the vertical wooden division between the two middle sections of the window. It was as if a stiff brush had been passed horizontally round the two inner corners of the bar at the level of the bottom of the quadrant openings. That on the left was more pronounced, and examination with a lens showed faint marks across the flat of the bar, connecting those at the corners.

174

For a few moments Fenning looked at the marks in a puzzled way. Then his expression changed and he gave vent to a mild oath. 'Got it again, chief,' he cried. 'There can't be much doubt about that.'

'No,' French agreed, trying to hide his excitement. 'We may take it that's the murderer's visiting card which he left after his call on Minter. A pity we can't read his name.'

'We'll get him,' Fenning returned with more enthusiasm than he had yet shown. 'This opens a completely new line.'

'I hope so,' said French more soberly. 'Let's put it into words, super. Sometimes doing that shows you a snag you've missed in your mind. Here, I take it, we have a mark made by drawing a rope round the mullion. It suggests to me that the murderer made his getaway by means of a rope which he brought in through one of the quadrant windows and out through the other, both ends hanging down to the ground. The height of the scratch suggests that the rope was resting on the top bars of the lower fixed panes in those centre sections. You agree?'

Fenning nodded. 'I agree. And the deeper mark on the left shows that when he had got down he pulled the rope out through the left window.'

'Quite; the deeper mark was on the last corner it passed round.'

'That seems all O.K.' Fenning thought for a while, then went on with more hesitation; 'But, look here, how do you think he got in?'

'Why not up the rope?'

'Oh, yes, that's right enough—provided the rope was there. But how did he get it there?'

'Well, so far as I can see, if he didn't use a wooden ladder, he could only have put it there from the inside. But if he had a wooden ladder, he wouldn't have wanted the rope. Therefore, he had no wooden ladder. Therefore, he fixed the rope from the inside of the house—after the curtains were drawn. Therefore, does it not follow that he was Norne or one of the visitors?'

Fenning somewhat doubtfully thought that that was so. Then they rang once again for the long-suffering Alice to ask when the curtains had been pulled, and learned that it was about half past six.

After a good deal of further discussion they agreed that their discovery proved the following facts:

1. That Minter had not been murdered by Norne when he went up to see him about ten.

2. That he had been murdered by some person or persons unknown shortly after that visit of Norne's.

3. That the unknown escaped to the ground by means of a rope.

4. That when he had climbed down he pulled it after him and removed the rope.

5. That in order to get the rope in position, he or an accomplice had placed it from inside the room.

6. That this had either been done by an unknown between 6.30, when the curtains were pulled, and Minter's arrival at 9.15, or by Norne when he went up to see Minter at 10.

7. That Norne (or Osenden or Ricardo, if either of these had left the room) *might* have climbed the rope and committed the murder at 10.30, though this was unlikely owing to their age.

Before leaving Severno French rang up the Yard, where for once he had left Carter, instructing that worthy to get in touch with Osenden and Ricardo and ask whether they had remained in the library while Norne was getting his print. Then he and Fenning inquired into the question of who could have known the room Minter was to occupy, satisfying themselves that unless Osenden or Ricardo had asked Norne—which was unlikely—neither could possibly have done so.

Considerably puzzled, the officers drove back to head-quarters. There French found waiting for him a message from the Yard. The Ely police reported that while Ricardo lived well at Garth House, he was known to be very hard up. Inquiries had shown that he was trying to raise money on his estate and finding it extremely difficult, for the simple reason that it was already mortgaged to nearly its full value. The police informant had said that he wouldn't be surprised at any time to see the place in the market.

This information at once opened a new vista for specu-lation. If Ricardo was so hard up as all this, could he have committed the theft? Could he have committed both theft and murder? Could his affair with Mrs Minter have only been a strengthening of a motive already in existence? French put the point to Fenning and they discussed it for some time. Finally French summed up their conclusions.

'It comes to this, then, super. The evidence of the rope shows that Minter was murdered by someone inside the house. Now, that someone was unlikely to have been a servant.'

'Agreed. In my judgment not one of them could be guilty.'

'That leaves Norne, Osenden and Ricardo. Now, Norne's unlikely for the same reason as we thought it unlikely that he had committed the murder at ten o'clock: that he allowed it to be known that he was alone there with Minter. You remember we agreed that if he had been intending to commit the murder at ten, he would have gone to the room secretly. That argument applies equally to a visit at ten-thirty.'

'Agreed again.'

'Osenden is to my mind the very last type of man who would commit murder and robbery. Besides our report from the Ryde police pictures him as altogether unlikely. That leaves Ricardo.'

'Agreed again.'

'Ricardo was running after Minter's wife and probably wanted Minter out of the way. And now we learn he was hard up and probably going to have to sell his family place. This business of which he was a director was about to crash, so that would be the last straw that would tip Ricardo into the soup—so to speak.'

'A good phrase, chief,' Fenning said with unction. 'I congratulate you.'

'Well, here's financial ruin and the loss of Mrs Minter on the one hand, and on the other a fortune and the possibility of an honourable marriage on the other—so to speak again. Yes, super, there's no doubt about motive.'

'And opportunity.'

'We've already discussed that. Ricardo somehow finds out which is Minter's room, and while supposed to be dressing for dinner, he slips in and fixes his rope. When Norne leaves the room to get his print, let's assume Ricardo does so also. Why should he not have gone out of the front door and round to Minter's window?'

'It's a question of time.'

'Then let's estimate. It would take him, say, a minute to shut the door and run round to the window.'

'One minute.'

'Say three or four minutes to climb up the rope, open the window, and get into the room.'

'Say five minutes altogether.'

'Five minutes to smother Minter.'

'Ten minutes.'

'A minute to get the keys and take an impression.'

'Eleven minutes.'

'Three minutes to get down to the ground, pull down the rope and hide it in some prearranged place near by.'

'Fourteen minutes.'

'A minute to get back to the door and let himself in.'

'Say fifteen minutes altogether. It seems tight.'

'It might have taken him less than fifteen minutes. Minter in his poor state of health might have died in less than five. Ricardo could have slid down the rope in a matter of seconds. Besides, Norne said ten or twelve minutes. It might have been fifteen.'

'I suppose,' Fenning admitted, 'it would have been just possible.'

'If that didn't happen, something equally unlikely must have.'

Fenning moved as if reaching a conclusion. 'Well, I'll tell you how it would look to me,' he declared. 'You think his fundamental motive would have been to get the key?'

'An impression of it. It seems to me that if he couldn't get money, he couldn't get Mrs Minter either.'

'You're assuming also that he had already got Norne's key?'

'We must assume that, whoever was guilty.'

'Very well. Then his guilt or innocence of the murder would seem to me to hinge on whether he robbed the safe or whether he didn't.'

179

This led to a further argument, but at length it was decided that French should go into the possibilities of Ricardo being guilty of the robbery. According to the results of that inquiry would depend their future conduct of the case.

When French reached the Yard he found that one, at least, of the difficulties he had anticipated was nonexistent. Carter had rung up Osenden at his home near Ryde and put his question. On Norne's leaving the room to get his print, Osenden had also gone out for a few minutes, leaving Ricardo alone. When he returned, Ricardo was not there, though he came in just before Norne.

So far, so good! There had then been an opportunity for the murder. Now for the question of the theft.

After dinner that night French filled his pipe and sat down to consider his programme for the next day.

The period of Ricardo's time which he had to investigate was from about four o'clock on Sunday afternoon, when the man was set down by Sloley at Piccadilly Circus, and ten next morning, when the robbery was discovered.

For some time he considered whether Ricardo might not have had an accomplice who would have done the actual robbing of the safe. Then he saw that, whether or not, Ricardo would have been present at its opening. What was the universal feeling between conspirators? Distrust! Ricardo would never have allowed his partner in crime a free hand to take what he liked from the safe.

How, then, were the man's actions during the critical period to be ascertained? French could only think of one way. He must ask him the question. It would, of course, have the drawback of putting him on his guard, but that couldn't be helped.

French uneasily looked at his watch. It was but little past nine. Then with a sigh he went to the telephone and rang up The Counties, Ricardo's club. Was Mr Ricardo in the building, and if so could he see Mr French, if the latter were to call?

Ricardo, it appeared, was there, and would expect Mr French. French, thereupon, called up Carter, and half an hour later the two men were shown into a visitors' room, where presently Ricardo joined them.

'Good evening, chief-inspector. I hope there's nothing wrong?'

'Nothing fresh, sir. I'm still on my search for information. I must apologise for coming at such a time, but I thought I would probably annoy you less now than if I called in the day time.'

Ricardo threw himself into an armchair. 'Sit down and go ahead,' he invited.

'We have got, sir, to the stage in our investigation at which we ask everyone connected with the company to account for his or her time during the period between the death of Mr Minter and the discovery of the theft. This is routine, but we're bound to state that no one need answer the questions and that anything said may be used in evidence. I'm sorry to be a nuisance, sir, but I've come to ask if you will give this information, of course, under the official warning.'

'Suppose I take advantage of your offer, and refuse to speak?'

'That is open to you, though it has objections. I'm not threatening, of course, but if you refuse to answer we naturally assume you have something to hide, and we then set to work to find it out in other ways; or if that proves impossible, we can take you to court and there you would have to answer.'

French had been unobtrusively watching the man's reaction to all this. Ricardo's manner had changed. Instead of his easy off-hand bearing, he was now looking anxious and wary. For a moment he made no reply, then he shrugged. 'You're not threatening, of course. Very well: what do you want to know?'

'You have had the official warning and speak of your own free will?' French went on imperturbably.

Ricardo laughed scornfully. 'Well, what do you think?' he retorted. 'Never mind; I've heard you. Go ahead.'

'It's a simple matter, sir. One question, I think, will cover all I want to know. You've already told me how you spent your time on that Sunday of Mr Minter's death up till about four o'clock, when you were set down by Mr Sloley at Piccadilly Circus. Will you please tell me how you spent your time from that hour until, say, ten o'clock next morning?'

Ricardo continued to look worried. For some moments he sat silent, and when he did speak, it was not to answer, but to grumble about the question.

'I don't see what business of yours this is,' he countered. 'Do you accuse me of stealing the blessed jewels? If so, you shouldn't ask such a question. If you don't, what does it matter?'

'I certainly don't accuse you of anything,' French returned, hiding as best he could his irritation. How well he knew that gambit! Sometimes it indicated merely a fool with a swelled head, but usually it was to gain time to think out a plausible statement. He answered Ricardo's objections with patience and politeness, and at last the man gave way.

182

'I haven't the slightest objection to telling you where I was and what I was doing,' he declared testily, 'but no one likes being jumped into things and made a fool of. Four o'clock, Piccadilly Circus. What I did was this, if you must know. I came straight from Piccadilly here and had tea. Then—'

'Just a moment, sir. You drove through this street on your way to Piccadilly Circus, if I've understood you correctly, and set Sir Ralph Osenden down at his club, which is nearly next door. Why did you not get out here?'

'Well, I think you might guess that. I wanted to be alone. Osenden's a good fellow, and we're quite friends, but I was fed up with the whole party. If I'd got out here, Osenden would have suggested my having tea with him.'

'You told Mr Sloley you wanted to go somewhere by tube?'

'Yes, I had to explain my destination. It was with the same object.'

'Very good, sir. Please go on.'

'I got here, as I say, and had tea. Then I went up to my room, took up a book, and lay down on the bed, hoping I'd get a bit of a sleep. I was deadly tired, if you understand, but restless also. It was that confounded morning at Norne's.'

'I can well understand it, sir.'

'Oh, you can, can you? Well, I stayed there till about half-past six. Then I could stand it no longer. I went out for a walk through the streets. Presently I felt I wanted some food. I couldn't face the heavy club dinner: I wanted something light. I went into the Corner House in Coventry Street and had some coffee and an omelette. Then between eight and nine I came out and was once

183

more at a loose end. For a time I strolled about, and in the end I did what I seldom do, I went to see the show at the Tivoli. I stuck it for a couple of hours, then walked back to the club. I got here about half-past ten and went to bed. Shortly afterwards,' he concluded with elaborate sarcasm, 'I became drowsy and presently fell asleep. I slept well and awoke on the following morning, when I got up, dressed, had my breakfast, and went to the office. Does that content you?'

'Yes, sir, I think that about covers the ground. Had you a good film at the Tivoli?'

'I don't know. I arrived after the thing had started, and I never got the hang of what it was all about. As a matter of fact, I didn't try. I couldn't get Minter and the smash of our business out of my head, and all those fools plunging about on the screen seemed a sort of anti-climax. I don't know if you can well understand that?'

'I think I can, sir,' said French innocently. 'You walked to and from the club?'

'I said so.'

French rose. 'Well, sir, I'm much obliged to you. I think that's all I require. I may wish you goodnight.'

'You may,' retorted Ricardo, 'and if you don't believe what I say, you may ask the club servants.'

French paused. 'You mean that, sir?'

'Of course I mean it. And what matter whether I mean it or not? Won't you do it in any case?'

'I shall, sir. It's my routine duty. But I'd much rather do it with your will than against it. May I send for your bedroom attendant now? Or perhaps you would?'

With a bad grace Ricardo rang the bell and told the page to ask Henderson to come down.

184

'Perhaps, sir, if you'd tell him that we're trying to get times checked up in conection with a street accident you saw, and then allow me to ask the questions, it would be easier.'

'Tactful, what? Very well, I'll do so.'

Presently a highly respectable gentleman's gentleman entered, and stood just inside the door, respectfully curious.

'Oh, Henderson,' said Ricardo, 'this is a chief-inspector of police. He's been asking me about an accident I saw last Sunday week, and we want to get some times checked up. Can you help me at all? You'd better ask him, chief-inspector.'

'Mr Ricardo isn't certain of the time he saw the thing,' French explained, 'and we are trying to estimate it. We want the time he left the club and arrived back, if you can help us with either. That's right, isn't it, sir?'

'That's right,' Ricardo agreed.

Whether Henderson took this at its face value or suspected something very different could not be learnt from his eminently correct demeanour. He thought he could oblige. Mr Ricardo had left his bedroom at just half-past six, after spending a couple of hours therein. He had returned about half-past ten. His, Henderson's, box was beside the lift, and he made a point of seeing the gentlemen coming in and going out.

Thorough always, French next saw the porter. He happened to have seen Ricardo leave and return and he was able to confirm the statements already made. He also certified that Ricardo could not possibly have left the club during the night.

The critical period was now all accounted for except the four hours from 6.30 to 10.30. But during this time French saw that Ricardo could very well have cut the key and opened the safe. How was he to check those four hours?

He felt there was little use in making inquiries at either the Corner House or the Tivoli, though he dare not omit to do it. If Ricardo had wanted to find the two places in which his presence would be least likely to be noted, he could scarcely have chosen better. And so it proved. As French had expected, several hours' work at each place drew blank.

French was a good deal worried. It wasn't going to be easy to check the matter up, and yet somehow it must be done.

There seemed to be just one possible line of inquiry. If Ricardo had cut the key and burgled the safe, he would not have had any too much time to do it in. If so, he would scarcely have walked to wherever he was going. There was no tube station near the middle of Pall Mall. What would he have done?

He had stated he had walked to and from the building, and this the porter had confirmed. But that would be a natural precaution. As soon as he was a few yards down the street, would he not take a taxi? French thought so. He, therefore, circularised all taxi drivers on the matter.

For some time there was no reply, and he began to fear that his clue was also petering out. Then, to his surprise and delight, a man called with some information.

He had, he said, been passing through Pall Mall on the day and at the time mentioned. When about halfway down the street he was hailed by an elderly man of the given description. And on being handed a sheaf of photographs, the taximan obligingly picked out Ricardo's.

'Where did you drive him to?' French asked eagerly.

'An 'ouse in Rennington Street, Maida Vale. I don't remember the number.'

573 Rennington Street! French felt he ought to have thought of it. That would be his obvious retreat if he wanted to cut the key in secret. 'Mr Parkinson' could use his own rooms for what purpose he chose, and there would be nothing to connect his action with Mr Anthony Ricardo of Ely.

'You might drive there again,' said French, calling Carter and jumping into the vehicle. Instead of starting, however, the man climbed laboriously out of his seat and came to the door.

'Come to think of it,' he said, 'I didn't go direct that night. I called at a restaurant in Piccadilly. The gentleman 'e went in, and then 'e came back with a boy carrying some parcels. They put 'em in and 'e got in and told me to go ahead to Rennington Street.'

'Go to the restaurant,' said French.

It proved to be a place in which, in addition to serving meals, cold lunches and suppers were provided ready cooked and packed so that they could be taken away and eaten elsewhere. French produced his photograph, but no one could remember Ricardo's call. However, this was not very surprising, as the place was large and, so the manager assured French, very busy at that hour on Sunday evenings.

In Rennington Street they pulled up, as French had expected, at No. 573. French dismissed the taxi and he and Carter rang.

'Good evening, Mrs Mickleham,' he greeted the diminutive landlady. 'Can I have another word with you?'

With somewhat less suspicion than on the first occasion, she admitted him and replied to his questions. As he listened to her the misgivings French had been feeling deepened to a sense of profound disappointment. There was no longer any question as to what had occurred.

On that Sunday evening 'Mr Parkinson' had arrived shortly before seven and had carried up several parcels to his rooms. Not five minutes later 'Mrs Parkinson' had come. They had remained upstairs until about ten, when they had left together. Afterwards Mrs Mickleham had cleared away the remains of a very dainty supper.

French thought bitterly that he ought to have foreseen this development. It fully explained Ricardo's manner and false statements. Not knowing that French was aware of his secret, he would naturally try to keep Mrs Minter's name out of things. Indeed, considering the time he had had to invent his story, French thought grimly that he hadn't done badly.

But it was when he began to consider the bearing of the discovery on the case as a whole, that French grew really despondent. He didn't wish evil to Ricardo, but he had to find the thief. If he failed, it would count rather seriously against him. His credit and reputation, and, in the last resort, his bread and butter were at stake. He *must* find not only the guilty man but the stolen jewels. There had been a nasty hitch in the early part of that Southampton Water case, and he couldn't risk another hold-up.

That night he settled down to go once again over all the facts that he had so far learned, in the hope that by a miracle he had overlooked some point which might give him a fresh start. For three solid hours he worried over his notes, sifting, comparing, weighing, trying to find some further deduction; but all to no purpose. His usual bedtime came and went, but he threw some more logs on the fire and continued working. And then at last he remembered one point which he had considered previously, but which he had dismissed as unimportant.

It was a tiny discrepancy between the evidence of Mrs Turbot, the office charwoman, and that of Sloley and Sheen. Mrs Turbot had stated that Minter had arrived at the office first, by himself, and that Sloley and Sheen had come a few minutes later and together. Sloley and Sheen on the other hand had said that they had arrived together to find the office empty, and that Minter had presently joined them.

At the time French had dismissed the discrepancy, supposing that Mrs Turbot had made a mistake. But now he was in such a state of anxiety over the case, that he determined that even so slight an element of doubt must be set at rest. Next morning, he decided, he would see Mrs Turbot again and try to get the point cleared up.

His plans for the immediate future settled, French suddenly felt sleepy. Glancing at the clock and finding that it was twenty minutes past two, he muttered an annoyed oath and went up to bed.

14

Enter a Yellow Box

French was not destined next morning to carry out his plan to see Mrs Turbot. Something quite unexpected occurred to prevent it. A man called at the Yard and said he had been sent to make a statement which might have something to do with the case.

French smiled grimly when he was told. He knew that sort of statement. Some fool with a cock and bull story which would give any amount of work and lead nowhere! He had been had that way so often!

More than perhaps in any other walk of life the detective has reason to cry, 'Save me from my friends!' In any major case which has taken the fancy of the public, countless offers of help pour in. If a suspect is wanted, he is seen all over the country, perhaps in a score of widely divided places at the same time. Many people have theories of the crime which they are only too ready to furnish to the police. Even the conscientious man is a nuisance, because his well-intentioned, but irrelevant disclosures have to be investigated like the rest, leading to more lost work and time. For the occasional result achieved by publicity the detective officer has to pay dear.

'Who is he?' French said in an aggrieved way to the announcing constable.

'Gives his name as John Seaton, post office lineman, sir,' the man replied. 'Says his engineer sent him along.'

French made a gesture of resignation. 'Oh, well, I'll see him. Send him in.'

Seaton proved to be a youngish man, respectable and dependable-looking, but with a rather stupid expression. 'A man who'll be sure of what he saw or heard,' French thought, 'and won't be full of flights of fancy. So much to the good.' Aloud he said; 'Good morning. You're John Seaton, are you? You think you've got some information for me?'

'Yes, sir. It was the boss sent me along.'

'Good,' French returned cheerily. 'Then sit down and let's hear all about it.'

The man slowly crossed the room, twisting his cap in his powerful hands, and sat down awkwardly on the corner of the chair French had indicated. French was accustomed to these signs. They meant nothing but the general uneasiness which to so many minds accompanied a visit to the police-station.

'You're in the post office service?' French went on in the hope of getting the statement under way.

'Yes, sir; telephone lineman. Been in the job six years.'

'It's a good service.' French grinned. 'A better service by a long chalk than the police, eh?'

'I don't know about that, sir,' the man said seriously. 'I'd rather be a constable myself.'

'Don't you believe it. You know everyone wants someone

191

else's job. Well now, just start in and let's hear what you have to tell me.'

Seaton, evidently relieved in his mind by French's talk, settled himself on a larger area of his chair and began his story.

'Last Sunday five weeks we were doing a bit of a change over. Mostly that can be done on week-days, but where lines have to be put out of use, like this time, we generally do it on Sunday. Saves inconvenience, you see.'

'That's right. Sunday five weeks.' French made play of looking up a calendar, though all the dates of this period were burned into his memory. 'Let's see, that was the 30th of September?'

'That's right, sir. I was changing some lines from chimneys and odd places to a new pole that had been set up on the roof. I was with the squad, but was working alone on the pole, if you understand?'

'I think so,' said French. 'Your squad were all on the job, but you were separate from the others in that you were up this pole.'

'That's right, sir.'

'Where was this roof and pole?'

'In Ronder Lane, off Kingsway.'

French felt a sudden thrill. Perhaps this visit was going to mean something after all!

'Yes?' he said, with a subtle change of manner.

'The pole was on the roof of Kirkby-Orr's building, that's on the Oxford Street side of Ronder Lane. There was a big building just opposite across the lane. I didn't know what it was at the time, but I found out later. It was Norne's.'

'Yes?'

192

'The Norne building's higher than Kirkby-Orr's, but where I was on the pole I was level with the roof of Norne's, if you understand?'

French nodded.

'I could see into the top room of the Norne building, or one of them. It wasn't very clear, you understand, but still I could see a bit. There was a table and a safe and a sort of green painted press I took to be a letter file.'

Norne's room! All the boredom had now vanished from French's manner. He nodded again.

'There were two men in the room. I could see them moving about. They had a sort of flat yellow box in their hands, or one of them had. I couldn't see what it was. But they spent a deal of time fiddling with it.'

'What size was it?'

The man hesitated. 'I couldn't rightly say. So long perhaps.' He held his hands eighteen inches apart. 'And flat; not more than three or four inches deep.'

'Yes?'

'I wasn't watching them particularly, of course, for I had my own job to do. But every now and then I took a look in. The window was just before me, if you understand, and I could see without raising my head. One of them put the yellow box on the large green one, and then stood leaning over it and fiddling with it, while the other went forward to the safe and seemed to be putting in the key to open it. But he didn't open it, or, at least, I didn't see it open. They did that several times. I couldn't tell what they were doing.'

French nodded. 'That's quite interesting, Seaton. Yes?'

'Well, that was all I saw. I had to turn round to fix the wires on the other end of the arms, and it was some time before I turned back. When I did look in again, they were gone.'

At this French felt a little shock of disappointment. The statement had led off so well and come to such a fine climax that he had hoped for something more definite. However, there might be more. 'Yes?' he repeated.

'Well, I didn't think nothing of it. Why should I? It wasn't my business and, in any case, they hadn't done nothing out of the way. Then I read in the paper about this here Norne robbery. Still I didn't think nothing of it until last Sunday. And then in one of the Sunday papers I saw a photograph of the room in Norne's where the robbery had been done, and the safe the stuff had been taken out of, and it was the same room and safe. So I told the gaffer yesterday, that was Monday, but he only laughed at me. But he must have told the engineer for he sent for me this morning and asked me about it and then told me to come down and tell you about it here.'

'Quite right,' French approved. 'I'm interested in your story. Now, I'll have to ask you one or two questions. Take a cigarette, Seaton.' He pushed a box over. There was a little pause and then he went on: 'Could you describe the men?'

Seaton shook his head. 'No, sir, I could not. They were a bit shadowy through the glass, if you understand.'

'What about their height?'

'One seemed to be a middling tall man and one about medium.'

'How were they dressed?'

'Dark clothes, both of them. I couldn't tell more than that.'

'That'll do. Any hair on their faces?'

Seaton shook his head again. He had not seen. Nor could

194

French's efforts achieve any further results. He turned to another point.

'What time in the day did all this occur?'

'Between eleven and twelve in the morning.'

French then went back to the question of what the men were doing, but here Seaton couldn't amplify his statement at all. In fact, he was unable to give any further particulars of any kind.

'I think we'll go along to the office,' French decided. 'I'd like you to point out where the men stood, so there'll be no mistake.'

Seaton indicated that this was a matter for the chief-inspector, and in a couple of minutes they were in a taxi driving eastwards. A few more minutes and they pushed open the door of Miss Barber's room.

'Mr Norne in?' French asked after an adequate greeting.

The young woman shook her head. 'He's gone out. I don't know when he'll be back.'

'Unfortunate,' returned French, while congratulating himself on this good fortune. 'Well, I'd like my friend to have a look at the safe. May we go in?'

Miss Barber graciously gave the permission and the two men passed into Norne's room. French rather unkindly shut the door.

'Now, Seaton; go ahead.'

The man was obviously anxious to help, but he was unable to add to his previous statement. One of the men had put his yellow box on the top of the letter file, and stood as it were leaning on it, and looking towards the safe. The other had gone through the motions of putting in and withdrawing keys. But they had not opened the safe, at least, while Seaton was watching them.

One point the lineman did make a little clearer. Work at the box had occupied by far the longer time. The man at the file had fiddled with it for one or two minutes, then he had remained steady, apparently watching, while the second man had put his hand to the safe and withdrawn it again. The second man had then, as it were, stood aside, and the first had spent another one or two minutes working with his apparatus. This was repeated again and again: one or two minutes at the box and ten seconds at the safe alternately for as long as Seaton watched.

That this information was of first-class importance French had now no doubt. It certainly looked as if these two men were the thieves and that they were making preparations for their *coup*. French's routine inquiries had established the fact that no authorised work was going on in the office on that Sunday, and in any case the actions of the men were not consistent with authorised work. It seemed evident that their activities were connected with the fitting of a key, though how, French could not imagine.

It might be that they were using some new appliance unknown to him. Some block of soft metal, perhaps, which could be pushed against the lock levers, so as to take an impression of anything unyielding. Possibly by this means a blank key could be gradually cut down until it did the work. The yellow box might have been a kit of tools or a battery or a small power plant for cutting the wards.

One other thing was evident: that the men had not noticed that they were observed. For that French supposed he should consider himself lucky. Norne's room being higher than the houses across the street, no one in the ordinary course could see in through the windows. As a matter of fact there were no blinds. The window faced north and there was, therefore, never any inconvenience from sunlight. The telephone pole was new, and in any case, the men would never think of it.

All that day French pondered the problem: What could the men have been doing? Was it trying to make a key? Suppose they had that blank key of some soft substance which he had already considered, and that heat was required to make the substance plastic, could the yellow box be a means of generating this heat, something on the lines of an electric soldering iron?

Then it occurred to French that he was probably on the wrong track. Whatever they were doing, it was unlikely they were trying to fit a key. Had this been their object, the greater intervals of time would have been spent at the keyhole. In the few seconds during which attention was given to the safe, no such work could have been carried on.

No, the kernel of the affair was the yellow box. To that practically the whole of their attention had been directed.

But if the men weren't trying to fit a key, what under heaven were they doing? French could conceive of nothing.

During practically the whole of that night he lay awake wrestling with the problem. But no solution came to him. He got quite frantic towards the small hours. Hang it all, they were doing something! Naturally it was something intelligent and with a purpose. What other people had thought of, surely he should be able to think of too? But no ray of light came to him.

Next day in his office he settled down with the determination not to leave till he had reached some conclusion. He began by trying to reconstruct the conditions in Norne's room. First, he made a full-size model of the safe door and letter file. The file case he had no trouble in reproducing, because there was an exactly similar one in the adjoining office, and he had it brought in. The safe door he made out of a sheet of newspaper, which he pinned to the wall. On this he marked the keyhole in blue pencil. He was careful to get the relative positions correct.

Then he placed his emergency case on the top of the file. It was a little over a foot long, and as he did not know the exact shape or size of the yellow box, it would do well enough.

For some time he studied this combination, but without gaining any light. Then he tried to reproduce the actions of the men, so far as he knew them.

He stood in front of the file and leant over the emergency case. With the latter he pretended to fumble. Next he looked towards the safe door, and imagined he saw a friend putting his hand towards and away from the keyhole. Then he fumbled again at the case and again looked towards the keyhole. This he repeated several times.

After nearly three hours of intensive effort, he sat down slowly in his chair and began to swear. For a moment he let himself go and a stream of rather ugly blasphemy poured from his lips, a low growling murmur which would not penetrate to the adjoining room. Presently he grew ashamed of himself, took out his pipe, filled it slowly, and began to smoke.

But none of these expedients helped in the least. He couldn't imagine what had been done. In an exasperated mood, he went out for a solitary lunch.

It was on his way back to the office that light suddenly flashed into his mind. On the pavement was one of those optimistic cinematographers who film advancing individuals, and hand them a card to say that the film will be produced at such a theatre, and that if they attend they will see themselves on the screen. The man did not film French—French would have considered it a mortal insult if he had. He confined his attentions to those who seemed to him of a type likely to respond.

So far so good, the whole thing was a phenomenon too commonplace to excite French's interest. But as he approached he saw the man look down at his machine, and then glance up at his intended victim and down again.

Subconsciously the action struck a chord of memory. A ciné camera . . .

A ciné camera! Could it be?

French stood still as this idea smote him with a positive shock. He was right in the line of the lens, and his expression must have highly edified the patrons of the Elysian Cinema on the following day. But he wasn't thinking of cinema audiences.

A ciné camera! Why, *damn* it all, that was it! Why hadn't he thought of it before? A ciné camera! Of course!

The power of movement returned to his limbs and he began mechanically to walk on towards the Yard.

A ciné camera! Yes, he had got it at last! A ciné camera would photograph the key as it was being advanced towards and withdrawn from the lock. With such a photograph a skilful man should surely be able to cut a new key!*

Here at last was the idea he had been so long seeking! Given some way of disguising the camera—the yellow box—and a means of getting it unsuspiciously into position

---

* This is the idea referred to in the dedication.

on the file case while the safe was being opened, and the rest would be child's play.

For a while French was overjoyed with his discovery, and then the doubts usual under such circumstances began to assert themselves.

Could a ciné camera take a key in sufficient detail at a distance of five feet? If it could, was there anything to guide the locksmith as to its size? In short, was the whole proposition possible? Could a key really be out from a photograph?

On reaching the Yard French walked round to the photographic department and drew aside the photographer.

'I say, Cooper,' he began, 'I want your opinion on something. Do you remember that safe in Norne's office?'

Cooper nodded.

'You remember there was a letter file case standing beside it, about five feet from the keyhole?'

Cooper remembered this also.

'Suppose you stuck a ciné camera on the file and shot the key being put in, could you cut a key from the photo?'

Cooper stared, then swore. 'Fine you could,' he declared with enthusiasm. 'Is that what was done?'

'I think so. But it's only an idea so far.'

'I bet you're right, sir. It's a brainy notion for sure.' He grew less enthusiastic. 'But do you think they'd let anyone do that while the safe was open?'

'I've not got that length yet. What I wanted to know was, was it possible from the photographic point of view.'

Of this Cooper had no doubt whatever. 'And I'll tell you the camera for the purpose,' he went on. 'You know those little cameras that take on ciné film? No? Well, there are such cameras. They're pretty expensive, but they're scientific instruments of precision. With the light in that office you could get an enlargement amply big enough and clear enough for what you want. They'll show the leg of a bee on a flower from five feet away. A special lens, of course. Now the same people sell a ciné camera that'll do equally good work. It's a small thing, about eight or nine inches long and an inch or two high. You could hide it in anything and photo away to your heart's content.'

This was good news. But Cooper went on, as if in reply to French's thought.

'And another thing. There's a small raised moulding round the keyhole on that safe. I remember the trouble it gave Boyle when he was trying for fingerprints. That moulding would be photographed too. Now if you could get to the safe—as your people must have been able to do—they could measure the actual size of that moulding. If they then measured the moulding on their enlargement, that would give them the scale of the photo and they could cut the key the right size.'

'Ah,' said French with satisfaction, 'that point was bothering me.'

'Well, it needn't, sir.'

'Good! Now, Cooper, try again. What could they have been doing on that Sunday?' and he repeated Seaton's description of the men's movements.

Once again Cooper was equal to the occasion.

'I'll tell you what they could have been doing, sir, and I haven't the least doubt, were. They could have been finding the position for their yellow box. Incidentally it sounds to me like a despatch case with the camera hidden inside. I suggest they moved it a little at a time on the top of the file and took a note of the places. Then if they made a shot at each position, their developed film would show them the best one for covering the key. I'll bet what the other man was doing was moving a key backwards and forwards to the lock.'

'You mean that they wouldn't be able to judge the correct position of the camera without experiment?'

'Yes, that's just what I do mean. With the lens they'd have to use, the field would be small and they might easily miss the key altogether.'

'Quite. And they noted the position of each shot so as to be able to put the camera back into the correct one when they came to do the job in real earnest?'

'That's my notion, sir.'

French was impressed. This certainly did sound plausible. It was really beginning to look as if he were on the right track at last.

'That's very good. I'm obliged to you, Cooper.' He paused. 'Tell me, could you get hold of one of those cameras?'

Cooper grinned. 'Easily, sir, if you pass over the necessary fifty quid or thereabouts.'

'Hell, is it all that?'

'You'll have to have one, sir, if you're going to take this case into court,' Cooper said guilefully. 'We ought to have one anyhow for the department.'

French grunted. 'I'll consider it,' he said and returned to his own office.

Cooper, he saw, was right. If the case went to court an actual demonstration would be necessary. The police, properly witnessed, would have to cut a key to prove the method feasible. But before spending fifty pounds on a camera French saw that he had a good deal to do. He had to find out whether a photograph had been taken, who could have taken it, and how the camera could have been disguised.

He settled down at his desk to consider the matter systematically. Assuming his photographic theory were correct, it was clear that the man who operated the camera must have been well known to Norne. No stranger would have been allowed to put his case on the file and work with it while Norne and Minter were opening the safe. Secondly, it was improbable that the thief possessed a camera of the required type. If the photographic method became known, this would lead to instant suspicion. He would be more likely to buy a camera for the occasion and get rid of it again when it had served its purpose. Probably also he would buy it under a false name, so that the transaction should not be easily traced.

French's routine inquiries had established the fact that none of the senior members of the Norne staff was a photographer. This, however, as he had just seen, was no reason to assume their innocence. A line of research then would be an attempt to discover the purchase and disposal of a suitable camera.

French began by starting a number of men to go round the principal shops and pawnbrokers on this errand. They were armed with photographs of the Norne staff, which at the start of the inquiry French had made a point of procuring. He warned them not to overlook the possibility of someone having bought a camera on the hire purchase system, and relinquishing it after paying one or more instalments.

French went himself to the firm mentioned by Cooper and had a chat with the manager. He saw the beautiful little cameras they turned out, both ordinary and ciné, and also the work these did. He was soon satisfied that one of them would have been ideal for the thieves' purpose.

But when he tried to trace the postulated purchase, he found himself at once up against difficulties. A number of cameras of both kinds had been sold over the counter during the four weeks before the theft—the period which he had assumed would cover the transaction. But of these no note of the names of the purchasers had been kept. And none of the assistants could recall a customer resembling any of the photographs French produced.

After a careful inquiry French realised that his efforts had drawn blank. The thief might have bought his apparatus from this firm or he might not.

Of course the camera used—if one had been used—might not have been of this type. French saw his inquiry spreading to all shops which sold ciné instruments—half the photographers in London. He, therefore, began to consider whether he could do what was necessary by circular or advertisement. Neither, of course, was so satisfactory as a personal visit, but a personal visit to all dealers would be scarcely practicable.

However, information came to him much more quickly than he had anticipated. As he was drafting a circular, his telephone rang. It was one of his men, speaking from a public call office in Shaftesbury Avenue.

He had, he said, just come from Messrs Dobson & Hall, the very superior pawnbrokers of that street. They had there a ciné camera, of the special type mentioned by Cooper. It had been pledged on the Wednesday before the theft by a small thin man who had given his name as Hunt. The camera looked new, and the constable thought the chief-inspector might like to inquire into the transaction himself.

'Right,' French returned. 'I'll be there in ten minutes.'

Constable Hemingway was waiting for French at the pawnshop door, and without delay they saw the manager. The camera was new and valuable and they had allowed £20 on it. Their customer was small and thin, and though no one who had spoken to him could actually identify him as the original of any of the photographs, he was not unlike No. 17. No. 17 was that of Minter.

This was not at all what French had expected to hear. He had not imagined that Minter was guilty of the theft or had used a camera for an improper purpose. But, of course, the theory would work in well enough with the circumstances of the case. Minter had his own key, but not Norne's, and if he wanted to rob the safe the photograph would be a ready means.

That he was on the right track as to this being the camera which had been used, French soon became convinced. In the first place no one named Hunt was known at the address the customer had given, so that there was something fishy about the transaction. In the second, when he had taken the camera to the shop he had just left, they were there able to trace the sale. All these high-class cameras bore a serial number, and this one had been sold five weeks before the theft. And that, French noted, was just three days after the question of a possible bankruptcy had been mooted by Norne.

It looked then as if French was on to the truth in his photograph idea. The sequence of events seemed to prove it. Norne raises the question of the firm's dangerous position. Three days later Minter—if it was he—buys the camera. On the following Sunday he or someone else is seen experimenting in Norne's office. The key made, the camera would have served its turn, and three or four days before the theft, it is pawned. Probably there was never any intention of redeeming it: it was doubtless pledged simply to cut the loss on it as far as this could be done. Yes, it all worked in. French with growing excitement believed he was right so far.

He worked hard to establish the identity of the depositor, but without success. No one would state it was Minter, though when French learned that the unknown had spoken in a high-pitched voice, the assumption grew more likely. But it stopped short of proof.

In fact, at this point all advance along this line of research ceased. French did everything he could think of to connect up the purchase or sale of the camera with one of his suspects, and to find out who could have been experimenting in Norne's office. But he could get no more information of any kind.

This did not mean that he could relax his efforts. Being brought to a standstill in one direction merely meant starting in some other. He thought again of the discrepancy between the recollections of Mrs Turbot, the charlady, of what had taken place in the office on the Saturday night before the crime, and that of Sloley and Sheen. Here was something still to be cleared up. He determined he would really go into it this time.

15

Enter the Unknown

Mrs Turbot lived in a small court at the back of Fleet Street, a poor locality, though not as bad as some of the dreadful slums farther down the river. French thought he might get more from her if he saw her by herself, so once again he left Carter behind and sallied forth alone.

The good lady was out when he arrived, but an interested neighbour was able to run her to earth in an adjoining shop. She came hurrying, begged the gentleman's pardon for keeping him, and opening her room, showed him in.

French was not to be outdone in politeness. He expressed his regret for troubling her and trusted she could spare him a few minutes.

'That's all right, sir,' she answered. 'I'd be coming back for my dinner soon in any case.'

'What I want, Mrs Turbot,' French went on, these preliminaries satisfactorily completed, 'is to ask you for a little more information about what you saw on that Saturday evening before the robbery. You said, I think, that as you were preparing to go home, you saw Mr Minter come

207

upstairs and go into Miss Barber's room, and that a few moments later Mr Sloley and Mr Sheen followed him. Then you left the building. Is that correct?'

'Yes, sir, that's correct. That's what I said and that's the truth.'

'Quite. But I must tell you that there's some other evidence which doesn't square with it, and there must, therefore, be a mistake somewhere. It's really to find the mistake that I've come. I'd like to ask you a few more questions, but I don't want you to think I'm doubting your word.'

'That's all right, sir. Ask what you like and I'll answer it; if I can.'

'Well now, first, about the layout of the office and where you were when you saw the gentlemen arrive. The lift I have seen for myself is in the well of the staircase, and the flight of steps goes down at one side of it. That being the top floor there's no flight at the other side going up, as there is on all the floors below.'

Mrs Turbot agreed that that was so.

'Outside the stairs on that top floor a passage goes to the men's lavatory; I know that for I've been in it. Now, I understand a similar passage at the other side of the lift goes back into the ladies' lavatory?'

'That's right, sir.'

'And besides that ladies' lavatory there's a room which you use for your brushes and so forth?'

'That's right. It's in the ladies' lavatory, as you might say: a store room that I keeps locked up, with the brushes and buckets and the rest of the stuff.'

'Quite. Now, when you saw Mr Minter, where were you?'

'In the passage.'

'In the passage to the ladies' lavatory?'

'Yes, sir. I was in my store, tidying up before going home, when I heard soft steps on the stairs. There didn't ought to be anyone there at the time, so I went into the passage and looked out to the lobby. It was Mr Minter and he went into Miss Barber's room.'

'You had a good view from there?'

'I had a good view of his back, but I didn't see his face.'

'Quite. Miss Barber's door is facing the lift and so facing where you were standing, and there was nothing to make Mr Minter turn round. You didn't speak to him?'

'No, sir.'

'And he didn't see you?'

'No, sir, I'm sure he didn't.'

'You said soft steps. What did you mean by that?'

'He wasn't making much noise when he walked. It was only by chance I heard him.'

'Do you mean that he was walking on tiptoe?'

'No, sir, he was wearing rubber soled shoes.'

'I see. Now, what lights were on, Mrs Turbot?'

'There was the centre light in the lobby and the light in the ladies' lavatory.'

'He could see the lobby light, of course. Could he see the one in the ladies' lavatory?'

'No, sir. He could have seen the light from it, of course, if he had looked round. But he didn't look round.'

'He saw the light in the lobby and he didn't look round. That would suggest that he expected to find it turned on, wouldn't it?'

For the first time the woman hesitated. This was not a matter of observation but of deduction, and she wasn't so sure.

'Well, let's consider it,' French went on. 'You've explained that eight o'clock was not your usual time to be in the office. Therefore, Mr Minter couldn't have expected you to be there at that time?'

Mrs Turbot shook her head. She didn't think so, but she couldn't say for sure. The gentlemen wouldn't trouble their heads whether she was there or not.

'Don't you think that Mr Minter, seeing a light in the lobby, would have made a search to see who was in the building?'

Mrs Turbot admitted politely that she certainly should have thought so, though French felt her conviction was that under no circumstances could you tell what gentlemen would do.

He was not satisfied. It seemed to him that Minter, seeing the light, must have expected to find the other two in the office. If he had seen they were not in Miss Barber's office, would he not then have come to see who had turned on the light in the lobby? Did this evidence of Mrs Turbot's not contradict her own statement, and prove that Sloley and Sheen were really the first in the building, as they themselves had said? It almost looked like it.

'Now, let's turn to another point,' he went on presently. 'You first heard Mr Minter when he was coming up the stairs? Do you mean that he didn't use the lift?'

'No, sir. I wondered at it myself, a man in that weak state of health, climbing up all that way.'

'All that way? Eight double flights?'

'Yes, sir.'

'But you don't know he came up all that way, do you?'

'He must have, sir. The lift didn't move. I would have heard it if it had.'

French was genuinely puzzled at this. He hadn't realised

that Minter had climbed up from the ground floor. It was true that there was an attendant to operate the lift in the daytime, but it was of the automatic type, and the office staff could surely work it.

'Did the gentlemen not use the lift without the attendant?' he asked.

'Oh, yes, sir; often.'

French frowned. To climb eight double flights was no joke for any infirm person, and French couldn't conceive Minter doing it. However, Mrs Turbot was positive he had.

'Very well,' French said presently, 'Mr Minter walked upstairs and went into Miss Barber's room. Now, what was the next thing you saw?'

'The next thing I heard was the lift coming up. By that time I had finished squaring up and was ready to go. I looked out again, same as I had done before, and I saw Mr Sloley and Mr Sheen. They came out of the lift and went into Miss Barber's room.'

'Yes?'

'Well, I went home then.'

'By the lift?'

'Yes, sir.'

'Would the gentlemen have heard the lift in Miss Barber's room?'

Again Mrs Turbot hesitated. 'I don't think so. It's a very silent-running lift. I only heard it because I was beside it, but Miss Barber's office is a good step away. They'd have heard it if I'd banged the gates, but I didn't want to disturb the gentlemen and I shut them quietly.'

Here was a matter for experiment, and French noted it accordingly. He was not getting much by the inquiry. Indeed, except that Minter had walked all the way upstairs, he had learned nothing fresh whatever. Mrs Turbot had made a very clear statement both this time and previously, and she seemed quite certain of her facts. There was just one other point he wished to clear up.

'I'd like to get the times fixed when these gentlemen arrived. Can you do that for me? First of all, what time did you leave?'

'I can tell you that. I left about a quarter to eight. I'm sure, because I was hurrying to get home and I was watching the clock.'

'Quite. Now, how long was it before you left that Mr Sloley and Mr Sheen arrived?'

'Just no time at all: a minute or two, if you like. As soon as they went into Miss Barber's office I went into the lift. In fact, I would have been away a minute or two earlier only for hearing the lift coming up. I waited till it would be vacant.'

French nodded. 'I think this is my last question, Mrs Turbot. Can you tell me how long the other two were after Mr Minter?'

The charlady was not so sure of this. It might have been three minutes or four, or it might have been five or six. But she was sure it wasn't more than six at the outside.

'Now tell me,' French went on confidentially, when he had brought the routine inquiry to an end, 'it has been stated that the men arrived the other way round, that Mr Sloley and Mr Sheen went together first and that Mr Minter followed them. Are you perfectly sure that you haven't made a mistake about that? If you have, for goodness' sake say so, because a mistake's nothing, but for me to get mixed up on a point like that is very serious.'

Mrs Turbot was quite sure. Indeed, for the first time she

appeared a little indignant. She had said Minter had arrived first because that was the fact. He had done so, and that was all there was to it. Who had said the contrary?

French intimated that the misguided people who had said the contrary were not worth mentioning by name, and presently he took his leave.

The discrepancy then held. French went back to the Yard, and taking out his notes of his interviews with the misguided people who had said the contrary, he proceeded to study them once again.

Sheen had stated he had dined with Sloley at the Holborn after the children's party, and they had then walked down Kingsway to the office. Sheen had checked up all the times and had been positive they had reached the office about quarter to eight. Sloley independently had given the same testimony. But both had stated definitely that the office was empty when they arrived and that Minter had not come till a good five minutes later.

French noted with interest that the time of their arrival which they gave agreed with that stated by Mrs Turbot. After consideration he came to the deliberate conclusion that this time must be accepted as correct.

The discrepancy then lay in the time of Minter's arrival. French wondered if there was any further evidence on this point. At once he saw that there was. The taximan had given the time as ten minutes to eight. He had said he remembered this because he had waited outside the door for quarter of an hour, leaving for Waterloo at five minutes past eight.

The time of leaving Minter's house was also known. The times at which the taxi had left the garage, reached Peacehaven Avenue, and left it, were stated by the garage proprietor, the taximan, and Martha Belden respectively, and their various statements checked up.

French left his office and, calling a taxi, was driven to the end of Peacehaven Avenue. There he told the driver to go as fast as he could to Ronder Lane. He noted the time it took, discounting any traffic hold-ups on the ground that when Minter drove on the Saturday evening the streets would be clearer of traffic.

The result was conclusive. It was obviously impossible that Minter could have arrived at twenty minutes to eight. Ten minutes to eight, as stated by Sloley, Sheen and the taximan, was just about correct.

But the discrepancy involved an even more puzzling feature: the fact that Mrs Turbot stated she had seen Minter arrive, when in reality she had left the building before he turned up. French wondered what he could make of that?

As he turned the matter over in his mind he found himself gradually forced to a conclusion. These facts could only mean that Mrs Turbot had never seen Minter at all. She had seen someone else, someone whose back view was like that of the deceased accountant. This was the only explanation French could think of which met the situation.

But if it were true, it followed that four men, not three, had visited the Norne offices on that Saturday night. First an unknown, then Sloley and Sheen, and lastly Minter.

This theory at once cleared up that mysterious point about Minter's not using the lift. Apparently he had used the lift, and it was the unknown who had come softly up the stairs in rubber-soled shoes. Looked at from this point of view that first soft approach became stealthy and guilty. There was a suggestion of something secret, something to be hidden, a suggestion which was powerfully confirmed in the statements of Sloley and Sheen, which had omitted all reference to the silent-footed stranger.

Then French whistled as he saw the significance of his conclusion. If Sloley and Sheen had lied about what took place that night, were they guilty?

They were certainly not guilty of Minter's murder. Quite definitely they had been at the Aldwych Theatre when that had taken place. But were they guilty of the theft? Had they made a new key by photographing Norne's, and had they got Minter's from him during his visit to the office? Then French saw that they couldn't have got Minter's key from him unless the accountant was a party to the theft, which from his later actions seemed entirely unlikely. Besides, if they had been able to get Norne's key by photography, they could have got Minter's equally easily by the same method. Where, in fact, did Minter come into it?

French, who had been growing gradually more and more eager, swore at this check. For some minutes he concentrated fruitlessly on the problem. Then realising that for the moment he could get no further, he turned to another point: Who might that fourth man have been?

This, he saw at once, should be easier to solve. He knew quite a lot about that fourth man. He was small and slight of build, else Mrs Turbot couldn't have mistaken him for Minter. His back view must be somewhat like Minter's, though French didn't build much on this latter point. There was in Mrs Turbot's conclusion the fruits of suggestion. She expected to see some member of the staff. The unknown was unlike everyone except Minter: therefore he was Minter. However, roughly speaking, he must have been of the same type.

Then this man must have been an acquaintance of Sloley's, Sheen's, or Minter's. He must also have known the office, either from a previous visit or from a description by one of the others. Further, it looked as if an actual meeting had been arranged for that evening. If not, why did the parties head with one consent for Miss Barber's office?

Systematically, French went through the names and descriptions of every member of the firm who could possibly be suspected. French had himself met most of them, and he was satisfied that none of them quite filled the bill. For some time he pondered over the problem, then suddenly made a little gesture of comprehension.

Lyde! Might the fourth man not have been Lyde?

Lyde, French remembered, was very much the size and build of Minter. Lyde, moreover, was an actor, and if he had wished to pass for Minter, he could doubtless have done so. Lyde, again, was known intimately by Sheen: he was his brother-in-law and was living in his house.

French sat back in his chair and lit his pipe as he turned this idea over in his mind. Lyde! Yes, Lyde would undoubtedly fill the bill. Had Lyde gone to the office at 7.40 on that Saturday evening?

And if he had, why had he?

If he had, the visit was not innocent. There had been too much secrecy about it for that. Was it connected with the robbery, or with the murder, or with both?

Then French saw another point. The evidence of the pawnbroker had suggested that Minter had pawned the ciné camera. This had seemed unlikely at the time, and French had hesitated to accept it. But suppose the depositor had been Lyde? If French could prove this, it would show at once that Lyde, Sloley and Sheen were guilty of the theft!

But stay: was another vista not opening up? Though Sloley and Sheen could not have been guilty of the murder, what about Lyde? Could Lyde have gone down to Guildford, climbed somehow into that room after Norne had left it, and smothered the unhappy Minter? Was Lyde the man for whom Superintendent Fenning was looking?

Here was something to think over. French thought over it, and it did not take him long to reach the conclusion that his next business must be an investigation into the movements of Lyde.

Once again full of an eager enthusiasm, he settled down to work out his plans.

16

Enter a Passport

For a considerable time French pondered the problem of whether he could find out what he wanted to know about Lyde without approaching the man in person. To ask him to account for his movements on the Saturday evening was the obvious course, but it had the serious drawback of showing French's hand. Lyde would be put on his guard, and not only Lyde, but Sloley and Sheen also.

It was entirely undesirable that this information should be given away, but French could not see how to avoid it. Under the circumstances the only way to learn what Lyde had done was to ask him.

Accordingly, French made it his business to call with Carter at Sheen's house early next morning. Once again Mrs Sheen opened the door. She looked at the two officers without speaking. French explained their call.

It appeared Lyde was at home, and French and his companion were shown to the same room as on their previous visit. With a curt remark to her brother that the chief-inspector wished to see him, Mrs Sheen withdrew and left them to it.

'Good morning, Mr Lyde,' French began. 'I'm sorry to trouble you, but one or two further points have come up in this Norne inquiry, and I am in hopes that you will kindly help me with some information.'

'Still at it?' Lyde replied with a scarcely veiled sneer. 'Another serious crime unsolved by Scotland Yard? We read of a good many these days.'

'That's so,' French agreed amicably. 'But you will understand that we have to make a show of working at them. Otherwise we should lose our jobs.'

'Oh, I suppose it doesn't do any harm, if it doesn't seem to do much good.'

'Quite, and if one can make one's living harmlessly it's all to the good. Everyone doesn't achieve that, you know, Mr Lyde.'

Lyde shrugged impatiently, as if anxious to make an end of such foolish talk. 'Well, what do you want now?' he asked rudely.

'May we sit down?' French answered as he took a chair at the table and placed his open note book before him. Carter, with another note book, sat beside him.

'Make yourselves at home,' said Lyde, still standing on the hearthrug.

'Thank you, sir,' French rejoined innocently, 'I think we're all right now. It's about that Saturday night, the night before Mr Minter died. Now, you made a statement about your movements that evening, which I have here in my book. That statement was satisfactory as far as it went, but I'm hoping that you may be able to amplify it a little for me now.'

'What the hell do you mean by saying it was satisfactory?' Lyde asked roughly. 'Do you think I'm called upon to justify my actions to you?'

'Every citizen may be called upon to justify his actions before one of his country's courts,' French pointed out, 'but it's usually easier for him to talk matters over in private instead. I have come to you for this information, but it is my duty to inform you that you are not bound to answer my questions and that anything you say may be used in evidence. That is a formal warning which I am bound to give you.'

'Well, then,' Lyde said with a sneer, 'if I needn't answer your questions, I'm not going to.'

'That's a matter for yourself, sir, but in that case I shall have to ask you to come with me now to Scotland Yard where your views and attitude may be put on record.'

Lyde looked taken aback at this and some of the offensiveness went out of his manner. 'What's that?' he asked. 'Are you accusing me of some crime?'

'No, sir,' French said in an unmoved tone. 'But I've got to get my information, or account to my superiors for my failure to do so. It's immaterial to me which it is. You please yourself.'

Lyde looked at him venomously, then threw himself into an armchair and took out his pipe. 'Very well,' he said, 'but you know that information obtained by threats isn't usually worth much.'

'No threats at all, sir: only a statement of cause and effect. Well, I'm glad you've decided to let us have our talk here. As a matter of fact, it's more comfortable than at the Yard.'

'Oh, to hell!' the actor growled. 'Get on with your blasted

job, and get done with it and get out. And look here, I've an appointment with Otto Goldstein at twelve, so you can't be all day.'

'Right, sir, I'll not be long. As I said, I want a more detailed statement as to your movements on that Saturday evening. You said,' French rapidly turned over the pages of his book and read some items, 'that after the children's party you packed for France and went from here by tube to Victoria, where you caught the 8.20 Continental boat-train. Do you adhere to that statement?'

'Of course I adhere to it.'

'I suggest you think carefully before doing so. Suppose I told you that you were seen in the Norne building just before eight o'clock, would you still adhere to it?'

French was still consulting his notes, but he managed to steal a glance at the other. This was certainly a blow. Figuratively speaking, the man staggered under it. But he quickly recovered.

'I couldn't have been seen in the Norne building, for the simple reason that I wasn't there. If anyone says I was, he's mistaken.'

'Well, now,' French persisted, 'I'll give you something to think about. When you reached the top floor, the floor of Miss Barber's office, did you notice that the light was on?'

French now gave up any pretence of looking at his notebook and stared at the other full in the face. Lyde did not reply at once, and an expression of doubt, not unmingled with fear, grew in his eyes. French experienced a sudden thrill. Up to now he had been bluffing, a some-what dangerous game for a man in his position. But now suddenly he was satisfied. He knew. The man was lying and the bluff had been justified.

Lyde, however, quickly pulled himself together. 'Is that a usual trick in your abominable business?' he asked scornfully. 'I wasn't in the Norne building and I don't see how I could know about the light.'

'That would seem reasonable,' French admitted. 'At the same time consider the facts. The lobby light, as a matter of fact, was on. It was on before Mr Sloley or Mr Sheen reached the building. Who turned it on? Well, I'll tell you. There was another person in the building that night. This person has made a statement to the police, a statement to the effect that a certain person—who shall be nameless—climbed the stairs to the office—eight double flights—treading softly in rubber-soled shoes. He reached the top floor and went directly into Miss Barber's room.' French leaned forward confidentially. 'You see, Mr Lyde, all that can be proved in court.'

'But you can't prove it was me.'

French shrugged. 'Do you think if I couldn't, I would talk to you as I have? Do be reasonable, Mr Lyde. I expect you have a perfectly innocent explanation for your call and I'm giving you the chance to make it, if you care to do so. But, of course, my formal warning stands.'

French could follow the man's thoughts as if some kind of lid had been raised from his mind, leaving it bare and open to observers. It was the light being on in the lobby that had done the trick. Lyde had been there and he had noticed that the light was on. Whether or not this had given him furiously to think at the time, it had done so now. He realised that someone else must have been there, and this so weighted French's bluff as to make it invincible.

For some time silence reigned, then at last Lyde seemed to come to a decision.

'I told you the truth in my statement. I said I went from here to Victoria by tube and caught the 8.20, and so I did. I didn't say I didn't call at Norne's on the way. You didn't ask me.'

'Then you admit now that you called?'

'There's no "admitting" about it. On that previous occasion you didn't ask me the question.'

'Very well, sir, we'll put it this way. You now amplify your previous statement by saying you called at the Norne building on your way to Victoria.'

'I did, and I'd like to know why I shouldn't and why you're making such a song about it?'

French's heart was beginning to sink. It was unlikely, he thought, that the man would take this line if he were guilty.

'My reason for asking should be perfectly clear. We know that a crime was committed in Norne's during that weekend, and we must, therefore, inquire into everything that went on there. You yourself aroused my suspicions because you didn't mention your visit. I haven't said you did anything wrong: I said that I wanted an explanation of your call. Now, will you please give it.'

Lyde was obviously unwilling to speak, but he did so at length.

'The thing's perfectly simple,' he said in a sulky voice. 'When I was giving my last turn at the children's party, it suddenly occurred to me that my sister had borrowed a fiver from me that day to pay some bill. I wanted the money to go to France with, and I had taken a mental note to get it from Sheen when he came home. But I had forgotten all about it, and I was short for my journey. I spoke to Sheen, but by an unlucky chance he hadn't the money in the house. It was too late, of course, to get it at

223

the bank, so he said, "I'll tell you: come along round to Norne's and I'll get it for you out of the petty cash. I can return it on Monday." I said, "I'll not be ready to go with you and Sloley; I've got to wash this blasted paint off my face." "Then come direct to the office," he said. "Here's my key and I'll meet you in Miss Barber's room at quarter to eight." I knew the office slightly, for I had been there on one occasion with my brother-in-law.

'I went as he said, but when I came to the lift I didn't try to use it. I had noticed it was run by an attendant and I was afraid I might not be able to work it. So I did climb those damned stairs, as your observer said. And when I got to the top I wasn't on for any big man stuff. I just crept to Miss Barber's room as best I could and sat down to try and get my breath.'

'I follow. And what happened then?'

'In three or four minutes Sloley and the brother-in-law turned up. Sheen went out of the room and came back directly with five pounds. I took the money and cleared off to Victoria. Is that enough for you?'

'I think so,' French replied cautiously. 'But tell me: If there was so little in the thing as all that, why should you have made a mystery about it? Why couldn't you have mentioned it at first and saved all this trouble?'

Lyde's unpleasant manner returned. He laughed scornfully. 'Well, I think you might have seen that,' he said offensively. 'The brother-in-law wanted it kept dark. He didn't think it would look any too well if it were known that he borrowed from the office funds, even if he intended to pay back at once.'

French had to admit to himself that this was reasonable. In fact, the whole story was reasonable. He wondered if it were true. However, some tests were possible. Had Mrs Sheen borrowed that five pounds? Had Sheen obtained the sum on Monday, when presumably he had paid it back into the petty cash? Had there been five pounds in the petty cash on that evening; if so, where was the money kept and had Sheen access to it? Some work would be required on the story and French felt that he must put it in at once.

But his suspicion of Lyde was not confined to that visit to the office. Lyde might also have pawned the camera. Lyde might even have murdered Minter. It would be better, therefore, to see what proof there was that he did cross to France by that evening's train.

'That's excellent, Mr Lyde, so far as it goes,' French declared. 'Now, while we're at it I want you please to continue your story to cover the weekend. Except that you went to France I know nothing about it.'

'And why should you?' Lyde asked truculently.

'If you must know,' French returned bluntly, 'I want to be sure of two things. The first is that you really did go. The second, that you didn't come back on Sunday.'

'Oh, so that's it, is it? You still think I burgled that safe?'

'I never said anything of the kind. But it's obvious that if you were in France during the weekend, I can be no longer interested in your movements.'

For some moments Lyde digested this, then sulky once again, he repeated his original question. 'Well, what do you want?'

'Some proof that you were in France over the weekend. Tell you what; if you'll say just what you did when you were there, it should do the trick. You can't have moved about for two days without meeting people who would remember it.'

225

'And you are going over to see them?'

'Not if your statement is satisfactory. But I might do so.'

'Well, you're candid at all events. I suppose I may as well tell you. I crossed over by the 8.20 from Victoria, that is, via Newhaven and Dieppe. I got into Paris early in the morning, about six. I hadn't slept very well, so I went to the bathrooms at St Lazare and had a bath. I had a good slow soak in hot water, which rested me and I felt fine again. I was hungry when I came out of it and I went round to the restaurant at the station and had my breakfast. By the time I had finished it was getting on to eight o'clock. I took the Metro then to the P. L. M. station and got a train for Fontainebleau about quarter to nine. I should explain that some years ago, when I was living in Paris, I used to go a good deal to Fontainebleau, and I wanted to take advantage of this visit to France to have a day's tramp over my old haunts. Sentimental, I dare say, but one does these things.'

'I've done it myself,' French agreed, 'though unhappily not at Fontainebleau. It's one of the places I'm still hoping to visit before I die.'

Lyde looked as if he would prefer French to die first, but he continued without putting this into words.

'I bought some lunch at the P. L. M. buffet, left my suitcase in the *consigne* and took the train. I don't know just at what time I arrived at Fontainebleau, but it must have been about ten. Then I set off for my tramp. I visited the places I wanted to see, had lunch in the forest, and returned to the station. I don't remember the exact time of the train, though if it's important you can look it up: it was getting on to five. I got back to Paris about six, and then I took the Metro to my hotel, the Hotel de Belleville, in the Rue Mallet, off the Boul' Miche. I changed and had some dinner, and then I went out to keep my appointment.'

'Excuse me, why didn't you go to the hotel in the morning and leave your things there?'

'Why should I have? It was out of my way, and all I wanted was a bath and breakfast, which I could get at the station I arrived at.'

This also seemed reasonable, and French nodded. 'Your appointment then?'

'Yes, do you want to know all about it too?'

'I want to know, sir, whom you met and when and where you met him or her or them. I don't want to know your business.'

'Oh, you don't, don't you? I'm surprised at that. Well, I'll tell you all the same. I went over to see M. André Brissonnet, the film producer. I had worked with him before in historical stuff, and I had heard that he was starting a big Empire film. I went to see if I could get a job.'

'Thank you, sir, but you needn't have told me that. What I want to know is where you saw him and when.'

'I saw him at the Elysée Palace, where he lives. My appointment was for nine o'clock, and you may bet I was on time.'

If this story were true, it finally disposed of Lyde as a participant in the crime. But here again, was it true? It had one rather significant feature, or so French thought. From the moment at which Lyde had left the Norne building, about eight o'clock on Saturday night, until he reached his hotel in Paris between six and seven on Sunday, it contained no single item capable of confirmation. It was exceedingly unlikely that any of the railway or steamer officials would have noticed him, and the same applied to the Customs and passport men on both sides of the Channel. The bath attendant at St Lazare might remember him, as might also the waiter at the station restaurant, but again they might not. At all events, if they did not, it would be no proof that he hadn't been there. Nor, apparently, was there anyone at Fontainebleau to whom he, French, could apply. No, whether by accident or design, Lyde's movements for the essential twenty-four hours could not be established by any of the ordinary means.

French pressed the man to give him some item which could be checked, or to mention someone whom he had met, but without success. Lyde had come across no one whom he knew. Again this was reasonable and might be true.

French sat thinking over the story. Then suddenly he could have kicked himself. There to his hand was all the proof he could possibly require, and he had missed it.

'Have you got your passport handy?' he asked.

With a bad grace Lyde got up and left the room. Presently he returned and threw down on the table a blue book of familiar shape. French took it up, satisfied himself that it really was Lyde's, and turned to the last page of the visés.

'It got knocked out of my hand by a lunatic who thought he was going to miss the train at Newhaven,' Lyde explained. 'It fell face downwards in the mud.'

It was indeed in a mess. Smears of brown mud ran across it and in the crease between the pages small grains of sand still lodged. These, however, had not wholly obscured what French wanted to see. On the pages were four recent stamps, covered by smears, but still readable. There was one leaving Newhaven on the 20th October, one arriving at Dieppe on the 21st, and two leaving Dieppe and arriving at Newhaven on the 22nd. That was to say the bearer had left Newhaven on the Saturday, arrived at Dieppe on the Sunday, and returned to England on the Monday.

These dates completely substantiated Lyde's story. Travellers by the 8.20 from Victoria reached Newhaven before midnight and Dieppe after it. Unless someone else had travelled on the passport, Lyde was innocent. And this was unlikely, for the photograph of Lyde was particularly distinctive.

'Tell me, did M. Brissonnet ask you to go over to meet him?'

Lyde laughed scornfully. 'No blooming fear. I thought he was doing well enough when he agreed to see me. He's a big bug in the film world.'

Though French was not very satisfied with the interview, he did not see what more he could do. Lyde had answered his questions, and though his manner had been unpleasant, French was accustomed to rudeness and thought little of it. Many people adopted a blustering manner when interrogated by the police. If they were innocent, they thought the questions insulting: if guilty, it was due to the fear of seeming afraid. French decided he would get the Paris men to check up on the interview with M. Brissonnet, and if that were satisfactory, as he was sure it would be, he would have to accept the alibi. Accordingly, he returned to the Yard and put through a call to the Sureté, asking for the required information.

He felt rather badly up against it. He had been on to what had seemed a promising clue, and now it looked like petering out. If Lyde had been in France during that critical weekend, he might as well dismiss him from his thoughts at once, for the man could not have been guilty of either murder or theft.

However, before putting the idea of Lyde's guilt finally out of his mind, French decided he would arrange a meeting between him and the pawnshop assistant with whom the camera had been pledged. This must be done unknown to Lyde, and French began to work out a suitable scheme.

For a moment he did not see how it was to be accomplished, then he realised that Lyde himself had given him the hint. The man had said that he had an appointment with Otto Goldstein for twelve noon that day. Goldstein was a well-known man in the film world, and a glance at the directory showed that his office was in Stephen Street, a narrow street off Regent Street. French saw that he had just time for his plan, and running down from his office, he found Carter and bundled him into a taxi.

'Messrs Dobson & Hall, Shaftesbury Avenue,' he told the driver, and then to Carter: 'Identification of man who popped the camera. If that blighter Lyde was telling the truth, he's due at Goldstein's in Stephen Street in half an hour. We'll have the pawnbroker's assistant to see him.'

The manager of Dobson & Hall's was accommodating, as French knew he would be. At once he arranged leave for his assistant, George Glave.

'It's that case I was speaking to you about before,' French explained to Glave as they drove towards Regent Street. 'The pledging of the ciné camera. I've a notion the man who did it will walk this morning through Stephen Street. I want you to sit back in the taxi and watch the people passing. If you see him don't make a song about it, but point him out quietly to me.'

Glave was obviously interested. He would be pleased, he said, to do what the chief-inspector wanted, and if the man passed he would certainly recognise him.

Stephen Street was a narrow lane which carried but little moving traffic. Indeed, it was almost filled with commercial vehicles parking outside warehouses and offices. French arranged for their taxi to take its place outside a merchant tailor's, from where a clear view could be obtained of persons entering Goldstein's office.

'Better move in behind, Carter,' he went on. 'We couldn't risk the shock of him suddenly seeing anything like your face. If you can't squeeze in between us, Mr Glave will give you his place and he can sit on your knee.'

By the time their dispositions were complete it was ten minutes to twelve. French was not entirely hopeful as to the result of the experiment. If Glave were to pick out Lyde, he might take it as proof that the actor was mixed up in the crime. But the converse did not apply. If Lyde passed unnoticed, it did not follow that he was innocent. And, of course, there was a third contingency, perhaps more likely than either: that Lyde would not pass at all.

However, there was nothing for it but to wait and see, and as twelve approached even French grew more eager and watched more intently the pavement in front of them.

Suddenly he noticed Lyde turn into the street and walk towards Goldstein's office. His direction of approach was the best that he could have taken for French's plans, for he faced the taxi as he came forward. Now for it! Would Glave spot him?

It made French more confident in the man's evidence that he did so at once. Lyde had scarcely taken three steps forward when he whispered, 'There he is.'

'Don't be in a hurry,' French advised. 'Look at him carefully as he passes and be quite sure before you speak.'

When Lyde had turned into Goldstein's door Glave

expressed himself in no uncertain terms. Lyde was the man who had popped the camera. Of that he was absolutely assured. The chief-inspector could count on his evidence if he wanted it.

French was entirely delighted. Here was the greatest single step towards a solution that he had yet made. Lyde definitely was in the theft, and in all probability Sloley and Sheen were in it too. Knowing what he now knew, it should not be hard to get his proof.

Inevitably French's thoughts went back to the alibi. If Lyde were in the theft, had he really done no more than call at the office on that Saturday night? Before the man's plausible explanation, there had been his denials. Had Lyde really gone to France? In the light of this new discovery all French's doubts revived.

Then suddenly he could have kicked himself. He had been a fool! He believed now that he had been tricked.

From his room at the Yard he rang up the Meteorological Office. Could they tell him what the weather had been like in Northern France and Southern England during the weekend of the 20th-22nd ultimo and for some days before it?

Soon there was reply. Those days and the preceding week had been fine.

Lyde, then, if he had dropped his passport on the Newhaven quay at all, had done it at the end of a week of fine weather. What about the mud with which it had been so thickly coated?

French swore. That mud would usefully cover unsightly scrapes on the paper!

He sent a man to Sheen's house to watch for the return of Lyde, and when the constable rang up to say the quarry

232

had arrived, he hurried out. He saw that if Lyde had been fully awake to his position he would have burnt the passport. French's own evidence would have cleared him of participation in the crime. He could only hope the man had not been so acute.

'I'm extremely sorry to trouble you again, Mr Lyde,' French apologised when once more he and Carter were seated in the dining room. 'This time I shall not keep you a moment. It's just something I forgot this morning. I omitted to take the number and date of your passport. May I have these, as the regulations require that I check up that it was really issued to you.'

Lyde at the beginning of this address had seemed to regain all his nervousness, but the latter portion reassured him and he became sarcastic about the way the Yard did its business. However, his tone changed once again when French slipped the book into his pocket and said that he was going to keep it for a day or so, and here was a receipt.

Eagerly French took the book to the department which dealt with forgery of documents.

'Have a look at that Newhaven stamp,' he said, 'and tell me if it's quite all right?'

'Looks all right,' the officer in charge answered, 'to the naked eye. But we'll not try the naked eye on it.' He slipped it beneath a low-powered microscope, fidgeted and focused till French could have screamed, and then went on coolly: 'No, I guess you've got it this time, whatever it is. That date is a very neat forgery. It looks as if it had been changed from 21st to 20th. Would that help you any?'

French choked. 'That would about set me up for life,' he said at length. 'Blessings on you, my son! Incidentally, you've probably hanged three men!'

17

Enter a Picture

So Lyde didn't go to Paris on the Saturday night after all!
For once in this difficult case French had attained something
more than guesswork or theory: this was fact; fact definitely
and adequately proven.

On this Newhaven-Dieppe route there were only two
outward services in the day, passing Newhaven shortly
before midday and midnight respectively. The passport
stamp showed that Lyde had crossed on the Sunday, and
the fact that he had had an appointment in Paris on the
Sunday evening—for French was sure he had kept it—
proved that it was the morning service he had used.

As if to set French's mind at rest on this matter of the
appointment, a call came in from the Paris police at that
very moment. It appeared that M. Brissonnet had been
interviewed and had confirmed on every point the statement made by Lyde.

French felt equally certain that if inquiries were made
at the Hotel de Belleville, a similar confirmation of Lyde's
story would be obtained. These were matters on which the

man would be bound to tell the truth, for the simple reason that if he lied, the fact would at once become known.

Lyde then had been in England on Saturday night and Sunday morning. What had he been doing during that time? It looked as if it must have been something criminal, since he had taken such trouble to provide himself with an alibi.

French's mind at once reverted to the murder. Had Lyde killed Minter, taken an impression of his key, cut a new key somewhere during the night, and burgled the safe on Sunday morning before starting for France?

This was a promising idea as far as it went, but it didn't go quite far enough. If Norne's key had been made by photographic methods, why not Minter's also? Then how could Lyde have reached the deceased's room? And how could he have got back to Town, since there were no trains at that hour and it was unlikely that he would have borrowed a car?

Another difficulty concerned the alibi. All that matter of the visit to France and the forging of the passport stamp must have been premeditated, indeed, must have been worked out some time beforehand. The interview with the film magnate in particular—which French now supposed had been arranged simply to provide a motive for the journey—could not have been achieved without preparation.

But when Lyde had arranged his alibi, he couldn't possibly have known that the other circumstances in the case would work in. Even with the help of Sloley and Sheen French didn't believe he could have overcome this difficulty. There were too many details which he couldn't have foreseen. Minter's illness, involving a last minute change of plans, was one of these. The room at Norne's which Minter would be given was another.

While French believed there had been a partnership between Lyde, Sloley and Sheen, he felt this theory did not cover the whole ground. He might be, and probably was, close to the truth, but he was sure he hadn't yet reached it. There must be some other factor, as yet unknown, which would throw a light on to these puzzling facts, and draw them into place in a comprehensive and consecutive whole.

French puzzled over the affair till he grew stupid. Then realising that for the time being further concentration would get him nowhere, he decided to give up for the day.

Before stopping, however, he planned his next piece of work. One obvious line of inquiry in connection with the photographing of the key was still untouched, and the sooner it was done, the better.

Accordingly, next morning he called Carter and set off to the Ronder Lane office, where he asked for Norne. He began by saying he had not seen the managing-director for some time, and though unhappily he had no special progress to report, he thought it might be a help to talk over one or two aspects of the case. When he had touched on a number of points, and so had confused Norne as to the object of his visit, he turned to the matter at issue.

'I want you,' he said in as off-hand a manner as he could achieve, 'to look back during the past few weeks and tell me if you can recall any occasion on which anyone put a despatch case or other yellowish box-like object on the top of your letter file, and stood beside it, probably leaning his arms on it, while the safe was being opened or closed?'

Norne was at once curious. 'What does that mean, chief-inspector?' he asked. 'Are you on to some clue?'

'I don't suppose it means anything,' French returned, 'but all the same I'd like the information. I should explain,' he went on with a slight falling off from his usual veracity, 'that what I have described was seen through the window.'

'Through the window? No one can see in through the window.'

'Yes, sir. It was seen by a lineman and he was up that telephone pole.'

'Good heavens, I never should have thought of that. But how does it affect this case?'

'I don't say it does affect it, sir. I'm asking out of curiosity.'

Norne's expression changed to something like disappointment. 'Yes, I remember what your lineman saw, but it won't help you any.'

'Perhaps not, sir. All the same, I'd be obliged if you'd answer the question.'

Norne shrugged. 'Well, it seems to me a bit of nonsense; however, if you insist . . . It was Mr Sloley.' French's hopes suddenly soared. 'He was in here, oh, perhaps six weeks ago. He said he had just come from his solicitor and that he had the deeds of his house and some other important papers in his pocket. "Shove them into the safe for me, will you?" he said. "I'm going to a match and I don't want to carry them about in my pocket." He had the papers in a sealed envelope and he handed them to me. I was opening the safe shortly afterwards and I put them in.

'Then on this occasion some week or so later, he came back. "You have some papers of mine in the safe," he said; "I wonder could I have them now?" I called Minter and we opened the safe and gave them to him. I remember he had with him a yellow despatch case, and he put it on the

237

top of the letter file and opened it there. It was a suitable height, you understand, when he was standing up. He put the papers in the case and then went out. Is that what you want to know?'

French shook his head. 'That's not much help,' he admitted in a crestfallen way. 'Was that the only time anyone did such a thing?'

'Yes, so far as I can remember.'

French made a gesture of disappointment. 'I'm afraid you were right after all,' he declared. 'There's nothing there in the way of a clue. Were there many others present at the time?'

'No: only Sloley, Minter and myself.' Norne spoke with some impatience. 'If that's all, chief-inspector,' he added, 'I'd like to get on with my work.'

'That's all, sir, and thank you very much.'

French got up, but a sudden idea struck him. 'I suppose, sir, that wasn't the day that Mr Sloley was a little—what shall I say?—jolly?'

Norne frowned. 'Jolly?' he said coldly.

'Well, inclined to sing a bit, for instance?'

'If you must know, he did hum some tune while he was waiting for the papers,' Norne said disagreeably. 'But I don't know what you mean by jolly. If you mean was Mr Sloley drunk? I may tell you he was not.'

French was shocked that such an idea should have been imputed to him. If anything he had said had seemed to suggest it, he withdrew it unreservedly. He hoped Mr Norne would say nothing about this not very happy inquiry. 'I mean that, if you please, sir. It's important that nothing should be said about it to anyone. May I count on you?'

Norne said he was not sufficiently interested in the subject to wish to speak of it again, and French, thinking this a good opportunity to withdraw, did so.

He was wholly delighted with his interview. This really was extraordinarily important information; as important as any he had yet received. It now seemed certain that Sloley was in the thing with Lyde. And if so, Sheen must have been in it too. Lyde, making himself up to represent Minter, had bought the ciné camera. He and Sloley, or Sloley and Sheen, had experimented with the despatch case, so as to get the camera into the correct position. Then a method had to be devised of getting the safe open in Sloley's presence, and one also which would account for his working with the despatch case at the time. This had been quite skilfully done with the story of the valuable papers and the visit to the match. And lest the faint sound of the filming mechanism might be heard, Sloley had simulated a little refreshment and had sung during the critical period. The photographs taken, the camera became a danger, and Lyde once more took over and got rid of it in a way which cut the loss as far as could be done.

So much for Sloley and Lyde. What about Sheen?

The list of shareholders recurred to French. He had already wondered if this had been got out with the sole object of getting Minter to the office on the fatal evening. Now this idea suddenly seemed much more likely.

Then French remembered the glimpse he had had out of Sheen's dining room window when he called to interview Mrs Sheen. Besides grass, shrubs, a mellow brick wall and a sleeping cat, he had seen a shed containing a bench and rack of tools. Suppose Sheen were a metal worker?

Suppose, as well as getting Minter to the office, his part had been to cut the keys?

So far French was well satisfied with his progress, but now he seemed to come to a full stop. Even if all this were true, it did not account for the murder of Minter. It did not explain exactly how the theft had been committed. Still less did it indicate where the missing stones were to be found. It did not give him the proof he required for court.

This wasn't good enough. He must do a lot better if he wasn't going to make a hash of the entire case.

He returned to his room thinking deeply. What must be his next step?

Could he prove that the camera had been in Sloley's case at the critical time?

Unless he could find the case, he doubted it. If his theory were correct, the case must have had some arrangement whereby the light could have reached the lens. Either a hole had been cut in the side which was filled or covered in some way except when the pictures were actually being taken, or the raising of the lid must in some way have raised the camera also. At all events, some structural alteration to the case must have been made.

But if so, Sloley would have been certain to destroy such tell-tale evidence as soon as the pictures were taken. He, French, could have a look about Sloley's house, but he didn't hope for any result therefrom.

Deductions from Sheen's list were, of course, even more nebulous. The man had made the list openly, and no human being could say what had been in his mind at the time.

There remained the question of whether Sheen had or

240

had not cut the keys. Was there any way in which this could be ascertained?

French thought that if he could gain access to Sheen's workshop he might find something suggestive. If Sheen had been as careful as everyone else seemed to have been in this confounded affair, there would be nothing. But he might conceivably have fallen below the general level and made a mistake. A very small slip might be enough to give him away. Suppose he had experimented on some blank keys before cutting the final models, and suppose one of these had slipped down out of sight and been forgotten, its discovery might be just what was required. French felt he must have a look.

But to gain access to the place wouldn't be easy. He could not simply break in. He could only be there by the permission of someone in the Sheen household. But this would put Sheen on his guard, the thing of all others which he, French, wished to avoid. To get a search warrant would have the same defect.

For some time he sat worrying over the problem, and then he thought he saw his way. The scheme required a wet Saturday afternoon, and here the fates seemed extraordinarily propitious, for this was Saturday and it was beginning to rain. French decided that no time was like the present.

The plan depended on there being a lane behind the wall at the bottom of Sheen's garden, preferably with a door leading from the garden. If this door were old and cracked, so much the better; but if not, a suitably sized gimlet would doubtless meet the case.

By lunch time French had arrived on the site, taking with him not only Sergeant Carter, but also an energetic young constable named Lowe. A reconnaisance in force disclosed the fact that the lane existed just as French had expected, moreover, that Sheen's door was well stricken in years and had cracks of gratifying dimensions. All of which was very satisfactory.

Sheen's house was near the end of the cross-road from which the lane started. French posted Constable Lowe down the lane with instructions to watch Sheen's ground through the cracks, and signal to him if Sheen went into his workshop. Meantime he and Carter took up their positions at the end of the lane. From where they stood Sheen's house could be reached in a couple of minutes.

The rain grew steadily heavier. Unpleasant as it made their task, French was overjoyed by it. It was much more likely that Sheen would go to his workshop for relaxation on a wet afternoon than on a fine one.

French wanted to remain dry for his call on Sheen, lest drops of moisture deposited on the floor of the workshop might suggest activities which otherwise would remain decently hidden. He had therefore provided himself and Carter with two extra large umbrellas, and under these the two men crouched just far enough into the lane to avoid being seen from the adjoining houses.

Time passed extraordinarily slowly as they stood listening to the patter of the drops on the umbrellas and keeping a watchful eye on Lowe. Carter was not a brilliant conversationalist at the best of times, and now his sources of inspiration seemed to have failed him entirely. However, French didn't mind. He had plenty to think about.

When about an hour had dragged drearily by, Lowe made a sudden signal. This was equivalent to the 'Stand by!' which the captain of a steamer rings down to his engineer, when variations in the movements of the engines are imminent. The two men stiffened and got ready to furl their umbrellas, while keeping a still more eager eye on their scout.

Ten seconds more and there came another wave. This signified that Sheen had entered his workshop. French and Carter leaving their umbrellas standing against the wall, hurried out of the lane and round to Sheen's front door. French rang. As before, Mrs Sheen answered.

'I called for just a word with Mr Sheen, madam,' French explained, 'and as we were coming to the door I saw him go into his workshop. If you'll allow us to follow him there direct, we needn't trouble you further.'

'Yes,' Mrs Sheen answered, 'he's just gone out. Can you find your way?'

'Yes, thank you, madam.' French took off his hat and moved quickly round the house, so as to give the lady no time to revoke her permission.

The workshop was a small wooden building about twelve feet by five. There was just room for a narrow bench along the front, with a still narrower passage behind. Sheen had already taken off his coat and was screwing up a small casting in the vice. He stopped as the officers appeared, greeted them without enthusiasm, and asked them to come in out of the rain.

'Mrs Sheen said we'd find you here, sir,' French explained. 'I'm sorry to trouble you, but if you would be so kind as to answer a question or two I won't keep you long.'

'It's all right, chief-inspector,' Sheen answered. 'I'm not busy. Would you like to come into the house?'

'Not at all, sir,' French answered with truth. 'All I want can be done here. As I say, I won't keep you any time.'

He glanced round. 'A nice little shop you have here, if I may say so. I do a little bit at the same kind of work, but I haven't a place like this.'

Sheen was not expansive. He was polite, but only just. French felt he must get to business.

'It's a small point that has arisen about your meeting in the office on the Saturday evening before the theft,' he went on. 'I'm afraid, sir, that you didn't tell me all that you might have about that.'

'What do you mean?'

'Well, I dare say Mr Lyde has spoken to you about it, has he not?'

'Oh, you mean about his calling at the office that evening? No, I didn't mention it. Why should I? It had nothing to do with the crime, and you didn't ask me the question.'

'I asked you, sir, for a full account of what happened.'

'About the crime, yes. Not about irrelevant matters. I didn't tell you that I had wound my watch before going to bed that night. Why not? For the same reason that I didn't mention Lyde's call: it had nothing to do with the case.'

'That's not quite correct, sir. If I had known Mr Lyde was there I would have asked him if he had seen anyone else in the building. He might have, you know.'

'He didn't.'

'Well, there was another person there, all the same. And that brings me to the object of my call. I want to know, sir, whether the light on the landing outside Miss Barber's door was on or off when you and Mr Sloley got out of the lift. Can you remember?'

'Yes; it was on.'

'Did that suggest anything to your mind when you saw that it was on?'

'In what way?'

'Did you wonder who had turned it on?'

French anxiously tried to estimate the time. Constable Lowe had been told that after the expiration of four minutes he was to ring Sheen up and keep him at the telephone as long as he could. This interrogation was going very well so far, but as there was nothing that French really wanted to know, he could not keep it up indefinitely. Sheen, more-over, was getting annoyed.

'I didn't wonder,' the man returned. 'I supposed Lyde had arrived before us. It was the natural thing to suppose, wasn't it?'

'Quite. But when Mr Lyde reached the landing, the light was also on. Who did he think had turned it on?'

Sheen shook his head impatiently. 'I don't know what he thought. If you want to know, I'm afraid you'll have to ask him. Where's all this getting to, anyway, chief-inspector?'

'Confound Lowe,' French thought. 'Can't he ring the blessed telephone?' But what he said aloud was: 'I wanted to know if he said anything to you or Mr Sloley on the subject?'

'No.'

'It wasn't discussed at all?'

'Haven't I said no?'

'Then just tell me this, Mr Sheen. Did you and Mr Sloley not know that it had been on when Mr Lyde entered?'

With an instantly suppressed sigh of relief French heard Mrs Sheen's voice from the house. 'Harry! Harry!' it called, and when Sheen had opened the door and shouted back, it went on: 'Telephone!'

'The telephone,' Sheen said to French. 'Excuse me a moment. I'll not be long.'

'Thank you, sir; no hurry,' French answered politely, and then as the man vanished he went on to Carter. 'Now, Carter, we've about three minutes. Wire into it. You take the bench and I'll do the floor.'

They had closed the door after Sheen as if to prevent the rain beating in. Carter now set himself to run over the tools and *débris* on the bench, while French, dropping on his knees, began to shine his powerful wide-angled electric torch over the floor.

It was laid rather roughly with old railway sleepers. They were about ten inches wide and were fairly level on the tops, but between them there were spaces of from a quarter to three-quarters of an inch. A glance showed that the floor, for a workshop, was clean; it had certainly been swept recently, and there was nothing to be seen on it which was in the slightest degree suspicious. French therefore concentrated on the cracks between the sleepers, shining the torch into them, and rapidly running along each from one end of the shed to the other.

Both men worked at their highest capacity, for they knew their time was severely limited. Lowe was a smart man, but even he was not likely to keep Sheen talking about non-existent business for more than two or three minutes. Up and down the floor French ran his torch, but though the cracks were full of all kinds of *débris*, he couldn't see anything helpful.

Then suddenly he drew in his breath. 'Got it, I believe, Carter,' he whispered eagerly, and plunged his hand into his pocket for a forceps which would reach down into the crack.

But as he did so Carter whispered. 'Here he is, sir! Look out!'

'Keep him out for heaven's sake,' French gasped. 'A moment'll do it.'

Carter slipped out of the shed and French heard him say smoothly, 'I think Mrs Sheen was calling you, sir: just this moment.' Then came Sheen's voice: 'Couldn't have been. She heard me at the telephone.' Then Carter's again: 'Is that so, sir? Funny how one makes mistakes. I could have sworn I heard her calling you.'

French by this time had picked up his treasure trove, dusted his knees, extinguished his torch, and banished the eager expression from his face. Then he opened the door slowly.

'I told you you were wrong, Carter,' he said rather unkindly. 'You're far too cocksure.'

'Sorry, sir,' Carter returned with becoming sulkiness of manner.

'Idiots there are in this world,' announced Sheen, whose temper had evidently not improved. 'That was some fool saying he wanted to buy my house. My house, if you please! Said he had seen an advertisement of it and that the agents had told him it was for sale. Argued about it as if I didn't know who owned my own house! Then after questioning him for about an hour I discovered it was in another street. He'd got hold of the wrong address. Well, are you satisfied now about the light on the landing?'

'I think so,' French returned. 'You have told me the matter was not discussed. I'm much obliged to you, sir.'

'But what was at the back of it all?'

'Nothing, sir, except that the point was raised by my superiors. They said, "Those three men must have seen the

247

light on and must have known some other person was in the building. They haven't told you about it. Get on to them." But the thing's quite easy to understand. You and Mr Sloley would subconsciously assume that Mr Lyde had turned on the light, and he, being a stranger to the office, wouldn't think about it. Yes, sir, I think that's all and quite satisfactory.'

French was now only anxious to get away, and as this seemed to be the idea in Sheen's mind also, the withdrawal was achieved without further difficulty.

'What did you get, sir?' Carter asked as soon as they were out of sound of the house.

'Show you in my room. Can't take it out here. That was good, Carter. Lowe did that well and you weren't too bad yourself. If I'm right about what's in my pocket, we've got those fellows!'

In his room French very carefully removed his find from his pocket and laid it on a sheet of glass, putting a second over it.

It was a tiny piece of cinematograph film, bearing about half of one picture.

'They've been trimming their work, and this piece has dropped off the bench,' said French, carefully raising the glasses to the light. 'Ah,' he went on, 'that's about what we wanted!'

The picture was a microscopic view of part of Norne's office with a hand holding the end of something like a key. The key and the safe had been cut off.

18

Enter Light

French was agreeably surprised to find that Cooper, the photographer, was still in the building. Congratulating himself on his good luck, he went up to see him. Cooper greeted him as jovially as their respective ranks would allow.

'I've got something to show you, sir,' he burst out without waiting for French to speak. 'Look here.' He held out a key with extremely complicated wards.

'What is it?' French asked.

'Key of the A.C.'s safe!' Cooper returned with a grin. 'You weren't far wrong about that ciné camera idea. Let me show you.'

He took from a drawer a roll of cinematograph film and a small ciné camera of the type he had recommended. 'Here's the machine and here's what it does. Look, sir, through this glass.' Rapidly he rigged the film in a frame, switched on a light below it, and motioned French to look through an eye-piece.

'By Jove,' French observed as he applied his eye to the

lens, 'you've actually been and bought a machine? I thought you said they were a prohibitive price?'

'Something like seventy quid all this outfit cost,' Cooper replied. 'I didn't think the A.C. would stand for it, but he did. Thought we should have one for other purposes as well. But you see the key, sir. Like a tiny black spot on the film, and magnifies up till you can see every ward as clear as you'd want.'

'Very interesting,' said French presently. 'And the key was cut from the photo?'

'Yes, sir. Jackson did it. He made a good job. Fitted first shot and opened the safe as easy as the A.C.'s own.'

'When did you try it?' French went on. He thought he might have been told what was in the wind.

'Only just now, sir. It's queer that you should come up at this moment. The A.C.'s still talking to Jackson, or was a moment ago.'

'H'm; very interesting,' French repeated. 'Now, young feller me lad, take that film out of your apparatus and put this in.' Carefully he took from his pocket-book his treasure trove.

Cooper had been keen enough before, but when he saw the fragment of film his enthusiasm grew greater than ever. 'By Jove, sir, you've got 'em on the spot this time! Where'd you get this, if I may ask?'

'Sheen's workshop. I could see screw-holes all round the windows, which suggested that frames had been fitted.'

'Using it as a dark room?'

'Secrecy was what I imagined. I didn't think these films were developed in the dark?'

'They are, sir, as a rule. They're generally wound spirally round a glass cylinder hung over the dish of developer, so that the film gets wet all along as the cylinder is turned. You see it developing and know when to stop. But I don't think they would have used the cylinder.'

'Why not?'

Cooper pointed to French's find. 'They've cut the film. You see, sir, that shows the key well forward, though probably not yet in the lock. I mean it's a view out of the middle of the series. They must, therefore, have cut the film.'

'I don't follow. What for?'

'To develop it in an ordinary dish. I suggest they used ordinary whole-plate dishes and cut the film in strips about eight inches long. You see, for this job you wouldn't want every picture. Two or three from different angles, got as the key was moved forward, would be enough. When cutting before development they might cut through a picture, but that wouldn't matter. They'd simply trim the ruined picture off, as soon as the development had shown where its edge came. They evidently did cut it as I suggest, and this bit got knocked down and they overlooked it.'

'It was in a crack in the floor.'

'Just so, sir. They would have a lot of cuttings and they wouldn't have missed it.'

Though it would be true to say that French was delighted by his find, he could not but realise that he was still far from the end of his case. To him this piece of film was proof that so far as the robbery was concerned he had got his men. But he doubted whether it was sufficient proof for court. And, of course, in the case of the murder, he was no nearer a solution than ever. It was, therefore, with qualified optimism that he went in to report to the Assistant Commissioner.

251

The interview he found satisfactory on the whole. Sir Mortimer Ellison did not minimise the progress which had been made, but he harped rather more than French appreciated on the amount that still remained to be done. French knew who had robbed the safe? Good! But what about the proof? And where was the stuff which had been stolen? Also had the thieves committed the murder? Never mind about the murder being a local police job. The crimes were probably connected and French should know all about both. Had French been inclined to rest on his oars—which, indeed, he had not—the A.C.'s views would have made such an attitude highly undesirable.

That night, though it was his weekend holiday, French set himself for the *n*th time to struggle with his difficulties. Obviously the best proof of the guilt of the trio would be the discovery of the swag. But it was exceedingly unlikely that this would be found—if found at all—until after the arrest. A search of the men's belongings would probably indicate where it had been hidden, or the channels by which it was hoped to convert it into money. But an arrest could scarcely be made until clearer proof of the robbery had been obtained. The thing was a vicious circle. French was fed up with it.

He turned from the theft, as he had turned so many times before, to the murder. If the three could be arrested for the murder, the necessary search would follow just the same. *Could* he not get anything on these lines?

Suppose Lyde had murdered Minter in that bedroom at Norne's. If so, he had left by a rope from the window. What had become of him?

French wondered if this line of investigation had been fully explored. He picked up his telephone, got through to Fenning's house, and asked the super what he had done about it?

Fenning said that he had made a general inquiry as to whether anyone had been seen leaving the neighbourhood on the fatal night, but this had produced no result. Could French suggest anything better?

French suggested assuming that Lyde was the murderer, and repeating the question with the inclusion of Lyde's description. Fenning, eager for anything which might help him out of his difficulties, said he would have the fullest inquiries made.

On Monday morning Fenning rang up. He believed that Lyde had been seen. He wondered if it would suit the chief-inspector to run down to Guildford, when he could hear the report for himself?

Two hours later French was seated with Fenning in the latter's room at police headquarters.

'I think it was Lyde all right,' Fenning said after greetings. 'He passed two of our patrols who had met at the end of their respective beats. I have the men here. You'd better hear what they have to say.'

Two stalwart constables were summoned and reported that they had met as Superintendent Fenning had stated and were exchanging a few remarks when a man appeared coming towards them. When he saw them he seemed to hesitate, and looked quickly to each side, as if searching for a road down which he might turn. There was none, and after that momentary hesitation, he came on past them. He walked quickly as with a purpose, and both supposed he was simply hurrying home. He was like Lyde in height and build, and also walked with the rising motion in his gait which had been mentioned in the description. He had passed on out of sight and they had thought no more of the matter, not of course, connecting him with the murder.

'Where did you see him?' French asked.

'On the new bridge where the by-pass goes over the railway to Reading.'

'Perhaps that doesn't convey as much to you as it does to anyone knowing the town, chief-inspector,' said Fenning. He got down a large-scale map from a shelf and spread it on his desk. 'See here,' he went on, 'here's the Hog's Back and the main Guildford-Farnham road. Here,' he pointed to a parallel track, 'is the old road, one of the oldest roads in England, believed indeed to be prehistoric. It carries on from the Guildford High Street along the top of the Hog's Back spine, and is joined by the new road a couple of miles out. Here is a steep hill, which the newer road avoids.'

French nodded.

'Now, here beside that old track is Guildown where Norne's house is built. The house is not shown on this map, but it's there.' He made a pencil cross. 'Now, there's a footpath here, nearly opposite Norne's house, from the old track to the newer road, so that anyone leaving Norne's could get quickly down to the newer road at that point. You follow?'

French followed.

'Very well. Here, on the opposite side of the newer road, the path runs on through Guildford Park, which is not completely shown on the map. It covers this area, and is well laid out with roads and largely built over. So that a man leaving Norne's could cross the newer road and pass northwards through this area. Now here, to the north side of this area, runs the Guildford-Reading railway, and here, not shown, of course, is the new by-pass bridge. So you see that if a man were heading north from Norne's he would pass over this bridge.'

'That's very suggestive, super. And where would he get to if he had gone on in that direction?'

Fenning shrugged. 'Woking? Bagshot? Town? Unless it was a roundabout to confuse a possible scent.'

'If it was Lyde, he crossed by Newhaven and Dieppe on the Sunday morning. Have you tried any of those places you mention?'

'All of them. So far there's been no reply.'

'It looks a pretty sure thing,' French mused. 'Tell me, what time was the man seen?'

'That's the only thing that doesn't work in so well,' Fenning said. 'It was about one-fifteen in the morning.'

'Good Lord!' French exclaimed. 'There's a snag there right enough. If the murder was committed about ten, as the medical evidence proves, what would Lyde have been doing for three hours? How long should it have taken him to walk from Norne's to the bridge?'

Fenning looked at his men. 'Quarter of an hour?' he suggested, with which both agreed. 'Well,' he went on to French, 'there you have it. I take it you've done with these men?'

French and Fenning continued discussing the affair after the constables had left. Here was another case of strong probability, but no more. There was none of that absolute proof for which French's soul yearned.

'What about letting those two men of yours see Lyde?' French said presently. 'If they picked him out, it should be good enough for court.'

'I expect you're right. Will you make the necessary arrangements?'

'I'll do so if you send them up.'

This was agreed on, and French soon left, having promised to telephone Fenning when he had arranged the identification.

Seated in the train, he continued thinking over what he had just learnt. This information would have been highly satisfactory, had it not been for that hitch about the time. But it was inconceivable that the murderer would have remained on the scene of his crime for three hours longer than was necessary. Therefore, surely the man seen was not Lyde? French began to fear this discovery of the super's wasn't going to be much of a help.

Then another point struck him. Suppose Lyde had travelled down to Norne's with Sloley and Sheen and then set off to walk, the time would have worked in exactly. Could he have done so?

French thought not. If Lyde had come with the others he couldn't have committed the murder, and if he hadn't committed the murder, what had he come for? Again it looked as if the man wasn't Lyde. Well he must fix up that identification as quickly as possible.

Reaching the office, he got in touch with the divisional officer responsible for the area containing Sheen's house, and secured his co-operation. Then he rang up Fenning and asked him to send his men up on the following morning. Having seen them rigged out in Metropolitan uniform, he posted them, as if on beat, near the house. He himself remained close by, sometimes in a police car, usually strolling aimlessly along, occasionally pausing at shop windows. He had a very boring morning, but towards lunch his patience was rewarded.

About half-past twelve one of the constables made the

prearranged sign and indicated a short thin man who was walking with quick nervous steps away from Sheen's. French, who was then in his car, drove slowly past and had a look at the man. It was Lyde.

Quickly French picked up the second constable and drove past Lyde again. This man pointed out the actor at once, though when he came closer he admitted he could not swear to him. But the first officer made no bones about swearing to him. He was, he said, absolutely certain.

So that was Lyde! Lyde had gone down to Guildford. But when? And what for? The affair was confoundedly puzzling.

French thought again of his idea that Lyde might have driven down with Sloley and Sheen. Was there any way, he wondered, in which he could settle the point?

He remembered that Sloley had said he had parked opposite the office door in Ronder Lane. Was there the slightest hope that their start had been observed?

He thought it unlikely though just possible. Still the matter offered another line of inquiry. In the absence of anything more promising, he decided he would do his best with it.

In the ordinary routine of inquiry the constable on patrol duty on that Saturday night in the area containing the Norne building had been interrogated. He had stated that he had noticed a car standing immediately in front of the Norne door, of a similar type to Sloley's. He did not remember the number, but there could have been no doubt it was Sloley's. He had remarked it particularly because it had remained there longer than any of the others. He had seen it after the theatres had emptied, the one car in the street, and he had gone back specially a few minutes later to see if it was still there. It had, however, then gone.

French decided he would go down to Ronder Lane that evening and have a look round. At these temporary car parks it often happened that some out-of-work hung about in the hope of picking up a few coppers. It was not a very hopeful proposition, but it was just worth trying.

As theatre time approached the cul-de-sac began to fill up. French, dressed in his oldest lounge suit and smoking his shortest pipe, lounged about, keeping a watchful eye on the proceedings. For half an hour he killed time, then his interest in the scene suddenly quickened.

An old man was trying to get a job as watchman. He was opening the doors of parking cars, touching his hat to the occupants, and evidently offering his services. Though French had his own troubles, he could not but feel sorry for the old fellow, as he watched the ill-mannered way in which nine out of ten motorists turned him down, and imagined the continual disappointment he must feel.

Presently it became apparent that all the cars which were coming to park had arrived. The old man had had no luck, and now he was beginning to shuffle despondently off. French followed him and touched him on the shoulder.

'Just a minute,' he said. 'I've been watching you. No luck?'

The old fellow, though obviously in the last stages of poverty, looked decent and as clean as his circumstances would permit. There was no whine in his voice or obsequiousness in his manner as he replied respectfully, 'No, sir, no luck tonight.'

French felt for half a crown. 'Put that in your pocket,' he

said, 'in place of the job you didn't get. But I want something in return.'

The man stood holding the coin. 'I thank you, sir,' he said doubtfully. 'What is it that you wish?'

'I'm a police officer,' French returned, 'and as such I'm not allowed to give money like this. So that's an unofficial gift and we'll both forget it.'

At the mention of French's calling an expression of alarm came over the man's face. 'I wasn't doing any harm, sir,' he said earnestly. 'I was only asking the gentlemen if I might watch their cars. Sometimes things are stolen from cars. I would have watched that.'

French shook his head. 'I'm not saying you were doing any harm. In any case, I'm not interested in that. What I want is some information that you may be able to give me. Do you come round here every night?'

'Yes, sir, I do. Sometimes someone lets me look after a car: just once in a while.'

'Do you remember last Saturday evening three weeks? It was the evening before the robbery was discovered in Norne's. You heard about the robbery, I suppose?'

The man nodded with some eagerness. 'That I did, sir. I heard about it on the Monday. Everyone was talking about it.'

'Well, it's about the robbery I'm interested, not about anything that you were doing. Were you out here that evening?'

'Yes, sir, I was.'

'Did you get a job?'

'Yes, sir, I had a bit of luck that night. A gentleman with an open car let me watch it for him. There were two rugs in it and some parcels. I watched it for him from close on eight till eleven and he gave me a bob. Yes, I had a stroke of luck that night.'

French wondered was he going to have a stroke of luck on this night. 'Where was the man's car parked?' he went on. 'Come and show me the place.'

It proved to have been along the wall of Norne's building, some three cars' length from the entrance. From it Sloley's car must have been clearly visible.

'Did you see a car parked just opposite the entrance door?'

'Yes, sir, a dark saloon. I saw it. It must have come early, for it was there when I arrived.'

French was getting more and more interested. Quietly he asked the fateful question. 'Did you see that car start, the car that was before the door?'

The man seemed slow of replying. French tried to look bored, but in reality he hung on his words. Then the old man pronounced the thrilling words: 'Yes, sir, I saw it.'

For a moment French wondered if his half-crown was working too well. 'Oh,' he said, 'then did it leave before the one you were watching?'

But he saw he had been about to misjudge the other. 'No, sir,' the man said, 'it was the last to go. It waited three or four minutes after the rest.'

'Then how did you come to stay so long?'

'I could hardly say, sir. I just wasn't in a hurry. When you've no job you get info the way of spending as much time everywhere as you can. There's always too much of it.'

'Where were you when it left?'

'Just about to turn into Kingsway, sir. I happened to look back and I saw the men getting in and the car starting.'

'Oh, you saw the men getting in? Two men?'

'Three men, sir.'

French stared. Three men? Then Lyde had gone with the others after all!

'Three men, you say? Are you sure of that?'

'Oh, yes, sir, I'm sure. Perfectly sure. There's a lamp just beyond the door, and I saw them in the light quite distinctly.'

'Three men. Did you see where they came from?'

'Yes, sir, they came out of the building.'

Again French paused. This certainly was unexpected. Neither Sloley nor Sheen had mentioned that they had gone back into the office after the show. Then he saw that it was not unreasonable that they should have done so. Presumably they had suitcases, and because of possible thieves had left them inside the door rather than in the car.

'Had their suitcases in their hands?'

'No, sir.'

French grunted. 'Can you describe the men?' he went on.

For the first time the old fellow hesitated. 'I don't know that I can, sir,' he said slowly. 'I didn't see them so well as that. I saw the three figures, but I couldn't see their faces.'

'I don't suppose you could,' French admitted. 'They didn't seem to be carrying anything?'

The man shook his head. 'No, sir, I'm sure they weren't. I think I should have seen it. One of them didn't seem to be well and the other two were helping him.'

This also was unexpected and French asked for further particulars. One man, the old fellow repeated, had seemed either ill or drunk—though able to walk, he was staggering—and the others had assisted him across the pavement into the car. One had got in behind with the sick man and the other in front. They had then driven off.

261

This being all the old man could tell, French took his name and address, gave him another half-crown 'for luck,' and turned slowly away in the direction of his home.

So Lyde had gone down with the other two, and his appearance at the Guildford by-pass bridge worked in after all!

French swore slowly and comprehensively. If Lyde hadn't left Town till eleven, who had murdered Minter at ten? Curse it all, was he on the wrong track from the beginning? Was there a fourth man in the thing? Perhaps Norne after all? Perhaps Osenden? French trudged blindly on, finding his way by instinct, escaping death in the traffic by a miracle, puzzling over this new turn in the case.

The miracles persisted and he reached home in safety. In due course he went to bed, but not to sleep. The affair had taken a hold of him that he couldn't break. The possibility of having to start again at the beginning seemed so terrible that he could scarcely contemplate it.

The murderer must, he thought, be Norne. Norne must have killed the accountant when he visited him at ten. This after all was the likely thing, and it was simply due to Norne's cleverness that he, French, had acquitted him in his mind. Well, on the following day he would look again into the case of Norne. Fortunately most of the data he would require had already been obtained.

Then another idea flashed into French's mind, gripping him as in a vice. Suppose he were wrong! Suppose it were not Norne. Instead, suppose . . .

For a few moments he weighed the new idea. It looked promising, a real solution, a complete explanation of all these confusing facts. Then just as he was growing really excited, he saw he was wrong. There was a snag; an over-whelming snag. He quieted down again.

But his brain was working feverishly and he could not rest. He had seemed so near a solution, was he really getting nowhere? For another hour he tossed backwards and forwards.

Then suddenly he thought of something else and he wakened Mrs French with a yell of joy.

'I've got it! I've got it, my dear!' he shouted in reply to her protests. 'At last I've got the confounded thing! Bless my soul, that's something like a relief: more than I would have believed!'

For a while he was lyrical, then he turned over on his side and fell promptly asleep.

And in the darkness Mrs French smiled at this great boy that was her husband.

263

19

Enter a Demonstration

But in the sober light of day French's new idea looked a great deal less rosy than it had during the more fevered hours of the night. He saw now—or thought he did—what had been done. He had achieved a theory which covered all the facts, with one exception. That exception did not in any way invalidate the theory, but it made him, French, much less happy about staking his reputation on it. It was the important point that he did not see why Minter had been murdered at all. Given the need for the accountant's death, he could see how the unfortunate man had been killed. But he couldn't see why.

There was also the worrying fact that he couldn't prove his theory. He felt convinced of its truth himself, but of direct proof he had none. With increasing bitterness he began to see that he was not so very much farther on after all.

He was, moreover, at a loss as to what he should do. Should he see Sir Mortimer Ellison and put his theory before him? Or should he go down to Guildford and talk it over with Fenning? Or again should he keep his own counsel and work on alone?

Finally he decided on a combination of the last two alternatives. He would go and have a talk with Fenning, but he would not give his theory away unless it seemed good at the time.

After ringing Fenning up, he went down to Guildford. For a time the two men talked generalities, then French turned to his special business.

'A couple of points have occurred to me, super,' he began. 'I wondered whether you'd gone into them. The first is the arrival of Sloley's car at Norne's house on the Saturday night. Was that checked up?'

'No. I admit I didn't inquire specially, but I've heard nothing of its having been seen.'

'Well, it strikes me that it may be a pretty important matter. Could you have inquiries made?'

'Of course. But this is new, chief. You didn't say you were interested in that.'

'As a matter of fact, I've got a new theory of the entire crime,' French admitted. 'If we could find out anything about that car it might show me whether I'm right or wrong.'

'You're not saying what the theory is, are you?'

French grinned. 'I'd rather wait, if you don't mind. If you get something in the nature of a surprise about the car, then I'll know I'm right and I'll put the whole thing before you.'

'I'll have it gone into at once. Anything else?'

'There is one other point, but I don't hope for anything from it. Where are the clothes and contents of the pockets of the deceased?'

'I have them next door. We held them till the adjourned inquest should be finished. Now since the case has become one of murder, I suppose we'll hold them till it's complete too.'

'Good,' said French. 'Then do you mind my having another look at them?'

Superintendent Fenning led the way into an adjoining store room, and unlocking a cupboard, pointed to a heap of clothes and small objects such as a watch, money, fountain pen and handkerchief.

'I'm afraid,' French went on, eyeing the collection with a frown, 'we'll not get anything here. They've all been handled, I suppose?'

'Well, yes, they have. Why not?'

'Only that I had half-hoped we might get some prints on them.'

'Prints? We might have got Minter's, but what good would they have been?'

'Yes, that's right, of course. Still, super, I'd very much like to try.'

Fenning was obviously sceptical, but as obviously he wanted to be polite. He produced powders and the two men began dusting them on everything which might possibly bear finger-prints. They were soon rewarded. The prints had remained better than French could have believed possible. The watch and the smooth parts of the other hard objects were covered with impressions.

'That's a bit surprising, super,' French remarked.

'I've noticed it before about things stored here,' Fenning returned. 'I can't explain it—unless it is that this place is damp and may prevent the moisture of the prints drying up.'

'I expect you've hit it,' French agreed. 'Lucky for me anyway. Can you get these checked up?'

Fenning went to have the necessary arrangements made. The two men had concentrated on objects taken from the pockets, but now French turned to the clothes.

The clothes were more difficult to deal with. Thoughtfully French turned them over. No chance of prints on these! There were, indeed, only two possibilities, the shoes, of smooth black calf, and the collar, a wing collar of stiff well-laundered linen. Minter was somewhat old-fashioned in his sartorial ideas, and usually wore a black coat and waistcoat, dark grey striped trousers, this wing collar and a black bow tie.

French tried the shoes and collar. On the shoes he got nothing, the prints had evidently dried off. But there were several on the collar. French placed it with the others.

'Take a bit of time to go through all those,' Fenning remarked, returning. 'They'll have to be photographed and enlarged, then all our own men's prints taken and checked off. But I needn't tell you.'

For answer French took a photograph of a set of finger-prints from his pocket-book. 'Perhaps we could save some of that trouble,' he said. 'It's these prints I'm really interested in. Can we see if they're present on any of these objects? If we're sure they're not, I don't want anything further. Any possibilities I'd like photographed and checked up properly.'

Fenning agreed that this might be possible and they set to work. Object after object was examined with a lens and dismissed. French's photographs showed clearly marked whorls, and it was easy to dismiss prints on which no such appeared:

At last everything from the pockets had been rejected

and there remained only the collar. As Fenning picked it up, French's eagerness, which had been gradually getting keener, grew much more marked. He watched Fenning almost with excitement. Fenning took longer over the collar. He turned it backwards and forwards and scrutinised it carefully with a lens.

''Pon my soul, chief-inspector,' he remarked at last, 'I believe you've got a bull's eye this time. There are prints here uncommonly like your photographs.'

'I hope to heaven you're right, super. Let me see.'

French took the collar and lens and began slowly and systematically to compare. Yes, the prints were the same! His idea had been right, rather marvellously right! A long shot, but seemingly it had got the bull! It was on the collar that he had hoped to make the find. But he had doubted whether the prints would have remained so long. Was this at last really all the proof he required?

'You'll get them photographed and checked up, won't you, super? And for heaven's sake let someone do it who knows his job. It's your murder case that's at stake.'

Fenning stared. 'Then whose are the prints?' he demanded.

'Lyde's!' French answered dramatically. 'Do you see where that leads you?'

Fenning continued to stare. 'Lyde's?' he repeated. Then after a pause, 'Gosh!'

For a moment silence reigned. Then Fenning went on: 'But I don't see even now. Are you suggesting this proves Lyde is the murderer?'

French shook his head. 'No, not quite,' he returned. 'Don't ask me yet, super. If you've any luck about the car, you see the whole thing.'

'You're darned mysterious, I will say,' declared the

puzzled superintendent. 'May I at least ask if this is your case or mine you're on to?'

French laughed. 'Dash it, it's yours!' he said. 'I know how the safe was opened and I know who opened it, but I'm doubtful of my proof. And I know who murdered Minter and how it was done, but I can get no motive. So there you are, super. This print will help, but we're not out of the wood yet.'

'But damn it all, how were the jobs done? I'm afraid you've gone too far, chief, not to go the whole way.'

'I suppose I have,' French agreed. 'Since finding the print I don't mind. Come and sit down in your room and I'll tell you.'

They went back to Fenning's room and settled themselves as comfortably as the strictly utilitarian chairs would allow. Fenning held out a box of cigarettes, but French, who smoked cigarettes and a pipe as the humour took him, and cigars when he could get them, said that on this occasion he preferred a pipe. The super grunted and rang his bell, and when a constable appeared he gave orders that they were not to be disturbed.

'Now, for heaven's sake let's hear what's in your mind,' he went on.

'I'm not going through the case as a whole,' French began. 'You know it as well as I do, and we're both, I expect, equally sick of it. But I must just refer to a few matters in order to get the sequence of ideas.'

'What I'd like,' Fenning returned, 'is that you'd give the whole thing as you would in a report.'

'I'll do so as far as my theory is concerned. And it would be a help for that report when it comes, if you'd stop me if I'm not quite clear about anything.'

'No fear about that,' Fenning said with conviction.

'Well,' went on French, 'first of all we have the death of Minter. You are called in and the doctor says he is not satisfied about the affair. You have a postmortem, which shows the man was murdered by suffocation. You make inquiries and you find out all about the firm's difficulties and the meeting that was to be held on that Sunday. I needn't surely go over that?'

'No, we'll take that as read.'

'Then there's the discovery of the robbery, which for my sins brings me into the affair. I ask, I suppose, much the same questions as you, and find out about the firm's condition, the directors' meeting, and so on. When I hear about Minter's death I wonder if the crimes are connected. You are wondering the same thing. I come down and we talk it over and agree to work together as far as possible.'

'I'm glad we did,' Fenning exclaimed between two great puffs of smoke.

'So am I. Apart from it being a wise thing, we know now the crimes are connected, and we'd have to have got together sooner or later. The first thing we both saw was the obvious motive for the theft, but we noted further that the members of the firm had a stronger motive than outsiders. They would not only get immense wealth if they pulled off the robbery, but—and this was to my mind a much stronger consideration—they would avoid the ruin which was threatening them. A man might not want to be very much richer than he is, but he certainly will do his utmost not to be poorer.'

'I agree, of course. That already threw the balance of suspicion on someone in the Norne firm.'

270

'Yes, and there were other indications pointing in the same direction. There was the question of the keys, for example. It was difficult to see how an outsider could have got hold of the keys and cut new ones from their impressions, as at first we supposed had been done. Then the whole crime showed familiarity with the office and the working of the firm. It wasn't quite certain, but as you say, the probabilities pointed to someone connected with the concern. Add to that the facts that Minter was a member of the staff, and that the others in the house at the time of his death were connected with the business, and the entire case seems what I might call a Nornes Limited case.'

'Agreed. That was clear from the start.'

'Well, we both started from that, and we both went aside on blind issues, or at least, I did. I'm not going into that. Firstly, we thought Norne was guilty, then we thought he wasn't. We dabbled with the idea of Minter's being the thief. We suspected Sloley and Sheen, and cleared them in our minds. I thought Ricardo was our man, and found he wasn't. And so on. I'll not mention any of that.'

'It is, so to speak, a page of history that's best forgotten.'

'That's right. Then I'll come straight on to what I actually got. I know now that Sloley, Sheen and Lyde stole the stones jointly. They were all in it: those three and no one else.'

'I gathered that, and I've a notion how you proved it. What I want to know about is the murder.'

'I'm coming to that, but I must touch on the robbery first because some of the details of the murder hinge on it.'

Fenning nodded without speaking and French went on.

'The first thing that really put me on the trail was that lineman turning up. And that I have to admit was sheer luck. That he should have happened to be at a place from which he could see into the window, just when two of those boys were focusing their camera, was a piece of very pretty luck.'

Fenning moved uneasily. 'That's so, chief, in a way, but only in a way. In the first place, as you know yourself, things like that are always happening. Again and again a chance word overheard, or something seen quite by accident, has brought the solution of an otherwise baffling case. Look at the men who happened to be on the road in the middle of the night and saw Rouse after he had left his car. Just a chance, and it hanged Rouse.'

'Well, likely or unlikely, it was a pretty useful hint to me. I thought over it and thought over it, wondering what these two could have been doing. I made a lot of wrong guesses, which I needn't mention. But at last the idea of taking photographs of the keys shot into my mind and I believed I had it. I very soon saw that a single photograph wouldn't be enough—there were two keys to be taken. Then a ciné camera occurred to me. This also would give pictures of the keys from slightly different angles as they were being pushed forward, which would make it easier to copy them.'

'It was a good shot getting that, I will say,' Fenning declared.

'Oh, I don't know. It came by elimination. Nothing else seemed possible. Incidentally I saw that if I was right, it enormously strengthened the argument that the guilty man was one of the firm. More than that, he must be in a high position. The photographing would have to be done while

Norne and Minter were present, and to take a liberty like putting the despatch case on the letter file and standing over it while the safe was being opened, indicated a friend of Norne's.

'I, of course, made the obvious inquiries. I tried to check up the purchase of the camera. But that proved a wash-out, and I got my first bit of help from considering its disposal.'

'You told me about that,' Fenning interrupted. 'You argued that they would not have dared to keep the camera, but would have tried to cut their losses by popping it.'

'That's right. I found a man like Minter in appearance had popped one of the special cameras which would have been most suitable for the purpose, and that it had been bought shortly before. I couldn't actually connect the transactions with the affair, but the dates worked in so well that I thought I was probably on the right track. That at all events was Point No. 1.'

'And a very good one too.'

'Point No. 2 was better. I found out from Norne that Sloley had turned up in the office with a despatch case which he had put on the letter file, and had opened it and fumbled in it while the safe was being unlocked. That in itself was suggestive, but when I found that he had himself arranged for the safe to be opened at that time, I thought it was pretty nearly proof. But there was further evidence for it even than that. While he stood at the file he sang—a very unusual thing for him. In fact, he pretended to have taken a drop too much to account for it. That clinched the thing to me, though I still doubted I had enough evidence for court.'

'I don't quite get your point about the singing,' Fenning said doubtfully.

'These cameras make a slight noise when they're working. He couldn't risk it being heard.'

The super made a little gesture of comprehension. 'Bless my soul! Drown the sound?'

'That's what I took it to be. Well, there was the case for Sloley having "shot" the keys. Then I looked back over my notes and I found Point No. 3. It was Sloley who had brought about the meeting at Norne's on the Sunday. Sloley had managed it skilfully and indirectly, making suggestions which inevitably led the others to make the counter suggestions he wanted. This Point No. 3 not only confirmed my view that Sloley was at the bottom of the robbery, but it also indicated that the meeting down here at Guildford was an essential part of the scheme.'

Fenning nodded appreciatively. French continued.

'All this theory about photoing the keys was confirmed once and for all by the discovery I made at Sheen's, about which I've told you; I mean the finding of the cut film picture.'

'I should say so. I don't know what you're talking about in saying that's not good enough for court.'

'I'm glad you think so, super. I should have added that Sheen had a very decent little workshop with metal working tools: all on a small scale, of course. I mean, he could easily have cut the key.'

'I wish I was as far on with the murder as you are with that,' Fenning declared.

'As a matter of fact I think you are,' French answered. 'But before we leave the theft let me point out how completely all three men are in it. Lyde presumably bought and certainly pawned the camera. Sloley took the photographs. Sheen developed them and cut the key, or at least, the piece of film proves he was privy to it.'

'I see that. Short of finding someone who was with those fellows all the time watching what they did, I don't see that you could have got any more. Now, what about that murder?'

French laboriously and thoroughly changed his position. Then he re-lit his pipe, which in his intentness he had allowed to go out. Finally he turned over the pages of his notebook and glanced at some notes. Thus prepared, he went on with his exposition.

'Now, we had both begun by assuming that the theft and the murder were connected. Neither of us could prove it, but it seemed reasonable. I determined to continue to assume it and see where it led.

'If I were correct, it followed that Sloley, Sheen and Lyde, or certain of them, were guilty of the murder. Was there any evidence to support this theory?

'Well, in the first place, there was what I've already mentioned, that the meeting at Norne's was really engineered by Sloley. In the second, I saw equally clearly that Minter's call at the Norne office had been arranged by Sheen. You follow that, super?'

'You said you thought that shareholders' list that Sheen got out was only my eye?'

'That's it. I thought so, and you will notice that it was used to bring Minter to the office?'

'I follow that.'

'In the third place, and this perhaps is the most important of the three, Lyde faked an elaborate alibi. If it had been so necessary for him to prove he was in France that Saturday night, it surely pointed to him as the actual murderer?'

Again Fenning nodded without speaking.

275

'There was also the other point, that Lyde denied having been at the office that night. The tale about Sheen borrowing the five pounds from the petty cash may or may not have been true. I haven't had time to go into it yet, but I should imagine it was true, as they must have known it might be investigated.'

'You might find that Lyde or Sheen had brought about the loan to Mrs Sheen.'

French nodded in his turn. 'That's just what I should expect to find. However, we must leave that point, because it hasn't been gone into yet. Well, here was a certain amount of confirmation for the suspicion that those three might have murdered Minter. But here it stood. For a long time I couldn't get any further.

'Then I started another line. I tried to make an analysis of all the telephone messages which had passed on that afternoon, again with rather indifferent success.

'Sheen had stated that about half-past four he had 'phoned Minter to ask some questions which had just occurred to him in connection with his list of shareholders. When replying, Minter had mentioned that he was not going to Norne's till the 8.15 train, and it was then arranged that Minter would call at the office on his way. The receipt by Minter of a message at 4.30 was confirmed by the maid, so I took that call as having been cleared up. I presumed also that it was while then at the 'phone that Minter had called up Norne to say that he wouldn't go down till after dinner. I couldn't fix the exact time at which that message had been received, but it was somewhere about 4.30. That also worked in sufficiently well.

'But Minter had received another message at three o'clock, and this one I have been quite unable to trace. But immediately after receiving it he had rung up his garage and put back the time of his taxi from 4.45 to 7.30.

'Before I became suspicious about Minter's movements I had assumed that on this occasion also he had taken the opportunity of being at the telephone to make another call, this time to his garage. Now I thought it might be something more direct. I began to wonder whether that message he had received at three o'clock—and not illness—had been the real cause of the postponement of his journey? The relation in time between it and the message to the garage seemed suggestive. Here I couldn't see my way clear, so I left it for the moment and turned to review Minter's movements on that Saturday.

'Minter's servant, Martha Belden, who seemed quite reliable, had said that Minter had spent the afternoon in his house, leaving by taxi at 7.30. This time was confirmed directly by the taximan, and indirectly by the garage.

'Martha, however, hadn't known of Minter's illness. This, however, was not significant, as unless when very bad, he was not in the habit of complaining. On the other hand, the illness was supported by the fact—confirmed by the post-mortem—that he had no dinner.'

'But did you doubt the illness?'

'I doubted everything. I wanted to see just what there was proof for, and what there wasn't. I noted there was none for the illness.

'You may see that I was pretty suspicious by this time when I tell you that I particularly noted that Mrs Minter, who would undoubtedly have known whether her husband was or was not ill, was out for the afternoon. And I was more interested still when I remembered that that outing had been arranged by one of our three suspects—Sheen. Mrs Minter had been asked to Sheen's daughter's birthday party. I wondered if I was really on to something or was merely getting childish.

'Then I went on with Minter's movements. He had reached the office at 7.50. But what then? The evidence of what happened in the office might be washed out. But after that there was firm testimony that he had driven to Waterloo, travelled to Guildford, was driven to Norne's, went to bed, and was seen by Norne about ten.

'All this journey from the office to Norne's seemed conclusively proven till I began to look into it with scepticism, and then I saw that we really knew nothing about it at all. The taximan could really only state that he had driven a fare from the office to Waterloo. At Guildford, we were told, Minter was muffled up to the ears, and presumably he was the same at Waterloo. Besides the man would not observe him closely. The same applied in the case of Norne's chauffeur, and it should be remembered that this man had only seen Minter a few times at long intervals. Norne's butler, Jeffries, was a new man and had never seen Minter. Then with regard to Norne, two things were suggestive. First, Norne was greatly struck by the way the illness had changed Minter, and second, the headache had made Minter's eyes sensitive and only the light in the adjoining bathroom was on. We have to remember also that Minter was too ill to do more than give Norne Sheen's list; he didn't want to talk.'

An expression of intense amazement, not unmixed with excitement, was growing on Fenning's somewhat heavy features. French glanced at him and laughed.

'I see you've got it, super,' he remarked. 'That's it. If I'm right, Minter never travelled down by that 8.15

train from Waterloo. He came in the car with Sloley and Sheen.'

Fenning gave vent to an oath of some sturdiness. 'And that was Lyde?' he cried wonderingly. 'That sick man that we've been so sorry for and that was murdered later on!' He stopped and an expression of bewilderment passed across his face. Then it cleared and comprehension grew.

'I've got you at last. By heavens, chief, I should have seen that before. Of course! It all works in now. Lyde hadn't to get up into that room at Norne's because he was already there. And Minter was murdered, I suppose, before they were clear of London?'

'That's what I make of it,' French agreed. 'I take it what they did was this. Lyde—'

'Yes, go through it all. No; stop. Go on as you were and finish the tale.'

'As you like. Well, I was thinking over this evidence of Minter's journey when this idea that you've just got occurred to me: that Minter had never made it, but that Lyde had travelled in his place. At first I thought the idea absurd, but as I worried over it, certain things began to make it more likely.

'There was first of all the splendid opportunity it gave for the robbery. Suppose they had got Norne's key from the photographs and for some reason had failed to get Minter's. I may admit this is the point which still sticks me: I don't see why they should have failed. But suppose they did, everything becomes clear. They make Minter strip off his clothes and take his keys. Probably they tie or lock him up. Then Lyde, who is an actor and about the same size as Minter, and who has probably already made up to represent him, dresses in Minter's clothes. At the same time with Minter's key and the one they have made, Sloley and Lyde clear out the safe. They lock it, give Minter's key to Lyde and he starts off to Guildford. You will note that Sloley sees him into the taxi—all that whole way down from the top of the building. That, I take it, was to prevent Lyde having to speak to the taximan.'

Fenning nodded approvingly. 'That's it, as sure as we're alive. We ought to have got something from Sloley coming down all that way. I read your memo of it, but I missed the point.'

'So did I,' French admitted. 'Well, to follow Lyde's movements. I take it he went to Guildford, easily took in the chauffeur, hadn't to take in the butler, and succeeded in what must have been his hardest job, taking in Norne. There the illness was his salvation. He looked different, he couldn't talk, and he couldn't be seen in a decent light.'

'A bit lucky, that illness.'

French smiled slowly, but said nothing. Then Fenning swore again.

'Hell, do you mean that was a fake too? But of course! You've just pointed out that there's no evidence for it except from those three ruffians.'

Fenning thought for a moment, then added: 'But he 'phoned Norne?'

'But did he?'

Fenning made a furious gesture. 'Hell!' he cried again. 'I've been blind! That was Lyde?'

'I take it so. Actors are taught to mimic voices as well as appearances. I take it all the arrangements for that afternoon were made by our three friends.'

'But then why didn't Minter go down to Guildford at five o'clock as arranged?'

'I take it because of the message he received at three. I have no proof, but I suggest Lyde put through a message purporting to come from Norne, and postponing Minter's arrival. That's guesswork, of course.'

'Go ahead,' said Fenning in a small voice.

'As soon as Norne had left the bedroom, I suggest that Lyde got busy. He had brought the rope with him, and he lowered it from the window. Then he waited.'

'Waited for those other scoundrels from Town?'

'So I think. I imagine what took place in the office was this. When Minter arrived they forced him to drink that sleeping draught. It would probably have suited them best to murder him then and there, but they daren't do it for two reasons. First, it was only eight o'clock. It would have been too soon. The doctor's evidence would have blown the gaff. Secondly, they must keep him able to walk to the car—with assistance. If a constable had seen them carry him, they were done.'

'The dope would also make him stupid and prevent him from shouting out when getting into the car?'

'That's right. I think there may have been another reason also. They may not have faced keeping him alive from eight till eleven in full possession of his senses, and probably knowing that they were going to kill him. Hang it all, bad as they were, I scarcely think they'd have done that.'

Fenning shrugged. 'You think better of them than I do. But look here, chief, there's something wrong there, surely? The doctor said Minter was murdered at ten or thereabouts, he believed before eleven. But if you're right the doctor's wrong. You make the murder just when?'

'In the car immediately after leaving the office. About

281

quarter-past eleven. No, super, there's no discrepancy there. It's all right and this is one of the cleverest bits of the whole thing. Just recall the doctor's statement. He said the evidence was a bit conflicting. The evidence from the cooling of the body showed that death had taken place some considerable time earlier, he said from seven to ten or earlier. But all the other evidence pointed to a later time, from ten till midnight. He said such conflicting evidence was not unusual and that doctors usually took a sort of mean. He did so, and it made his result about ten.

'But look at what actually occurred and what he thought had occurred. He thought the deceased had been in bed, covered up by clothes. Radiation would be reduced to a minimum and cooling would be slow. But as a matter of fact the body, dressed probably in outer clothes only, was in a car, driving very quickly on a cold night. Cooling would be much more rapid than in bed. I'll bet if the doctor had known that, we'd have had a different time for the death.'

'I wonder if they intended that?'

'I don't know, but whether they did or not it worked out well for them. Well, they got Minter, stupefied, but able to walk with assistance, out of the office and into the car, and, of course, they brought also Lyde's clothes and probably an outfit to let him get off his make-up. They drove down to Guildford just as fast as wouldn't get them stopped, and ran up the old road on to the Hog's Back, behind Norne's house. They carried the dead man to the house, Lyde no doubt showing a convenient light so that they could identify the window. There at the bottom of the wall was Lyde's rope and they tied the body on and

Lyde drew it up. It wouldn't take him long to get it into bed and arrange everything as it was to be found. Then he no doubt changed the rope to the upper windows, got out on to the sill, closed the side window he had used, latched it through the upper quadrant, slipped down to the ground and drew the rope after him. We saw that all that would be possible.'

'And the glass?' Fenning murmured.

'About the glass I have no proof, but what I suggest took place was this. While all three doubtless hoped that the death would be taken to be either from natural causes or suicide, they must have realised that the murder might be discovered. To guard themselves in such a case, I suggest they decided to throw suspicion on Norne. The fact that he held one of the keys of the safe would suggest why Norne was chosen. This was by no means the least skilful part of the whole affair, in fact, it was carried out in a very subtle way, so that it wouldn't be discovered unless suspicion had already been aroused. Lyde got Norne up to the room alone and the last thing at night—at least, the last thing so far as Minter was ostensibly concerned. While there he tricked Norne into leaving his finger-prints on the glass, which he had cleaned for the purpose. Then Lyde again wiped the glass, carefully leaving a distinctive part of one of Norne's prints. Then when he had got the body into bed, he faked on Minter's prints, purposely turning the thumb to an impossible angle to show that it was a fake. That again, as I say, is only my suggestion.'

Fenning nodded heavily. He seemed too much overcome for words.

'While Sloley and Sheen drove round to the front door, Lyde must have dressed in his own clothes, got off his

283

make-up, and proceeded to make himself scarce. In this necessary part of the affair he passed your two constables at the new railway bridge. He made his way to Newhaven, crossed to Paris, and completed a quite decent alibi. When he got back he forged the passport stamp, smearing it with mud to try to hide his operations. But he made a bad mistake there. He forgot that the night he had crossed was dry.'

Still Fenning did not answer and French went on. 'All that reconstruction admittedly is guesswork, but you'll admit it fits the facts?'

At last Fenning moved. 'It's the truth,' he said with an oath. 'It's the truth as sure as we're here at this moment. But proof . . . That's another matter, I'm afraid.'

'The proof is the finger-print on the collar. To me it's complete, though I don't know how it would strike a jury. I thought there was just the off-chance that we might find that finger-print, for this reason. Lyde, I expect, wore gloves. He would be bound to do so, or he might have trapped himself with finger-prints. But a stiff linen collar's not an easy proposition to handle with gloves on. Therefore, the chances were that when he came to unbutton Minter's, which, of course, he had been wearing from the office to Norne's, he found he had to slip the gloves off. He either overlooked the fact that he had made prints, or thought no one would test for them.'

'Well, I admit I shouldn't have thought of testing for them myself. I don't see how the defence could explain those prints away.'

'They might say that Minter was taken faint in the office and that the other three loosened his collar for him.'

'And would that be an explanation?'

French shook his head. 'It wouldn't be to me. But you never know what view a jury'll take.'

'I don't think Lyde would get away with a tale of that sort.'

French knocked out his pipe. 'Well, super, there's the story. I don't think I've forgotten anything. I'm satisfied as to the truth; I'm doubtful as to the proof; and I'm *hanged* if I can see the motive. Can you?'

Fenning did not reply for some moments. 'It must have been what you say,' he answered presently, but there was doubt in his manner. 'They can't have got Minter's key with the camera.'

'But why not? If they got Norne's they should have got Minter's.'

Fenning shook his head. 'Well,' he said, 'we don't have to prove motive. There's enough in what you have for a conviction, and more than likely a search of the houses will give us more still. What about bringing those three fellows in before they get wise to our being on to them?'

French moved uneasily. Fenning was justified in demanding an arrest. In fact, he would have been remiss not to. But French didn't want an arrest: not yet.

'I dare say you're right, super,' he said diplomatically. 'At the same time I'd rather consider it a bit before making a move. The case isn't finished.'

'I know it's not. But we have enough for an arrest.'

'In your case, perhaps, yes: in mine, not by any means. As you know, I've only got ahead with half mine. What many people would call the most important half hasn't been touched yet.'

'You mean the swag?'

'That's just what I do mean. Without the swag the case is not finished. With the swag it's not only done, but we have the most complete proof that anyone could wish.'

'I agree. But have you any line on its probable position?'

'I'm afraid not.'

'Then how will postponing an arrest help matters. Aren't you more likely to come on it when you've got search warrants for the houses?'

'I doubt very much that it's in the houses. After all if you look carefully enough, you can find anything in a house. There have been a lot of first-class brains put into this job, and I believe the hiding-place will be equally well thought out. No, super, we'll not get anything in the houses.'

'Then what do you propose?'

French instinctively leant forward and sank his voice. 'I suggest we make them show us the hiding place.'

That Fenning was keenly interested was obvious. 'My word, if you could do that it would be something like. How would you set about it?'

'I've not thought out a proper scheme, but I suggest somehow giving them the tip that we were on to them. Not on to them exactly, but on to something that would necessarily lead to them. Suppose they saw that they had about a day to escape arrest for murder. Wouldn't that do the trick?'

'They'd do a bunk?'

'Yes, but not without the swag. They're not going to risk all they've risked and be cheated of the reward in the end.'

Fenning was impressed. All the same, he wondered if the chief's scheme would work. If it failed, he pointed out, they would be much worse off than before. 'They might get away,' he ended up, though in so half-hearted a way as to show French he had gained his point.

'They'll not get away,' French returned firmly. 'We can get them on the boats or 'planes, if we don't take them before.'

For another hour they discussed the affair. Finally it was settled that as French had provided what would be Fenning's case for murder, he was entitled to try any experiment he wanted to which would help him in the case for theft.

'What you've said to me was not said officially,' Fenning concluded, 'but in a private conversation. I can't act on it.'

French expressed warm approval, and after some further talk the two men parted. French was to put his proposals before Sir Mortimer Ellison. If the Assistant Commissioner approved, the experiment was to be carried out.

20

Exit Sloley

When French had worked out his plans for recovering the stones, he went in and put them before Sir Mortimer Ellison. The Assistant Commissioner listened without any sign of enthusiasm.

'It might be worth trying,' he said doubtfully when French had finished. 'You'd have to be careful they didn't give you the slip.'

'They'll not do that, sir,' French returned. 'We'll have them properly shadowed, and if by any chance they did break away, we'd get them again at the ports.'

'I hope you're right. You'll want a hell of a lot of help, for if they go, they'll all go different ways.'

'I thought of getting Tanner and Willis to help me, if you're agreeable. We'd each want one or two men to help us in the shadowing.'

Sir Mortimer turned back to the papers he was working on. 'All right, French,' he said. 'Go ahead, and good luck.'

With practically a free hand to do the best he knew, French set to work. First he despatched to all the ports, coastguards, police along the coasts, and air ports, detailed descriptions and photographs of the three men. Unless otherwise instructed, the fugitives were not to be allowed to leave the country. If found attempting to do so, they were to be detained until an officer arrived from the Yard to make formal arrests. To give them a sense of security, however, Lyde's passport was returned to him, after being marked secretly and carefully photographed. Then French got hold of Inspectors Tanner and Willis, Sergeant Carter, two other sergeants, and three constables. Having arranged that they should be relieved of their other work if and when they were required, he went down to the Norne building and saw Miss Barber.

It did not seem to that lady that French had much motive for his call. He stood there chatting about the weather and complaining about how hard he was worked, and occasionally touching on matters connected with the firm. He was surprised to learn that the directors had not yet come to a decision as to whether they would reconstruct their company, and wondered when they would do so. Miss Barber indicated that they were waiting to see whether French would recover the stolen booty, and delicately conveyed in her manner that if this was all they had to hope for they might as well go ahead and commit financial suicide at once. The next board was on the following Wednesday and the preliminary meeting was being held in two days.

On the second day French was again early on the scene, this time with his helpers. He watched till he saw Sloley and Ricardo go in, waited five minutes, and then went up once again to Miss Barber's room. Then he asked to see Norne.

Rather reluctantly, it seemed to him, she took in his message. Then she held the door open. 'Mr Norne will see you.' In her manner was a suggestion of faint surprise that Mr Norne had nothing better to do with his time.

When French saw Sloley and Ricardo he paused quickly as if he had expected Norne to be alone. Then immediately he went on. 'I'm sorry, sir, if I'm butting in on a conference. It was you, Mr Norne, I really came to see, but I think you other gentlemen will be equally interested in what I have to say. I've got some news at last.'

'If it's good news, we'll be glad of it,' Norne returned. 'We'd almost given up hope. Sit down, chief-inspector, and let's hear it.'

'I think, gentlemen, you'll be pleased with what I have to tell you. We've not completed our investigation, so you mustn't expect too much. But I was given to understand that your future policy as to your business would depend on whether or not you recovered your property, and I therefore thought I should advise you immediately if this began to seem likely.'

'Quite right. If we don't get the stuff back we'll be bankrupt. If you think you're going to get it, you're dead right to let us know' Norne looked at his codirectors, both of whom nodded.

French beamed. 'Well, gentlemen, I think we're going to get it. We've made a discovery that will, I think, have pretty far-reaching results. We've found how the thief got the keys.'

Norne and Ricardo seemed interested, but not greatly impressed. Sloley also seemed interested, but French noticed that he took out his handkerchief and on the excuse of blowing his nose, kept the lower part of his face covered. French took care to glance at him casually, but no more.

'It was done,' French went on, 'in a very novel and ingenious way. A ciné camera of very high type was arranged so as to photograph the keys being put forward into the lock, and photographs were enlarged, and new keys were cut from the enlargements.'

The three men stared. There was now no doubt of their interest. There were exclamations of surprise, then Norne struck a sceptical note. 'Oh, come now, chief-inspector, are you sure of that? I've been here every time the safe was opened and I've seen no camera.'

French smiled. 'You wouldn't be likely to do that, sir. I don't suppose anyone concerned was here when the thing was done. The camera was probably hidden somewhere near the safe and operated electrically from some adjoining room, or perhaps by an invisible ray when you approached the safe. Oh, no, you wouldn't be allowed to see it being done; neither you nor anyone else.'

'But how do you know it was done that way?' Sloley demanded. 'I must admit it doesn't strike me as very likely. As a matter of fact, would you get enough detail on such a photograph to cut a key from it? I should have said not.'

'So should I, sir. So I did, in fact. But our photographic department were convinced of it. They got a camera and tried it on the Assistant Commissioner's safe, and they surprised him by handing him a key that fitted. He was like you, Mr Sloley, sceptical before that. But he wasn't sceptical afterwards.'

'But you haven't answered my question,' Sloley persisted. 'You haven't explained how you know it was done in that way. I don't see how you could possibly tell that.'

'I'm afraid, sir, I can't answer that as fully as I should like,' French said with evident regret. 'It's from a personal statement, and we always treat such as confidential. But I may tell you this. Acting on information received, I made certain inquiries. I learned that four days before the robbery, a ciné camera was pledged in Dobson & Hall's pawnshop in Shaftesbury Avenue. These cameras bear a serial number, and I found that it had been bought on September 13th. That means that the thieves bought it early so as to allow time for experimenting, photographed the keys, and then, finding it would be too dangerous a thing to be found in their possession, they got rid of it in as profitable a way as they could. Now, you'll say, how do I know that this was the camera in question? I'll tell you. Apart from the significance of the dates, the man who pawned it was undoubtedly trying to pass as Mr Minter.'

'Minter?'

'Yes, sir. It wasn't Mr Minter, but it was very like him, and the clerk in the pawnshop noticed that he was made up.'

Ricardo moved uneasily. 'I'm sure it's all right if you say so, chief-inspector, but all that doesn't sound very convincing to me. How do you know it was Minter that the man was trying to represent?'

'Because, sir, he left an unsuspected clue to his identity. We are following it up, but so far we've not succeeded in getting our hands on him. But you may take it from me that it's only a question of a very short time. By tomorrow at latest we should have him under lock and key. And as there is reason to believe he was not acting alone, getting his associates also is a foregone conclusion.'

Norne looked at his co-directors. 'I'm sure it's very gratifying to hear all this,' he said with a slight trace of hesitation. 'I admit it doesn't sound very convincing to me either, but then I don't know the detective business. If the chief-inspector assures us that he is on these men's track, so very much the better. But there's one thing, Mr French, you haven't told us. Suppose you get the men: is that any reason to suppose you'll get the stones?'

'Yes, that's the point,' said Sloley, and Ricardo murmured his agreement.

French was now only anxious to leave. He didn't want to be asked too many questions, lest he should inadvertently betray his true suspicions. He therefore looked at his watch and said it was later than he had supposed and that he had an appointment which he had only just time to keep.

'I told you, gentlemen,' he said, standing up, 'that I couldn't guarantee anything absolutely. But I haven't myself the slightest doubt that we'll get the men within a few hours, and that when we get them we'll get the stones very soon after. I think you really may count on that. Certainly don't contemplate taking any immediate action about your affairs. This is Friday; if you haven't good news before Monday, I'll never back my opinion again.'

As he left the building French had to admit to a strong feeling of anxiety. The hook was now baited: would the fish bite? If they did, they would do so at once. The next few hours were likely to be fairly hectic.

French had decided that he, Carter and a constable would shadow Sloley, Tanner and Willis, each with a sergeant and constable, following Sheen and Lyde respectively. He and Carter now got into a police car which was waiting in Kingsway, while Constable Shaw, dressed inconspicuously as a rather respectable loafer, hung about the end of Ronder Lane. Tanner and his helpers were already in

293

position to freeze on to Sheen if and when he came out, and Willis and his men had gone out to Hampstead to watch Sheen's house for Lyde.

French did not expect any very immediate development. Sloley would probably not leave the office before the end of the meeting, though he might then make a bolt for it. Sheen would have to act even more slowly. It was unlikely that he would go before the evening. In the first place, Sloley would have to get the news to him, and then if Sheen were to start before working hours ended, some excuse for his doing so would have to be devised and put forward. Lyde could probably go at any time after the news had reached him.

It was equally possible, though French thought less likely, that Sloley would take his, French's, story as a bluff and do nothing. In that case the men would have to be arrested, and the chances of recovering the stones would be greatly lessened.

For upwards of an hour French and Carter sat in the car while Shaw hung about Ronder Lane. An indignant policeman came up to move them on, but vanished ignominiously on a word from French. The traffic flowed steadily past them and still there came no sign. Then suddenly Shaw came out into Kingsway and walked slowly towards the car.

This was the signal that things had begun to move. In a few seconds Sloley appeared, walking in a leisurely way. He also came out into Kingsway and stood watching the traffic. Presently a disengaged taxi hove in sight. Sloley hailed it and was driven off northwards.

Shaw having got into the police car, it followed. The driver was an experienced man, and he put on a spurt which brought his vehicle in close behind Sloley's when they were stopped at the head of Kingsway. The block ending, both cars moved forward into Southampton Row. The chase continued through Woburn Place, across Euston Road into Seymour Street, and then with a left and right into Euston Station.

French and Shaw left the car in Drummond Street, themselves hurrying after Sloley. They were in time to see him enter one of the telephone booths at the entrance to the central hall. French could see his movements through the glass well enough to note that he made two calls, both short.

When the man emerged French and Shaw were well hidden round the side of the bookstall. The possibility of pursuit did not, however, seem to have entered Sloley's mind, and without glancing round he disappeared down the Underground steps at the end of No. 6 Platform. The others followed, watched him book, and when he had passed round the next corner, hurried on.

Fortunately, at that time in the day but few people were travelling. French showed his card in at the booking window. 'Scotland Yard officer,' he said quickly. 'Where did that last passenger book to?'

'Hampstead,' the clerk said with a look of interest.

'Another of the same,' French went on.

He got the ticket, passed it to Shaw, whispered, 'I'll go by road,' and turned back to the main line station, while Shaw took the lift following Sloley's.

As Hampstead was not far from Sloley's house, French took the risk of assuming that he was going home. He hurried back to the car and told his man to go all out.

His decision was justified. As they came in sight of the

station Sloley emerged and without looking round turned towards his house. A moment later Shaw appeared and in another moment was back in his place on the front seat.

'Doesn't know we're on to him?' said French.

'Sure he doesn't, sir. But he's looking pretty thoughtful, as if he was up to something.'

'A bunk, I hope.'

French's earlier guess proved correct. Sloley went straight to his home. French and his helpers took up an inconspicuous position in a nearby lane to await developments.

The first of these came very soon. Scarcely had they got into place when Lyde appeared. He did not see the watchers, but walked to Sloley's house and entered.

A couple of minutes later Willis and his two men, looking for cover, entered the lane. This was unexpectedly satisfactory, as it enabled French to explain what was on foot. 'Sloley evidently called Lyde up from that booth at Euston,' he went on. 'He sent two calls and I expect the second was to Sheen. Some prearranged phrase would give the information, so that it wouldn't matter if the conversation was overheard.'

'If so, they're going at once.'

'It looks like it,' French agreed. 'What about the back of the house?'

With their six men they were able to surround the entire grounds. But no attempt was made to give them the slip. They settled down to wait.

Time soon began to drag. The conspirators were evidently in no hurry, and French began to think that his plan was miscarrying and that they were not going to make a bolt. So they waited till shortly after one o'clock.

Then suddenly Sloley and Lyde left the house together,

Sloley carrying a small suitcase. They walked to the end of the street, where Sloley turned towards Hampstead Station and Lyde in the opposite direction. French and his men hurriedly resumed their places in their car, while Willis and his helpers quietly faded away.

'Shaw, you better nip out and shadow him,' French directed. 'We'll get to the station before him.'

By an indirect route French had the car driven to Hampstead Station. They did not pass Sloley, so there was no risk of the man's seeing them. Reaching the Underground, French hurried to the booking-office, while Carter concealed himself on the emergency staircase.

'Inspector from Scotland Yard,' French said to the booking-clerk, holding out his card. 'I want to know where a man books. Let me come into the office, and when I point him out, give me a ticket to the same station.'

The manœuvre was quickly arranged. Sitting on the counter, himself unseen, French was able to recognise Sloley's voice when the man asked for a ticket to Victoria.

As the lift went down Shaw appeared. French thrust the ticket into his hand, saying 'Victoria,' and then beckoning Carter from his retreat, they returned to the car, which had been told to wait for fifteen minutes on chance.

'Victoria,' said French again.

He had little doubt what Sloley was about to do. Believing that he was still unsuspected, he was going to try for the Continent. Though it was true that extradition treaties had been entered into with most other countries, Sloley would scarcely be able to avoid the criminal's complex, that the farther he is from the scene of his crime, the safer he is from detection.

French fortunately knew the Continental trains. The next

left at two, and was an important train. In addition to Paris, it had direct connections to Brussels, Berlin and Central and Southern Europe generally. It was just the train that a criminal who believed himself unsuspected would make for.

So convinced was French as to Sloley's intentions, that at Victoria he repeated his Hampstead manœuvre. Explaining the matter to the booking-clerk, he got into the office, listened for Sloley's voice, and presently heard him ask for a second single to Brussels.

'That's via Dover, isn't it?' said French, who knew his timetable. 'Three returns, Dover.'

It was not until the train was just about to start that French and Carter joined Shaw at the barrier, and all three slipped into the last carriage. 'He's four coaches ahead,' Shaw explained as they took their places. 'I didn't see him looking round, and I don't think he knows we're on to him.'

'Did he come straight along?'

'He called at a post office between his house and Hampstead Station, I don't know what for. I thought I'd better not go in and there wasn't time to ask afterwards.'

'Was he long there?'

'No, sir; only a minute or two.'

'Then he didn't telephone?'

'No, not long enough for that.'

French was a little doubtful as to whether he should not have arrested the man then and there, instead of waiting till he reached the boat. It would have saved three journeys to and from Dover. However, there was just the possibility that Sloley was not going on board. Conceivably this taking of the ticket was a blind intended to throw off

298

a possible pursuit, and Sloley would strike out in some other direction from Dover.

However, at Dover he did nothing of the kind. He showed his passport with the other passengers and walked straight to the steamer. As he reached the gangway, French touched his arm.

'Excuse me, Mr Sloley,' he said gravely, 'but I'm afraid I must ask you to come with me. If you will do so quietly, there need be no publicity. I have two men with me,' he added meaningly.

Carter and Shaw had indeed already edged Sloley out of the queue approaching the gangway, and were standing on either side of him before he appeared to grasp what was happening. For a moment he seemed completely stunned, then rapidly he pulled himself together.

He turned slowly and began to walk with French. 'I don't know what you think you're doing,' he went on conversationally, 'but I presume I'll learn that later.'

French answered, 'Yes, sir,' in a dry voice and the little procession continued moving back along the wharf. Suddenly Sloley sneezed. Then from an inside pocket he pulled out a folded handkerchief and put it up to his face.

The action was commonplace and quite normal and French suspected nothing. Then as Sloley raised his arm, his eye caught the corner of a crumpled handkerchief protruding from the man's coat pocket.

In a way there was nothing remarkable in this and yet it gave French very furiously to think. Had the man really two handkerchiefs, and did he use a folded one when one that had been opened out was ready in his pocket? In the tenth of a second these thoughts passed through French's mind and in another tenth he reached a conclusion.

Swinging round, he seized Sloley's wrist just as the hand-kerchief approached his mouth. Carter and Shaw, seeing the movement, also grabbed the man.

They were just in time. From Sloley's hand they took a handkerchief, sewn as folded to make a pad. To the side which would have gone next Sloley's mouth was fixed a small white capsule. Nothing would have been easier than to have bitten this off and swallowed it. And it did not require much imagination to see that if Sloley had bitten it off and swallowed it, he would never have been charged with murder.

With the discovery of the capsule Sloley's self-control vanished. His face became convulsed with rage and fear, and he began struggling like a maniac. For a moment, indeed, it took all that the three men could do to hold him. Then French managed to slip on a pair of handcuffs, and calling a vehicle, they were driven to the local police station. There Sloley, now completely exhausted, was charged with being concerned in the murder and theft, and then came the moment for which French had waited so impatiently. The man was searched.

But French was disappointed, more bitterly disappointed than he cared to admit. Except for a small sum of money, there were no valuables on Sloley. French's scheme of recovering the stones had therefore failed, and he was as far as ever from the solution of this part of his problem.

With a bitter curse he turned to the telephone to report to the Yard.

21

Exeunt

Though the information French sent to the Yard was negative, he obtained some news in return which so filled his mind that his disappointment was forgotten and his revitalised energies were started off in a new channel.

It appeared that Lyde had also left Town. He had booked to Folkestone by the 3 p.m. from Charing Cross, and Willis and his helpers had travelled by the same train. Sheen, moreover was apparently contemplating a similar bolt. He had had a telephone call at the office to say that his wife had been run over by a car and was seriously hurt and asking him to go home at once. Tanner had shadowed him home, and incidentally had found out that Mrs Sheen, though out, was in perfect health. Sheen had now left his house, but no information as to his destination had as yet been received.

French found himself immediately confronted by a pressing problem. If the plan agreed on at the Yard were carried out, Willis would arrest Lyde if he attempted to go on board the boat at Folkestone. This had seemed the obvious thing to do when the affair was being discussed. But now the circumstances were altered. Additional information was available. One of the three men had already been arrested, and no jewels had been found on him. If so, was it not likely that the same would obtain in the cases of the other two?

French thought so. If they were going to take the stones out of the country on their persons, they would surely have divided them into three lots and each would have taken one. It now looked as if some other method of disposing of the booty had been adopted. Could the men still not be made to reveal it?

The immediate question then was whether Lyde and Sheen should be allowed to leave the country if they attempted to do so, being shadowed to their several destinations? The objection, of course, was that if they were once out of England, French's powers of arrest would be invalid. He would have to depend on the police of the country in which he found himself, and owing to unavoidable formal delays, the men might succeed in giving him the slip.

French tried to get through to Sir Mortimer Ellison, but unfortunately the A.C. was not in his office. And there was no one else in authority who understood the circumstances. French, therefore, decided to act on his own initiative. He thought he was justified, as he had been given practically a free hand.

A hurried dip into a timetable showed that the 3 p.m. train from Charing Cross was due at Folkestone Central at 5.03. It was now after half-past four, so that by taking a car there would be plenty of time to meet it. French rang up for a taxi, and he and his two men had already taken their places, when a furiously waving constable caused his driver to stop. French was once again wanted on the telephone.

It was another message from the Yard. Sheen, followed by Tanner and his men, had left Victoria by the 4.20 for Folkestone Harbour, having booked to Boulogne.

French found that Sir Mortimer had just returned to his office, and he consumed five of his precious remaining minutes in explaining what he proposed. To his great satisfaction he at once received the hierarchic blessing.

'I'll take over Sheen from Tanner at Folkestone, then,' he concluded. 'Would you be so good, sir, as to arrange for some help for me at Boulogne?' Sir Mortimer agreed to this also and rang off.

French urged his driver to speed, with the result that they arrived at Folkestone Central at a minute before five. There from behind a convenient pile of luggage French watched the train come in. Almost at once he saw Lyde, walking smartly from his compartment with a small suitcase in his hand. Then Willis hove in sight in a pullover and plus fours with a bag of golf clubs over his shoulder, the sporting Briton to the life. French edged up beside him.

'We pulled in Sloley and found nothing on him,' he murmured. 'You'd better follow Lyde to wherever he's going on the Continent. Keep in touch with me through the Yard.'

Willis nodded and passed on with the others, while French, after seeing that the coast was clear, followed discreetly to the Harbour Station. There he watched hare and hounds go on board the Boulogne boat, as he had expected they would.

When the 4.20 boat-train from Victoria arrived, French

had once more found a suitable cover from which to observe the descending passengers. Sheen got out of one of the first compartments, and passport in hand, moved off with the other travellers. Tanner was not far behind him, and in a moment French was beside him.

'The A.C. has 'phoned me to take over,' he said, and in a few words explained the situation. Tanner nodded and dropped behind, while French, also with his papers, followed Sheen to the passport officer. A moment later they were on board the boat.

Sheen had engaged a private cabin, and into this he immediately disappeared. French obtained another, from the slightly open door of which he could watch Sheen's, while himself remaining hidden from possible discovery by Lyde.

At Boulogne things worked out better than he could have hoped. From his porthole French could see Lyde among the first of those to pass down the gangway. Close behind him moved Willis' tall form and bag of golf clubs. Not until almost everyone else had gone ashore did Sheen appear, and he was clear of the immediate surroundings before French ventured to follow. Thanks to Sir Mortimer's use of the telephone, French found a plain-clothes member of the Boulogne police force awaiting him. With uncanny precision this man, who had lounged near the gangway while the passengers were disembarking, picked out French the moment he set foot on the quay. French pleased him by congratulating him on his skill, then rapidly explained what was wanted.

'Your man knows your appearance?' the Frenchman queried.

'Unfortunately he does.'

304

'Then, monsieur, if you will keep out of sight, I will find out where he goes and let you know.'

Nothing could have pleased French better. And in the end nothing could have proved more valuable. Indeed, had it not been for the Frenchman, it was not unlikely that the trail would have been lost altogether.

Sheen did not go forward by the boat-train. Instead, as soon as he was through the customs, he took a taxi and drove off. Neither French nor his helpers could have found out where the vehicle was bound, but the plain-clothes man ambling lazily past as the direction was given, heard all that passed. He ambled on till the taxi was out of sight, then hurried back to French.

'Your man has chartered a taxi for Etaples,' he explained. 'If you take another you'll be able to keep him in sight all the way.'

'Etaples?' French returned in surprise. 'What on earth is he going there for?'

The Frenchman shrugged politely. He supposed the chief-inspector had no idea of where his man might be heading?

'One of the trio booked to Brussels,' French suggested.

Again the other shrugged, shaking his head. He could make no suggestion, save that Brussels was a blind and that the reunion was to take place in Etaples. Here, however, was another taxi, and if French didn't want to lose his quarry, he advised that he should start at once.

French thanked him and jumped with his satellites into the vehicle, but before it could start, Willis appeared with hand upraised.

'Lyde's booked to Paris and has got into the front of the train,' he murmured and vanished. Five seconds later, sitting well back in the taxi, French was driving quickly towards the town.

After passing through Boulogne their driver put on a spurt. The road led inland, though they could see at intervals the sand dunes of the coast. Soon they noticed ahead another taxi and the driver slackened speed so as just to keep it in sight. It was not travelling fast, about thirty miles an hour or more.

From Boulogne to Etaples is only some eighteen miles, and in a little over half an hour they reached the outskirts of the latter town. Here the driver accelerated sharply, closing up on the quarry. Presently they reached the railway station, where they watched Sheen pay off his vehicle and disappear into the building. While French was settling with his driver, Shaw jumped out and followed Sheen.

French and Carter took cover behind a convenient lorry to await events. Presently they saw Sheen emerge from the station, cross the street, and disappear into an hotel. A moment later Shaw joined them.

'Went in to check up some trains that he had in a notebook,' said Shaw. 'He didn't see me.'

'You don't know what trains?'

'The local sheet: Calais to Paris.'

French nodded. 'Good cover in that station?'

'Not too bad.'

'We'll wait there.'

It was now half-past eight and growing very cold. The station was draughty and unattractive. French was a little doubtful as to his proper course. Sheen might well be going to spend the night in his hotel, and if so, there was no use in the others hanging about. Fortunately, they had had a meal. French had wisely had some supper sent to their cabin, on the boat.

'I don't want to go into that hotel,' French explained. 'If Sheen saw me it would be good-bye to getting the stones. And I don't want either of you to go either. So I'll ask the local police to send a man to make inquiries. You both wait where you are.'

This plan worked satisfactorily. A gendarme at once saw the manager of the hotel and reported to French. Sheen was not staying the night. He had explained that he was going to Calais by the eleven o'clock train.

There seemed then to be no need to wait at the station, and French and his party went to another hotel to kill time. But well before eleven they returned to the station, booked to Calais, and took cover.

French's anxieties were soon dispelled. Sheen entered the station about five minutes to eleven and booked. The train came in and he climbed on board. The others followed, taking the next coach.

At each stopping place they looked out guardedly, but till they reached Calais Sheen made no move. There he went quickly out of the station, and disappeared into the nearest hotel.

At such an hour—it was quarter past twelve—French didn't like applying for help to the local police. But there seemed nothing else to be done. He therefore found the police station and made his inquiries. From there a telephone to the manager of the hotel produced the needed information. Sheen had asked to be called early, as he was taking the 5.37 train to Lille.

Once again French repeated his manœuvre of the early evening. Choosing another hotel, he arranged with his men to keep watch in turn during the night, so as to ensure being at the railway in time in the morning. There they booked to Lille, took cover till Sheen had entered the train, and followed into the next coach. At each station—places many of them whose names are burnt into the heart of every Englishman: Hazebrouck, Bailleul, Armentières—they looked out and made sure that Sheen did not leave the train.

They reached Lille without incident, but here they were confronted by an unexpected difficulty. Sheen remained in his compartment. Fortunately there was a stop of eight minutes and French rushed to the booking-office and in a somewhat halting mixture of French and English, took the clerk into his confidence. Where was the train going on to?

The clerk quickly grasped the difficulty. The train went to Orchies, Valenciennes, Aulnoye for Paris and Brussels, and Hirson.

Brussels! Sloley had booked to Brussels! Could Brussels be the rendezvous?

To be on the safe side, French took three singles to Hirson, and sprinting for all he was worth, caught the train just as it was beginning to move.

The three men resumed their tactics of looking out at each stop, but it was not till they reached Aulnoye that they saw Sheen. There he alighted, and made his way to the north-bound platform.

There was some forty minutes to wait, and then at 11.29 the Paris-Brussels express thundered into the station. It stopped for seven minutes, so there was time to see what Sheen did before booking. But he acted as they expected. He climbed into the train and the others followed in due course.

It seemed evident, then, that Brussels really was the

meeting-place. Sheen's trip to Etaples and Lyde's to Paris were doubtless undertaken to cover any scent that might have been laid.

On reaching Brussels Midi slightly different tactics were employed. Shaw was sent forward to reconnoitre, while French and Carter kept in the background.

At a distance the last two followed Shaw. They were interested to see that the quarry didn't leave the station. Sheen headed to the booking-office, and they watched Shaw take his place behind him in the queue. Sheen booked and moved off, and French, fearful that while himself booking Shaw might lose the trail, hastened after Sheen. But in a couple of minutes Shaw overtook him, and French dropped back into his former obscurity.

Sheen appeared at ease and completely unconscious that he was being shadowed. He walked to the station restaurant and disappeared within. Shaw stopped at the door, and French hastened up to him.

'What about a second door?' he asked rapidly.

'He's booked to Amsterdam by the two-fifty,' Shaw answered in the same way. 'I think he's safe enough.'

'He might be on to us and it might be a trick,' French insisted. 'Better have a squint in and see that all's well.'

Shaw disappeared, but returned in a few seconds. Sheen was seated at a table and was discussing the menu with the waiter.

'I'm sure, sir,' Shaw declared, 'he's not on to us. He didn't see me at the booking window. I let a girl get in between us. He booked a second single to Amsterdam and asked if the train was fourteen-fifty. The clerk said yes, that it was the "Northern Star" pullman express, and that there was a supplement.'

'Did they talk English?'

Shaw grinned. 'I know enough French for that, sir.'

'Good for you. Did you book?'

'No, sir. I slipped out of the queue to follow him. I knew there'd be plenty of time.'

This news seemed extraordinarily satisfactory to French. Amsterdam! A name almost synonymous with precious stones! If these three had intended to meet in Amsterdam, the end was surely in sight.

There was a couple of hours till the train left. 'You book three singles,' he said to Carter, 'while I go to police head-quarters and get a message through to the Yard.'

He left the station and took a taxi. At the police station he met a polite and helpful officer who gave him some news in excellent English.

'Ah, monsieur, we have heard already of your chase. One of your men sent us a letter, it is not yet half an hour—' He took a paper from a file and glanced at it. 'Ouilli? Is it not?'

'That's right, monsieur,' French answered, 'Willis.'

'Ah, you call it Ouillize. Your English names!' He shrugged good-humouredly. 'This Ouillize, he has just left from the Gare du Midi by the 12.51 for Amsterdam. He has come this morning from Paris. He sent the letter by one of our men, and he asked us to inform your Scotland Yard of his movements. We did so immediately.'

'That's the best news you could have given me,' French declared heartily. 'It shows me I'm on the right track with my own inquiry. Will you do me the same favour you've already done my colleague—ring up Scotland Yard and ask them to advise Willis that I have traced Sheen here, that he has booked to Amsterdam by the two-fifty, and

310

that I'm going on by the same train. Also will you ask them to advise the Amsterdam men to give me the help I'll want. They know in London what that is.'

The officer promised he would do so at once.

'Fine,' said French heartily. 'I can't say how grateful I am. It's that case of the safe burglary in Kingsway, London. I think we've got the men.'

'I have read of the case. Congratulations, monsieur, on your success up to the present.'

French thanked the polite officer, then excusing himself on the ground that it was getting near his train time, he returned to the station.

Carter was waiting for him.

'He's in the train,' he said. 'Shaw's at the barrier. Here are the tickets.'

The train, with a single stop at Antwerp Est, ran express to Rosendaal, where they crossed the frontier. The journey across Dutch territory was equally quickly carried out, and at 6.50 to the minute they drew into the Central Station at Amsterdam.

Once again the burden of the chase fell on Shaw. He kept reasonably close to Sheen, while French and Carter followed far to the rear.

One of the first persons they saw on the platform was Willis.

'Just got word from the Yard you were coming in on this train,' he said. 'My bird's gone to roost in the Hotel des Pays Bas.'

'Fine,' French answered hurriedly. 'I wish you'd relieve Shaw. He's following Sheen, and he's done it so long that he might be recognised any time.'

Willis nodded. 'My room is 75 at the Pays Bas,' he

breathed, and slipped away. In a moment Shaw returned to the others.

'Inspector Willis has taken over?' he said interrogatively to French.

'That's right. Sheen has never seen him, while you've been on to him for about thirty hours. Let's go to this Hotel des Pays Bas.'

The omnibus hadn't left and they got on board. At the hotel Shaw was sent in to reconnoitre, and it was not till he reported all clear that the others followed. French showed his card to the reception clerk, and they were taken upstairs to wait in Willis's room.

Presently the telephone rang. French picked up the receiver.

It was Willis. Sheen, it appeared, had gone to the Hotel Amstel, booked a room, asked for letters and gone upstairs. What would French like Willis to do?

'Where did you leave Lyde?' French asked in return.

'In the smoking room of the des Pays Bas.'

'I'll put Shaw on to him and then I'll come round and see you. Where are you now?'

'At the Amstel. I'll meet you outside the door.'

'Right.'

Some careful reconnaisance on French's part revealed the fact that Lyde was still in the smoking room. Having pointed him out to Shaw, French set off for the Amstel, leaving Carter to assist Shaw, should his help be required. Willis, his hat pulled down and his collar up round his ears, was waiting in a convenient doorway.

'I expect they'll meet presently,' French began. 'Any trouble following Lyde?'

'None. He didn't suspect we were on to him.'

'Nor did Sheen. Extraordinary, but all the better for us. Go ahead with your story.'

'It was pretty plain sailing,' Willis declared. 'We got to Paris last night at 11.00. Lyde put up at the Terminus Hotel opposite the Gare de l'Est. We all left this morning at 7.00. A deuced slow train, but I suppose it was to avoid travelling with Sheen in the express. We had three-quarters of an hour in Brussels and came on here.'

'Much the same with us,' said French, and rapidly sketched the Etaples-Calais journey. 'The question now is what we're going to do? Better get the Dutch police on to them, I think, and shadow them till we see if they don't lift the stones or the equivalent money.'

'I've seen the police,' Willis answered. 'They've heard from the Yard and they're out to be helpful.'

'I expect so. Foreign police usually are.'

Willis slowly filled his pipe. 'There's one thing I've been thinking over, chief,' he went on, but French interrupted him.

'None of that here, old man,' he said. 'That's all right for the Yard, but when we're alone I'm French as before.'

Willis grinned. 'Right-o. I'll remember. But about what I was going to tell you. I wonder if you think there's anything in it. It's this. The first thing Lyde did when he got to the des Pays Bas was to ask if there were any letters. There weren't, but there was a parcel. It was a fairly large book, a bit larger than the ordinary-sized novel, but not so large as the usual encyclopædia; you know, about the size of those novels they sell for eight-and-six or ten shillings.'

French nodded.

'I know it was a book, because I got the police representative to question the hall porter, and he knew London and had noticed Foyle's label on it.'

French nodded again.

'Well, there was nothing in that, but here's what has made me think. When Sheen got here just now the first thing he asked for was letters. And here again there were none, but there was a book: come by post. This time I happened to see the man's face, and I'll swear the book was what he was after, and what's more, that it was of tremendous importance to him. I could see that from his expression.'

French turned and stared at his companion. 'Man alive!' he exclaimed with an oath. 'You tell me that as a sort of afterthought. Has nothing struck you about it?'

Willis laughed outright. 'Well, something did strike me, I'll admit,' he answered. 'But I didn't think there was any immediate hurry. I wasn't sure, of course. And I couldn't act without your authority.'

'We'll be sure before we're much older,' French returned. 'Valuable books, those two. We'll have a look inside them before we sleep tonight.'

'Just a minute, French: there's not that hurry. I've been thinking while you were walking over. Suppose the diamonds are in the books, as we both seem to think. Well, has this occurred to you: each man will have about a third of the lot in his book.'

French stared again. 'Well, suppose he has?'

'Then we'll only get two-thirds.'

'Two-thirds would be better than none.'

'Ah, but what about getting the other third as well?'

French's stare became fixed. He remained motionless so long that Willis began to grin.

'By heck, I see what you mean: and you're right. You mean there's another book lying here in some hotel awaiting Sloley's call?'

314

'I should guess that was about the size of it.'

'And so would I. You've not been asleep, Willis, I will say.' French considered for a moment, then went on: 'That reminds me, Sloley called at a post office on his way to the station when he was starting. What price posting a book?'

Willis nodded. 'That's the ticket. There's a big hotel near the Central Station, the Victoria. It looks the biggest and I should think the most likely. If you like to hare off there, I'll watch the mousehole till you get back.'

'Bless you, my son. I'll have to go to police headquarters to get a man.'

'You'll find them all right,' said Willis comfortably, as French turned away.

French found it hard to control his excitement as he considered the possibilities which might lie in this new development. The sending of the stones through the post in the form of books was just what might be expected from men of the mentality of these three thieves. How the trader's labels had been obtained—for if one bore a trader's label, it was probable the others did too—was not, of course, clear, but men who had shown such ingenuity as Sloley, Sheen and Lyde would have had no difficulty in arranging it.

But this was a minor point. What really mattered was that there was now a chance of arresting Sheen and Lyde with the stones actually in their possession. If so, it would bring his case to the most triumphant conclusion that he could possibly wish. It would not only be an overwhelming proof of guilt, but it would recover the swag: the two essentials for which he had been striving.

Sternly repressing his feelings so that he could exhibit

315

the detachment proper to so high an official of the British police, he presented himself at the Amsterdam headquarters. There he was received with politeness and asked, again in excellent English, what his Dutch confrères could have the pleasure of doing for him.

French was obliged for his courteous reception. If it would not be an inconvenience, he would like an officer to accompany him to the Victoria or other hotel, to try and find out if his third suspect had engaged a room there, and if so, to take over any correspondence which might be awaiting him. Would this be possible?

He was assured that nothing could be arranged more easily, and in a few minutes he left for the Victoria in company with a large, grave-faced and silent man named Slaats, who, he thought, but was not sure, occupied the position of an inspector. On the few occasions on which Slaats did speak, it was also in English.

French was too eager about his business to pay much attention to the streets through which they walked, but he could not fail to notice their distinctive and charming character. The outstanding features were, of course the 'grachten' or canals, whose waters shimmered peacefully, if somewhat coldly, under the electric lights, and the rows of well-grown elms, now unhappily bare of leaves, with behind them glimpses of the picturesque old seventeenth and eighteenth century houses for which the city is famous.

They soon reached the hotel and Slaats, having asked for the manager and explained to him the situation, suggested that French should be allowed to ask his questions. The manager, obviously anxious that whatever happened, it should be without scandal to the hotel, instantly agreed to give every possible facility.

'Can you tell me,' French began, 'if an Englishman booked a room here for tonight, and if he has failed to turn up?'

The manager could not, but he rang for a clerk, and presently it was found the suggestion of the visitor was correct. A Mr Johnson, of London, had made the reservation, but had not arrived to claim his room.

This looked well, but French was dashed by the answer to his next question. Asked if this Mr Johnson was a stranger, the clerk said not, that he had stayed in the hotel on one previous occasion, about a month earlier. He was, the clerk, understood, an engineer, and was interested in land reclamation; at least he had asked how he might get in touch with the engineers of the great works on the Zuider Zee.

This would seem to rule out Sloley, but French was taking no risks. He handed the clerk his bundle of photographs and asked if Mr Johnson was represented.

Then delight once more surged up in his mind. The clerk, without the slightest hesitation, picked out a photograph. 'Mr Johnson, sir,' he declared. It was Sloley's.

Crushing down unprofessional expressions of satisfaction, French nodded gravely and said that that was the man in whom he was interested. He would like to ask one other question. Had a parcel, a book in all probability, arrived for Mr Johnson? If so, might he see it?

The clerk returned to his office, but almost immediately reappeared with a parcel. French found himself utterly unable to hide his delight when he saw it was a book, wrapped up with the two ends left open, and bearing the label of Messrs Bumpus. It was addressed to Mr A. J. Johnson, Hotel Victoria, Amsterdam, and had not been opened by the Customs.

'That's what I was hoping to find,' said French. 'There were no other letters, I suppose?'

The clerk shook his head; this was the only thing. 'But,' he went on, looking at his manager, 'I don't know whether the gentleman would be interested, but I remember that on Mr Johnson's last visit he received an exactly similar package, a book from the same firm. I try to improve my English by reading, and I have bought books from Messrs Bumpus: that's how I know their name.'

'Interested?' French answered. 'I should think I am. I'm exceedingly obliged to you for telling me. I think it will help me quite a lot. Now,' he went on to the manager, 'I want to take charge of this book. I'll give you a receipt for it, of course.'

The manager was perfectly agreeable. Once again all he wanted was for French and everything connected with him to leave the hotel and vanish into oblivion. French gravely wrote his receipt, handed it over, and expressed his thanks.

'I want you to be witness that I take this parcel to headquarters,' he went on to Slaats, as they left the hotel. 'I think it may turn out to be valuable.'

At police headquarters French saw again the official with whom he had already dealt. 'I want one other favour of you, if you will be kind enough,' he asked, 'it won't take long. I want to open this parcel in your presence and the presence of Mynheer Slaats. Can that be arranged?'

Nothing, it appeared, would give the officer more pleasure than to assist his distinguished visitor. The parcel could be opened then and there. They would not be interrupted.

The three men sat round a table. French was almost, but not quite, trembling with excitement. Slowly, controlling himself, he took out his knife and cut the string. Then, equally slowly and carefully, he unwrapped the paper and took out the book.

It was Cripps' work on Old English Plate, a book measuring something like 9 inches by 6 inches by 2; a book, as French presently discovered, of over 500 pages, and weighing pretty heavily. He attempted to open it, and with a further thrill of pure joy found he could not do so. Pages and covers were stuck tightly together.

On seeing this, Slaats and his superior officer, who had seemed politely bored, waked up suddenly and began to take notice. French continued his operations. Placing the book flat on the table, he inserted his knife between the pages about quarter of the way from the upper cover, and began to cut between the leaves. He carried his cut right round the book except for the spine. then he lifted. This time the cover came up at his cut.

The inside of the book was hollow, and there packed in cotton wool lay a gleaming mass of gems! Diamonds, sapphires, emeralds, rubies: scintillating as if giving off flames of lambent fire. The two Dutchmen gazed with goggling eyes. Apart from the glory before them, here was a demonstration of the methods of the world-famed Scotland Yard which had more than fulfilled their highest expectations. Then at last they swore; at least it sounded like oaths. French beamed effusively. Under the circumstances he could permit himself a somewhat relaxed attitude.

'This,' he said, waving his hand over the *cache*, 'represents, if I'm correct, one-third of what was stolen. Those other two men about whom you've heard, each received books on arrival at their hotels. I suspected what they contained, but wasn't sure till this moment. It now remains for me to arrest those men before they can get rid of the swag. And there I am in your hands and must ask for your help.'

Help was soon forthcoming. The necessary formalities were quickly undertaken, and about two in the morning both the other hotels were visited, and Sheen and Lyde were taken into custody. Their books were also found to be hollow, and when the contents of the three were checked up, practically the whole of the loot was discovered.

A telephone to the Yard next morning soon obtained the information that Messrs Bumpus and the other firms concerned had sent their books to Amsterdam a month previously, and not within the last day or two. It was easy from that to see what had been done. The trio had sever-ally ordered books, and had gone out to Amsterdam to receive them—all three under assumed names. They had carefully removed the firms' addressed labels from the wrapping paper, and after hollowing out the leaves and packing the stones, had used them again on the new wrap-ping. Fortunately for them, the cancelling stamps had passed over the wrapping paper only, and so had left the labels clean. The packed books the trio had kept ready addressed, so that if a sudden flight became desirable, all they would have to do would be to post them. This unques-tionably accounted for Sloley's dive into the post office on his way to Victoria.

Taken red-handed with the loot in their possession, the men found it impossible to deny the theft, and when French described to them with minute accuracy the details of Minter's death, mentioning the finger-print on the dead man's collar and the helping of Minter from the office to the car after the theatre, they broke down and admitted the murder also.

The case, as French had put it together, proved to be substantially correct. Sloley and Sheen, foreseeing ruin if the firm closed down, decided to effect their own safety at the expense of the others concerned. They could, however, think of no method of getting at the stones. But, in a casual conversation Lyde happened to boast to Sheen, that given certain conditions, he could open any safe anywhere. Through ridiculing the statement, Sheen now got his brother-in-law to divulge his method. Sheen was impressed, and presently Lyde was introduced to Sloley and tentatively sounded. Lyde thereupon indicated his willingness to assist in any matters that might be going forward, for an adequate consideration. After discussion a firm partnership was entered into between the three and details were worked out. They intended photographically to copy both keys and to rob the safe at their leisure. The contents was to be divided equally between the three. All swore that at this time no thought of murder had entered their minds, and French believed them.

They obtained the camera without difficulty, Lyde making up as Minter as a safeguard in the event of suspicion being aroused. But the remainder of the photographic scheme they found much more difficult than they had anticipated. They had first intended to fix the camera in position, operating it electrically from outside the room while Norne and Minter were opening the safe. This, for several reasons, they had found impracticable, the chief being that they could find no place to put it which would be at once near enough the keyhole and out of sight—and therefore possible suspicion—of Norne and Minter. Then Sloley had tried shooting the keys by hand. He had carried the camera, hidden in various wrappings, and had attempted to direct the lens as one fires a gun from the hip. Four times he had tried this plan, and on each occasion he had missed his objective. The trio had then decided the camera must be properly focused, and this had led to the placing of the despatch case on the letter file. Four pins projecting from the bottom of the case formed a jig to enable Sloley to re-fit it to the file in exactly the right place, the pins being pushed in flush when out of use. The fixing of the camera in the case gave them more trouble than any other single detail of the plan. They dared not cut a hole in the side opposite the lens lest it should be noticed, so they had to arrange that springs would push the camera up into a frame when the lid was raised, thus bringing the lens above the level of the side. A woollen muffler carefully fixed to the camera rose with it and completely hid it, and they hoped that if the muffler were seen, its rising would be put down to the natural springiness of the wool. These fitments were made by Sheen, who was a skilful worker in metals.

When first they used this apparatus they thought that success had crowned their efforts. But a hideous disappointment awaited them. On developing their film, they found that Norne's key had come out splendidly, but that just as Minter was putting his forward, Norne had grasped the handle to be ready to open the safe when the second key was turned. Norne's hand had come in front of the key, completely obscuring it! And the very same thing happened during the withdrawal of the key: Norne had kept hold of the handle while Minter was locking up.

The conspirators were now in an awkward position. Either they would have to repeat their photographic effort, or they must try something else. Sloley, however declared that further photography was impossible. He had been chipped already by Norne for always turning up with a parcel or despatch case when the safe was being opened, as if he wanted to carry off the contents, and he felt that if he did this again, suspicion would inevitably be aroused when the theft was discovered. This suspicion would be increased by the fact, so far not appreciated, that on each of these occasions he, Sloley, had himself arranged for the safe to be opened.

Then Sheen came forward with an idea. Minter had the other key. If they could get Minter's key, clear out the safe, return the key to Minter, and then have Minter commit suicide, it would be assumed that Minter had stolen the stones, passed them on to someone else, and then, repenting of what he had done, had taken his life.

This meant murder, and at first Sloley and Lyde objected. But two considerations forced them on. The first was the offer for the stock which Norne had received. They feared the other directors would close with it. If this happened before the three had carried out their plan, it would mean their ruin. The second consideration was the fact that they had already overcome the major difficulty, the getting of Norne's key: and having done so much and seeing salvation from ruin so near them, they could not face losing their advantage.

Their new scheme was built on the visit to Guildford. Sloley had not consciously worked to get this visit arranged, being perfectly genuine in his arguments on the subject. But when it was arranged, the trio used it as the basis of their scheme.

In essentials it followed French's reconstruction. Sloley opened the ball at three o'clock by ringing up Minter. He gave Norne's name and mimicked Norne's voice, and said that he, Norne, had unexpectedly to come to Town that afternoon and therefore couldn't receive the party at Guildford; but would Minter join himself and the others at the office at 7.50, when they could dine together in Town and go down to Guildford later? Minter agreed, and ringing up his garage, altered the time of his taxi. Because of this message, also, he had not dined before starting.

At 4.30 Sheen took the next step. He had already got out his list of shareholders—purely in the interests of the robbery—and he now rang up Minter, told him of the list, and asked him if he would discuss it when they met in the evening. This was partly to make certain that there should be no hitch about Minter's turning up at the office, but it was principally to get him to the telephone at 4.30. For at that hour Lyde, mimicking Minter's voice, rang up Norne's house to say that he, Minter, was ill and couldn't go down till the 8.15 train. Inquiries, if such were made, would therefore show that Minter had been telephoning at the time his presumed message had reached Norne's. No doubt the criminals believed that the apparent checking of this message at each end would prevent inquiries at the telephone exchange, which might have shown that this call was received, not sent, by Minter—in which they were partly justified.

The meeting at the office took place as French had imagined. While Sloley and Sheen were robbing the safe, Lyde—already made up to resemble Minter—was dressing in the accountant's clothes. Minter was dressed in Lyde's clothes and given the dope with the assurance that this was just to enable an escape to be made, and that no further harm was intended him. Lyde then went off to

Guildford. After the theatre Minter was asleep, but he was aroused sufficiently for him to walk with assistance and in a state of semi-coma to the car. There while Sloley drove, Sheen gagged him, then tied him up, and finally suffocated him. Lyde had arranged the light in his window at Norne's and lowered his rope, and the body was arranged in bed, all as French had supposed.

One precaution Lyde suggested, on which the other two were not very keen. Lyde, however, had insisted on it. That was the matter of the glass. He had cleaned the glass and then got Norne to carry it to his bed. Breathing on it had brought up Norne's resulting prints, and he had skilfully wiped the glass so as to leave untouched an essential portion of one of these. His last act before leaving the room was to get Minter's prints on to it also, but he deliberately twisted the glass so that the thumb-print would not register with the others. He then left Norne's, walked to Woking, and caught an early train to Town, going on later to Paris.

An investigation by the Amsterdam police on another matter incidentally revealed the fact that the trio had arranged a sale of their gems to a firm of bad reputation in the city. The money was to have been paid the next day, and tickets and forged passports to South America were to have been part of the price.

After a three-day trial Sloley and Sheen were sentenced to death and Lyde to fifteen years penal servitude. Lyde's counsel ingeniously argued—and Lyde swore—that his client had not intended murder: that he had taken Minter's place on the understanding that Minter was only to be dosed with a drug which would destroy his memory of the period, and that he was to be taken down alive to

Guildford and left in the room at Norne's to recover. This introduced a sufficient element of doubt to evade the death sentence, though few really believed it.

For French there remained a certain amount of kudos— not referred to by anyone at the Yard—and a strong determination that his next holidays should be spent in Holland, with Amsterdam as a centre for his excursions. And till that happy time should arrive, he settled down with a half-sigh to carry out Sir Mortimer Ellison's desire that he should 'look into that poisoning affair down at Chelmsford.' At all events, if it didn't get him to Holland, it would get him into the country. Half a loaf, he thought, was better than no bread.

By the same author

Inspector French and the Starvel Hollow Tragedy

A chance invitation from friends saves Ruth Averill's life on the night her uncle's old house in Starvel Hollow is consumed by fire, killing him and incinerating the fortune he kept in cash. Dismissed at the inquest as a tragic accident, the case is closed—until Scotland Yard is alerted to the circulation of bank-notes supposedly destroyed in the inferno. Inspector Joseph French suspects that dark deeds were done in the Hollow that night and begins to uncover a brutal crime involving arson, murder and body snatching . . .

'*Freeman Wills Crofts is the only author who gives us intricate crime in fiction as it might really be, and not as the irreflective would like it to be.*'   *OBSERVER*

By the same author

Inspector French
and the Sea Mystery

Off the coast of Burry Port in south Wales, two fishermen
discover a shipping crate and manage to haul it ashore. Inside
is the decomposing body of a brutally murdered man. With
nothing to indicate who he is or where it came from, the
local police decide to call in Scotland Yard. Fortunately
Inspector Joseph French does not believe in insoluble cases—
there are always clues to be found if you know what to look
for. Testing his theories with his accustomed thoroughness,
French's ingenuity sets him off on another investigation . . .

'Inspector French is as near the real thing as any sleuth in
fiction.'   SUNDAY TIMES